Bloodshed in the Badlands

WREN AND RASCAL COZY MYSTERY, BOOK 1

JUDITH A. BARRETT

WOBBLY CREEK, LLC

BLOODSHED IN THE BADLANDS

WREN AND RASCAL COZY MYSTERY, BOOK 1

Published in the United States of America by Wobbly Creek, LLC

2023 Georgia

wobblycreek.com

Cover by Wobbly Creek, LLC

paperback ISBN 978-1-953870-42-1

Bloodshed in the Badlands is dedicated to the colors black and tan and to everyone who loves camping and dogs.

Chapter One

Wren glared at her phone as it rang. "I didn't even remember that my phone rang. Do I answer it?"

Wren's black and tan, mostly Labrador Retriever, Rascal, opened one eye and then went back to sleep.

"A lot of help you are."

After she answered, a man said, "Wren, my name is Charlie Hogue; I'm a friend of your mother's, and I've been following your writing for a while. I particularly enjoyed that piece you did for the culinary magazine on the Cajun chef who moved to Nebraska ten years ago and opened a restaurant. You have an entertaining way of engaging the reader with your refreshing viewpoint."

When Mr. Hogue didn't continue, Wren waited and then frowned. *It must be my turn to say something.*

"Thanks." *I'm definitely out of practice with phone etiquette.*

"Not at all; your mother told me you were between engagements. I'd like to offer you a position as a staff writer for my travel magazine. Check with your mother, then call me back so we can see if I have something that might interest you."

After Mr. Hogue disconnected, Wren sent her mom a text. "Charlie Hogue offered me a job. Legit?"

Mom responded, "Take it. Charlie's an old friend."

"Mom says he's okay, Rascal, but he must be eccentric; guess I'll have to get used to talking on the phone."

Wren flopped onto her broken-down sofa and put up her feet before she returned Mr. Hogue's call.

When Charlie answered, he said, "Carolina must have given me the old thumbs up."

"Sure did." Wren rolled her eyes. *That sounded lame.*

"A CEO of an RV manufacturing company is interested in having his camping trailers and vans tested by someone in their twenties. He wants honest feedback about his models because he'd like to expand his market to a younger population. Your mom used to be big on camping, so I called her for a recommendation, and she said you'd just completed a large project for a longtime client. Are you available?"

I need grocery money; that's pretty available.

"I'm listening."

"I pitched the idea of a series of articles on a theme, and he bought into my idea of a young woman driving across the country while she visits lesser-known haunted campgrounds, but his board of directors was concerned about asking someone to travel alone to possibly remote locations. I told him you had a dog; you still have your lab puppy, Rascal, don't you? I seem to recall he's a black and tan lab with a little husky mixed in."

Charlie chuckled. "Since you got him from the animal shelter, I assumed he wasn't one of those designer dogs."

I raised my eyebrows. *He really has read a few of my articles.*

"You have a good memory; Rascal's four now, so not as much of a puppy anymore."

Charlie chuckled. "I remember animals and their names; people, not so much."

Wren smiled, then realized they weren't on video chat, so she chuckled, too.

"What kind of feedback does the CEO want?" she asked. "Are there certain components he wants to be tested?"

"Tested might have been the wrong word, which was a terrible faux pas for a magazine publisher, wasn't it? My only excuse is that my magazine editor is on vacation. The campers and RVs have been designed for two different groups: retirees and families; so, for example, the retirees prefer extra living space and comfortable furniture for relaxing, while the families prefer two sleeping spaces separate from their living area, and both groups like a household-sized side-by-side refrigerator and freezer. Your assignment is to camp in different models and then share what worked and what would have made the camping more enjoyable for you."

"Got it; I don't think I've ever heard of a haunted campground."

"I was surprised at how many there were when I did some research last year. I've been kicking around the idea for a while, but I had to have the right person write it."

"Sounds interesting, but you've read my articles; I don't write fiction."

"I'm not looking for fiction. I'll email the details to you; read them over and get back to me with your questions. Your mom told me to find a private plane for you so you could take your carry pistol and ammunition. Your pistol would have to be in your suitcase in the luggage compartment, and all your ammunition would have to be in a locked box. Carolina told me you knew all that, but I wanted to remind you because if you can be ready in two days, I have a friend flying out from Atlanta to Phoenix; that might be the best option for Rascal because he won't have to stay in a crate."

After Wren read the email that Charlie Hogue sent her, she sipped on a glass of sweet tea while she listed her supplies to pack and the items she'd need in a camper on her phone, then researched the weather in Arizona and modified her lists.

"It's hot during the day and cold at night in the desert in September; even though we'll be there for only a week or two, I'll have to pack for summer, fall, and winter, Rascal."

Three days later

A slender young man with a buzzed haircut held a lined notecard in his hand as he stood at the gate near the runway for small jets.

"Miss Weaver and Rascal?" He read from the card when Wren and Rascal reached the gate for private plane passengers after they exited the plane.

"That's us." Wren squinted in the intense sunlight. *Sure is bright in Arizona.*

He smiled as he took her medium-sized suitcase. "There probably isn't another young woman with her dog landing here in a private plane today, but I was supposed to ask so you'd know I was hired to take you to the truck dealership; your truck is ready for you to pick up. Here are the keys."

Wren dropped the keys into her backpack and then pulled out her dusty rose ballcap and sunglasses.

As they walked to the young man's car, he said, "After you get your truck, you can follow me to the RV dealership."

He grinned. "Your boss told my boss you wouldn't know your way around Phoenix. I've lived here all my life, but they keep switching around those freeways, and I get lost half the time myself."

On the way to the dealership, he said, "Make sure you have a long rope; they come in handy when you need them, and when you don't, they store just fine. Do you have a water bottle? You'll need to drink lots of water here."

"Thanks; in Georgia, people say it isn't the heat, it's the humidity."

The young man chuckled. "Can't say that here."

When he pulled into the car dealership, the young man stopped next to a pickup that was parked in a spot close to the showroom.

"The red extended cab pickup with four doors is yours. It's plenty big and has a powerful engine, so you won't have one lick of trouble pulling any size trailer." He peered at her. "No offense, but are you okay with driving a big truck?"

Wren smiled at the concern on his face. "Sure am."

A slight, middle-aged man in a white short-sleeved dress shirt met her at the door. "Miss Weaver? We've been waiting for you. Follow me to the registration desk, and we'll take care of the last few details."

While Wren waited, she reviewed the directions from the RV dealership to the town of Hidden Gulch and the Forgotten Oasis Campground. In less than five minutes, Wren headed toward her red pickup; the young man opened the door to Wren's new truck for Rascal. Wren started the engine and familiarized herself with the pickup. When she waved, the young man headed toward the exit, and she followed him.

After Wren turned at the entrance to the RV dealership, she swung around and turned toward the exit.

Wren scanned the acres of large and small RVs, camping trailers, and fifth wheels. "Look at all these RVs, Rascal. Don't some of them look like city buses?"

After they went inside, Wren perched her sunglasses around her cap's brim so they'd be within easy reach when she went outside.

The receptionist glanced up. "Are you Ms. Weaver? We've been expecting you. I have your gift right here." She beamed as she held out a large, orange-tinted plastic water tumbler with a lid, straw, and the dealership logo.

"Thank you; this will help me remember to drink water."

"You're in Arizona now; that's critical to remember." She led Wren and Rascal to the service desk in the back of the expansive building.

The receptionist opened the service area door and shouted before leaving for her desk, "We got company."

A large man with a ruddy face came inside. He wore a gray shirt soaked with sweat. He stopped at a sink next to a door and scrubbed at the dark grease and grime on his hands.

After he dried them and tossed the paper towel toward the wastepaper basket and missed, he mumbled as he picked it up, "Timing's off."

The man smiled as he held out his hand. "Ms. Weaver, I'm the service manager, chief mechanic, and supply clerk around here. I'll give you a tour of your new trailer."

The service manager went through the camper with Wren, pointing out its major features and idiosyncrasies. He went into more detail as he explained the workings of the electrical and water systems.

Wren opened the refrigerator and then touched a rack. "It's cold."

He nodded. "Cold and ready to go."

After Wren locked the camper door, the service manager said, "Let's have you take it from here; bring your truck around."

When she returned, he handed her a three-ring binder. "We made up a few cheat sheets for you on the different systems and the answers to people's typical questions after they leave. We went over everything, but it was a lot to take in."

She backed the truck close to the trailer while he provided gentle words of encouragement and guidance until the truck could hook up. After she secured the trailer onto the truck's hitch, he showed her how to check the trailer lights without someone else helping.

"Do you want to take a short drive to get a feel for the truck and trailer before you go solo?" he asked.

"I'd like that."

When they returned, he handed her his business card before he climbed out of the truck. "You and Rascal are ready for the road. If you run into any problems or have any questions, remember to check your notebook, or feel free to call or text me or our service department; we'll be happy to help."

"The young man who picked me up at the airport told me to have a long rope in my truck," she said. "Is that important?"

"It isn't unless you need one, then there's no substitute; it will be stored in the compartment under your back seat and be your insurance that nothing will happen."

"I don't think I have a compartment under the back seat."

"I'm sure you do; tell you what: I'll give you a sturdy rope that can pull you out of the deepest mud as a gift from the dealership. I'll be right back."

When he returned with a coiled rope, he grinned. "This is the longest one we had." He showed her where the lever was to release the bottom of the seat so it flipped forward. "See how that looks like you have a flat surface? Lift that tab."

Wren pulled the tab, and the flat surface tipped back like opening the cover of a book. He dropped the rope into the boxlike space. Wren closed the lid and then locked the seat back into place. "That's really slick."

"You have another space on the passenger's side, just like it if you need it."

"Thanks again."

"You're quite welcome; let us know how your trip goes."

"I'll make sure the publisher sends you a magazine with my article."

"Make sure you mention the dashing, brilliant service manager at your first RV dealership." He chuckled.

After she started the engine, he tapped on the hood twice, stepped back, and saluted her with two fingers.

"That was a nice sendoff, wasn't it, Rascal?"

After she was on the freeway, Wren clutched the steering wheel as she maneuvered her way through the maze of the Phoenix interchanges and the fast-moving, nerve-wracking, bumper-to-bumper traffic. "This is rough; the truck handles the camper, but I'm afraid to breathe until we're on the open road."

Wren relaxed and gazed in wonder at her surroundings after they were away from the city and its freeways. "I thought Arizona was all brown when we circled to land; now that I have the chance for a closer look, I see different colors of brush: yellow-green, burnt orange, dusky gray, and dark purple; green cactus; gray rocks with streaks of red; and the bluest sky I've ever seen. The desert is beautiful."

As she drove through a small town, she noticed a tall sign on her right that announced she was approaching her favorite superstore.

"I just realized I meant to stop in Phoenix to get our basics for the trailer, but I was so focused on my driving that I forgot. I already have my list; I won't be long. I'll park in the shade if I can find any and leave the engine running. Don't let anyone steal the truck."

Rascal growled and then barked.

"Good boy, thanks."

When she walked into the store, she glanced to her left and raised her eyebrows in surprise at the grocery section. *The store's completely backward from what I'm used to; this might take longer than I expected.*

After finishing shopping and checking out, she pushed her full cart to the truck. She unlocked the camper to put away the refrigerated groceries, then locked the door.

She opened the truck's back door on the passenger's side and put the rest of the sacks on the floor. "I think I have everything we'll need for a few days. I'm sure I missed something, but I bought towels, a pillow, and sheets for me, and two bowls, dog food, and treats for you, so we'll get by."

She glanced at her suitcase. "I forgot to pull out my carry piece and some ammo. Mom would have a fit if she knew." Wren loaded her pistol, slid it into its holster, and snugged the inside waistband holster into place.

As she left the outskirts of the small town, Wren chuckled as a roadrunner briefly raced her and then disappeared into the brush. When the road with large rocks along the side twisted through the hills, she smiled as the truck's engine managed the climbs and easily maintained its steady speed on the downgrades.

Wren pulled over at a roadside rest area for a break; after she and Rascal climbed out of the truck, she poured water from the jug she'd bought into Rascal's bowl and into her cup. After she ate the small salad she'd bought for her lunch, Wren gave Rascal a treat.

When he abruptly darted after a jackrabbit, Wren gasped and then whistled; Rascal slowly returned.

She snatched up his leash from the truck and then attached it to his collar. "This was my fault; I forgot we weren't at home. We don't know our way around the desert, boy; we have to stay together."

Rascal led the way to the truck but glanced back with longing at the brush where the rabbit had disappeared.

Wren smiled when they reached the truck and opened the door behind the driver's seat. "That rabbit was scared you were going to catch up with it; you were impressive."

Rascal grinned and then hopped into the truck.

It was late afternoon when Wren passed a sign, "Hidden Gulch Town Limits." Three miles later, she turned at the Forgotten Oasis campground sign and slowly made her way to the small, wooden building with peeling once-red paint marked "Office."

Before she climbed out of the truck, Wren surveyed the campground. "I can't tell where the campground stops and the desert begins because it all blends together; I'll bet my eyes will adjust just like they did after we left Phoenix."

Wren snapped on the leash. "This is just for show because we're going into the office."

When they reached the office, Wren smiled at the large bowl of water with the sign, 'Dog Hydration Station'; after they were inside, Wren sighed at the refreshing coolness of the small office that contrasted so sharply with the intense, dry heat outside.

A woman in her fifties with soft brown hair highlighted with streaks of golden blond smiled as she set a box of ice cream treats into the ice cream chest and hurried to the desk. "Welcome to the Forgotten Oasis."

Another woman popped up from behind an aisle where she'd been stocking camping supplies, and Rascal wagged his tail. She was at least ten years younger than the first woman; she wore a tight, bright turquoise T-shirt that accentuated her curvy figure and was a perfect complement to her pale brown skin, dark brown eyes, and flyaway hair that she had unsuccessfully tried to entrap into a ponytail.

"Feels good, doesn't it? I'm Socorro Mendez, and you must be Wren Weaver; who's your handsome companion?"

"Rascal."

Rascal wagged his tail even faster at the mention of his name, then grinned at Socorro's throaty chuckle.

She held out her hand for him to sniff, then scratched his ear, and he leaned against her hand. "You are such a good boy," she cooed.

Rascal followed her and Wren to the desk.

"Socorro, I pulled up Miss Weaver's registration," the woman at the desk said.

"Thank you, Betsy."

While Socorro motioned for Wren to stand next to her, Betsy asked, "Rascal, are you a good boy?"

Rascal scrambled around to the side of the desk where Betsy stood and sat. She chuckled and gave him a treat. "Any time you need to go into town for research, Miss Weaver, you're welcome to leave Rascal with me."

"Please call me Wren, and I think he might enjoy that; thank you."

Betsy pointed to the sign on the desk. "That's our motto: Dogs Welcome, People Tolerated."

"We take our motto seriously." Socorro smiled. "We have you registered for a week with the option of a second week. Here's the campground map."

While Wren looked on, Socorro pointed as she spoke. "Restrooms are here, and this is the code to the door; the laundry is in the same building. We have a pool that is refreshing, especially in the afternoons and a fenced-in dog park that our canine visitors enjoy, but Rascal may prefer to investigate the grounds. Our campground is completely fenced except for the entrance. If we ever decide to expand, this back section is part of the campground, but so far, we enjoy having our personal desert. We do have roaming predators at night, so you may want to stay relatively close to your camper and the buildings after dark."

Socorro marked an X with a black marker next to a rectangle on the map. "Here is your site; our rows are one-way." She drew a line from the office to Wren's spot.

"This is my cell phone; text me anytime." Socorro circled the number on the map. "I live in the little house near the entrance, so I'm always onsite except when I go into town once a week on Tuesdays for supplies."

"I hadn't thought about whether anyone would be onsite; I should have because that's important."

Socorro raised an eyebrow. "It would be for me if I was traveling solo. Your magazine publisher, Mr. Hogue, told us you were coming here because the campground has a long-standing reputation for being haunted. I've owned and managed the campground for fifteen years; I bought it after my worthless ex-husband ran off with that hussy."

Socorro fanned her face with a brochure from a local tire company that was on the counter. "I don't think about that sleazy scumbag very often, but when I do, I still get a little worked up. Anyway, I haven't seen or heard anything that was remotely haunting, other than this odd feeling I've had lately that someone was watching me..."

Socorro peered past Wren and surveyed the parking lot before she cleared her throat. Socorro continued, "The hot wind from the desert gets on my nerves now and then and makes me jumpy; it's nothing. I meant to say I won't be able to help you with anything about the campground being haunted, but I know where the old-timers hang out, and they're quick to tell stories about the Old West. If you're interested in local color, you can join me for breakfast at the Watering Hole, our only diner."

"I hadn't thought about local color, but that would definitely help my article come alive; thank you. I can go anytime; I don't have a set schedule yet."

"Let's go tomorrow morning; can you be ready to leave around seven, or is that too early?"

"I'll still be on Eastern time, so seven won't be early at all for us."

As Wren and Rascal headed toward the door, Socorro added, "When you and Rascal go exploring, be careful around the wooden structures out back; they were here when I bought the place, and I haven't had the motivation or funds to fix them up."

"I've called Butch; he'll show you the way to your site," Betsy said.

When Wren and Rascal went outside, a wiry man with gray at his temples and dimples that deepened when he smiled waited next to her truck in a golf cart that had been repurposed into a maintenance vehicle.

"Follow me." He led her to her site and then signaled for her to stop when the trailer was in line with the utility hookups. When she stopped, he nodded and then sped away.

After unhooking and leveling the trailer, Wren plugged the electrical cord into the outlet and attached her water hose to the faucet next to her camper. She carried the rest of her shopping bags into the trailer; Rascal went inside with her.

"It's a cute camper, isn't it? Nice and compact." She turned on the air conditioner, pulled out her sheets, towels, and other items, and dropped them into her new laundry basket. "Let's stop by the laundry and get a load into the washer, and then we can explore."

Wren's eyes widened when they went into the laundry room. "It's spotless, Rascal."

She tossed her laundry into the washer, poured in her detergent, then fed coins into the washer's slots. When the washer started, they left.

Rascal trotted ahead and then waited for Wren before he raced ahead for a rabbit that scurried away.

"Don't go too far," Wren called out.

Rascal trotted back to her; the two of them continued to the fence and followed it to the back.

When they reached a wooden structure, Wren raised her eyebrows.

"Would you look at that?" she whispered almost reverently.

The façade of an old Western saloon was on a wooden stage almost five feet from the ground. The windowsills were sagging, and the one remaining swinging door hung by a single hinge. The stage was missing a few boards, and the entire structure leaned precariously to the right.

"Wow; they must have presented Old West shows here at one time."

"They sure 'nuf did, but don't you go thinkin' they was real," a young man said.

"Who said that?" Wren looked around and glanced at Rascal, who was staring at the top of the old saloon.

When Wren looked up, she saw the frail young man perched at the roof's peak; he wore a battered hat, a shirt with a large hole in the chest, and oversized britches held up by suspenders.

"What are you doing up there?" she asked.

"Doin' my job. Wait up there a minute. You heard me? You can see me? I been talkin' to people for ages, and ain't nobody ever heard me before. What's your name? Are you a ghost or somethin'?"

"My name is Wren. I'm not a ghost, are you?"

The young man stood up and stuck out his chest. "Nope; I'm Thomas, the guard for the stagecoach. My first job, and the man gave me a real silver dollar and told me to keep the lady safe. When the stagecoach robbers chased us, they shot me, but I always remembered it was my job to keep the lady safe." Thomas patted his nonexistent shirt pocket.

While Wren stared at Thomas, he disappeared.

"You saw him, right, Rascal?" Wren whispered.

"Of course, he did; dogs is smart," Thomas said from the far end of the facade. "Smarter than people."

"Who's the president, Thomas?" Wren asked.

"Ask your dog; he's smarter than you are, silly girl," Thomas chortled. "Everybody knows it's James Monroe."

"Of course, I was testing you."

Thomas snorted. "That's a girl answer if I ever heard one."

Wren glared at him and then stomped back to her trailer; Rascal trotted along behind her.

Wren watched a small dust devil dance across the field near the campground as she sat at the picnic table next to her camper.

She reached down and stroked Rascal's chin. "Did I just get into an argument with a ghost?"

A gust of wind blew off her cap.

"Okay, a stagecoach guard." Wren laughed as she dusted off her ball cap and jammed it onto her head.

"Let's go inside and put away our groceries, then check to see if our laundry is ready for the dryer, Rascal."

After they returned from the laundry room, Wren fed Rascal and pulled out the fried chicken she had bought. She wrapped it in foil, stood in front of the stove, and stared. "There's no oven, Rascal. I don't want mushy chicken, which is exactly what I'd get if I tried to warm it up in the microwave."

Wren sighed, warmed her dinner roll in the microwave, and ate her cold fried chicken, coleslaw, and roll.

She rinsed her plate and fork in the small sink and left them in the drainer to wash when she had more dirty dishes.

"The cold fried chicken wasn't bad, but it would have been better crispy. No oven is definitely complaint number one. I suppose I'll have to get a toaster oven or something like that if I want anything to be crispy or browned like the frozen biscuits I bought."

When they returned from the laundry room, Wren folded the bath, hand, and dish towels and then stared at the bed. "There's nowhere to stand next to the bed to make it. I'm going to have to climb onto the bed, tuck in the top of the fitted sheet, then climb off the bed and hope the elastic doesn't pop loose."

When she crawled onto the bed, she growled, "This bed is not just impossible to make; it's rock hard. A person would have to be exhausted every night to sleep."

After the bottom sheet was on the bed, she flipped the top sheet over it. "That was terrible; I'll fix it when I go to bed."

She exhaled. "That won't work; I'll need a blanket."

She slipped under the sheet and pulled it up; after she climbed out of bed, she threw the blanket on top of the sheet and groaned. "I should have done both of them at once. I'll wait to pull up the blanket."

She put the pillowcase on her new pillow and tossed it on the bed; it landed in the middle. "At least that worked, and I have my next two issues to report."

She set up her laptop at the small dining table and typed the details of her three complaints.

"Charlie and his CEO don't need the details, but it felt good to get the frustration out of my system."

Rascal whined; Wren finished her last sentence, then rose from her seat and stretched. "There was an outlet next to the table right where I needed one: that's a bonus point for the manufacturer. I'll add the good features in a different section. We need a walk before it gets dark. I think more RVs and trailers pulled in; let's see what everybody else has." She clipped his leash onto his collar.

As they strolled to the office building, Wren gazed at the orange-streaked sky with reds so brilliant near the horizon that it looked on fire.

After she and Rascal were near the drive in front of the office, they went from one row to the next until they eventually came to the end of the row of trailers and RVs. Wren inhaled the sweetly distinct aroma of the sagebrush that surrounded the campground. *I love camping in new places.*

Most of their neighbors relaxed in camping chairs while enjoying a cold drink. Wren returned waves and greetings; Rascal grinned to the delight of his new fans.

After they were back inside their camper, Wren said, "Everybody had camping chairs that looked a lot more comfortable than sitting on a hard picnic bench; I'll add one to our shopping list, then we can sit outside and wave when people walk by too."

Wren made a pitcher of sweet tea and then opened her laptop to research stagecoach lines from El Paso to Tucson in the 1800s; after half an hour, she switched to researching the area's history.

Another hour later, she yawned and added western boots to her list before setting up her coffee maker for the morning.

Rascal stayed on the rag rug she had purchased impulsively because of the colors: red, turquoise, tan, and black.

"I'm glad you like our Arizona rug. I'll see you in the morning."

Chapter Two

Wren was shivering when she woke. *What time is it? I'm freezing.*

She reached for her phone in the dark and peered at it then blinked to focus her bleary eyes. *Five o'clock.* She wrapped the thin blanket around her then crawled to the edge of the bed. *This bed is still rock-hard, and my hip hurts.*

She squealed when she stepped onto the ice-cold floor, and Rascal gave a low growl then padded to her bed.

"I didn't turn on the heat before we went to sleep." She opened the cabinet next to her bed and rummaged around until she found a pair of socks. "I need slippers."

Wren turned off the air conditioner then turned on the furnace and the coffee maker before she quickly dressed. She put on her warmest coat before she and Rascal went outside. When she scanned the surrounding area, she noticed several campers with the lights on inside. The enticing aroma of bacon came from the old trailer that was the closest to her site; her stomach rumbled, and Rascal whined.

"Bacon smells good, doesn't it? I didn't pick up any at the grocery store yesterday; I'll add it to our list. Desert air must make me hungry."

She stared at the sky and the stars. *Still dark, but the horizon in the east looks dark blue.*

"How about a dog park visit?" she asked. Rascal vocalized his agreement with a joyful moan.

After she clipped on his leash, they went to the fenced-in dog park. When they were inside the area, Wren removed the leash, and Rascal raced around the park while Wren yawned then stretched.

She clicked the clip on the leash, and Rascal trotted to her. While Rascal ate his breakfast, Wren sipped her coffee and recorded her impressions of the campground. She rose from her seat and stood at the window to watch the pickup trucks as they left; the sunlight spread across the eastern horizon.

"I don't feel like mentioning Thomas, but I'm not sure why."

Wren refilled her cup then sat at her computer and stared at her last sentence. After she added the parade of trucks, she reread what she'd written so far.

She furrowed her brow. "The word haunted sounds spooky and ominous; Thomas is annoying, but he's not spooky. I'm glad we'll get to hear some local stories because I'd like to know what makes the campground haunted." She sighed. "We have half an hour before we leave; I'll take a quick shower here. I was too tired last night to bother, and I'm not interested in running back to the camper in the cold after taking a nice, warm shower."

Wren quickly undressed; she turned on the water and stepped into the small shower then shrieked as she jumped out. "The water is freezing!"

She waited a few minutes for it to warm up then stuck her hand under the water and quickly jerked her hand back. After she turned off the water, she glanced at the time and hurriedly dressed.

"If I can't figure out what's wrong with the water after we get back, I'll call the RV dealership service department."

Before Wren and Rascal left for breakfast, Wren's phone rang.

When she answered, her mother asked, "How's the camper? Do you love the truck?"

"The camper isn't bad, but the truck is great; it's absolutely perfect for pulling a camper of any size."

"I'm glad to hear that because I talked to Charlie right after he offered you the job, and the truck is yours. Are you surprised?"

"I really am, but you didn't..."

"Yes, we did. Your dad wanted you to have a comfortable, safe pickup of your own; he's such a worry wart sometimes. Anyway, he picked it out, and we paid for it with your inheritance. You can blame us for that after we're gone, and you're stuck with an ancient truck and no money."

"Thanks, Mom, and tell Dad I love it."

After she hung up, Wren said, "Did you hear that? The pickup is ours; I don't have to feel like we'd be stranded somewhere if the job goes sour for any reason; I wonder if that's really why Dad wanted us to have it. We'll have to ask him sometime."

When Wren drove her truck to the office, Betsy waved as she swept the front porch; Socorro motioned from her pickup for Wren to follow her.

As she turned onto the highway, Wren glanced at a sign facing the campground. *Must be one of those cute check your steps and antenna signs. I'll have to look at it later.*

The parking lot at the Watering Hole was full, so Socorro parked in the vacant lot next to the diner; Wren parked next to her.

"I'll leave the back windows down for you. It's too warm to run the heater but too cool to run the air conditioner," Wren said.

Rascal grinned then flopped on the back seat and closed his eyes.

As Socorro and Wren hurried to the diner, Wren asked, "Is it always this crowded during the week?"

Socorro nodded. "Year round. The earlier workers already left. It clears out fast, though, because a lot of the people who are here right now have to be at work by eight-thirty. We'll have a lull until nine." She chuckled. "We all have our assigned shifts. There will be a table in there for us because it's Tuesday, which is my regular day. Just stay as close as you can to me, or I'll be eating alone. The tourists show up around ten then leave glowing reviews about the food and how quiet the diner is."

When they went inside the diner, their ears were assaulted by loud voices and laughter. Socorro motioned for Wren to follow her then pushed her way past men who stood in the aisle with their cups of coffee while they talked to a table of friends. Wren stayed so close to Socorro that when Socorro stopped,

Wren bumped into her, and Socorro laughed then pointed at the empty table next to them.

After they sat, two empty cups appeared on their table out of the sea of bodies in the aisle, then a server stopped with a full pot of coffee and filled the cups. Socorro held up two fingers, and the server nodded. Wren turned to watch as the small woman disappeared in the crush of large men.

"Amazing," Wren mouthed.

Socorro nodded then motioned for Wren to watch the door. Almost as if someone had sounded a loud signal, men began pouring out of the diner, and the roar of truck engines rivaled the roar of the conversations.

After the trucks left and the noise had quieted down, Wren asked, "Why didn't we wait and come inside after they left?"

"Because the nine o'clock crowd is even larger," Socorro said. "We'll have plenty of time for our breakfast and to hear a few stories before we have to vacate."

Wren glanced around. "Is there a menu?"

"The menus don't come out until ten; I already ordered for you, anyway. Both of us are having a chorizo, egg, and cheese burrito for breakfast."

"That's exactly what I would have ordered." Wren rolled her eyes then cocked her head. "What's a chorizo?"

"Some say it's like hot pork sausage, but with more personality. Ready for a story?"

Wren nodded.

Socorro leaned across the aisle to talk to the four men who sat at the table closest to her. "My friend Wren is a journalist. She's writing an article about the Forgotten Oasis being haunted."

A man with a scruffy, gray beard cocked his head. "Is that right? You may not have heard the story..."

Another man at the table snorted, and the first man said, "I know you heard it different, but your version is wrong. Wren, the town of Hidden Gulch was originally settled right there on Socorro's campground property. The Forgotten Oasis has been haunted since a crooked, self-appointed town marshal from back east brought his thugs into Hidden Gulch and took over. He was making all the merchants pay what he called protection money, but it was downright extortion."

The second man shook his head, and the first man glared at him then continued, "The saloon keeper didn't want to pay, so the so-called marshal had him disappear sudden-like; the whole town knew the saloon keeper's body was somewhere out in the desert, so nobody else tried to buck the phony marshal. The saloon keeper's wife took over the saloon, and when the goons showed up for their protection money, she and her two girls ambushed them, then the widow marched into the marshal's office and shot him in the head with her shotgun. Done blew it off, but there was one thug who hadn't gone to the saloon because he was too hung over; he shot her in the back then left town as fast as he could. The name of the saloon was the Forgotten Oasis, and the widow never left because she's waiting for her husband to return."

"Yeah, well, nice story," the second man said, "but this is what really happened."

"You was an eyewitness, was you?" the first man sneered.

The second man drained his cup; the server refilled it then vanished.

I wonder if all the townsfolk are ghosts. Wren peered at Socorro. *Naw, not Socorro.*

"The Forgotten Oasis was an...establishment run by a lady who was tossed off a stagecoach outside of town. She walked straight to the town marshal's office and asked if there was a store that she could buy. The old hotel was up for sale because it was in rotten shape. The marshal was kind of sweet on the purdy lady, so he wouldn't let the hotel owner swindle her. She paid a fair price for the hotel considering the condition it was in; she fixed it up, then some girls she knew showed up, and she was open for business."

"Yep," the first man chuckled, "eyewitness."

"You're crass," the second man said.

The first man narrowed his eyes. "What did you call me?"

"Look it up in the dictionary. Some of the merchants in town began grumbling because her business was booming. Every single one of them claimed he was about to buy the hotel, but she snatched it away from him. One man tried to get his wife to rile up the church ladies, but she asked him how he knew what business the nice hotel lady had, and he shut up."

"Well, that's unbelievable," the first man said.

"You might think so, but the hotel lady had all her girls going to Bible study, so they could learn to read. You done interrupting?"

The first man put money on the table and left.

When Wren's eyes widened, Socorro whispered, "They take turns walking out on each other; they're brothers."

"It was all going good for the town and the hotel lady until a gang of outlaws decided she was easy pickings and tried to rob her. Twelve of them rode into town and ambushed her outside the church. What they didn't know was after the daily Bible study, the hotel lady took all her girls and the church ladies outside of town and taught them to shoot. There were sixteen sharpshooters in that church, and while the hotel lady lay on the ground mortally wounded, they came barreling out and cut down all twelve of the cowardly killers."

"I love this story," Socorro said.

Wren nodded.

"The outlaw leader thought he'd gotten away, but the church ladies and all the girls swore they saw the hotel lady manage to get herself on a horse and ride after him. Two days later, they found him alongside the road dead with a bullet right between his eyes. They never found the hotel lady or her body. Some say the church ladies and the girls secretly buried her in the church cemetery, but others say they saw her in an upstairs window at the Forgotten Oasis while she made sure her girls and the church ladies were safe."

"I always enjoy the stories." Socorro rose. "I've got shopping to do."

"I appreciate the help." Wren snatched up their ticket from the table then hurried after Socorro.

"Expense account," Wren said as she paid their bill.

"Then that's okay."

On their way to their trucks, Socorro asked, "Did you have any shopping to do?"

Wren showed her list to Socorro.

"We go right past a hardware store that has boots, and they have a decent supply of camping equipment too; I don't know about the toaster oven, but the grocery store might have a couple of models stuck on a shelf. In the old days, our grocery store would have been called a general store. We can stop at the hardware store first, then you can follow me to the grocery store."

"You don't have to..."

"Stop right there; you'll see why I love any excuse to go to the hardware store soon enough. I can't wait to see whether you're immune." Socorro laughed.

Wren furrowed her brow as she climbed into her truck and followed Socorro.

"We're going to the hardware store. Socorro hinted there's a hunky, charming guy at the hardware store that she has a crush on." Wren snorted. "I learned my lesson in college."

After Wren parked and opened the back door for Rascal, they followed Socorro into the store.

Rascal whined, and Wren laughed when three puppies wiggled their way to Rascal then rolled onto their backs while Rascal inspected them. After Rascal licked then nosed them, they jumped up and danced around him. Rascal beamed as he strutted toward Socorro with his trail of puppies who yipped and jockeyed for the closest position to Rascal.

A middle-aged man, who looked like he had played football in college but remained in shape over the years, came out from the back. His dark hair had a touch of gray around his temples, and his smile revealed deep dimples in his cheeks.

"Sheridan, this is Rascal, and he brought his friend, Wren, with him," Socorro said.

Sheridan showed Rascal the treat he had in his hand, and Rascal immediately sat.

When the puppies copied him, Sheridan chuckled. "Thank you, Rascal. It would have taken me two months to teach those scatterbrained pups to sit."

After Sheridan gave Rascal his treat, Rascal maintained his regal posture until all the puppies had their treats.

"You're the best, Rascal," Socorro said.

When Wren knelt, Rascal yipped, and the puppies scrambled to her; she rubbed bellies and giggled at the kisses.

After she rose, Sheridan wiped his hands on his once-white cobbler's apron before he offered his hand. "Welcome, Wren. What can I do for you today?"

Wren smiled as they shook hands. "I need western boots, a toaster oven for my camper, and probably other things I haven't thought about."

"Boots are on your right; you know to shake out your boots in case any scorpions crawled in, don't you?"

"I guess I do now."

Sheridan smiled. "The camping equipment is in the back left corner. I have a few small electric appliances next to the camping equipment, so see if there's anything that would work for you. Look around, take all the time you need, and holler if you have any questions or need any help. I don't have any shopping carts, so stack what you find on the counter. The pups and I will be in the back while I shelve my latest shipment that came in this morning." Rascal followed Sheridan; the puppies followed Rascal.

"I think Rascal has a promising future in puppy training; I guess you can't resist puppies either." Socorro smiled.

"He's always been laid back unless another dog is aggressive," Wren said.

"I'm the same way; my bite is far worse than my bark," Socorro said. "Butch gave me a list of a few things he needs for repairs, so I won't hover unless you need my help. Do you have a cooler in your truck? You might want a medium-sized one for your groceries. When you're looking at boots, I've found the round-toed boots are more comfortable for day-to-day wear."

Socorro pointed to her boots, and Wren examined them then nodded. *I wouldn't have thought of that.*

Wren stared at the different styles and prices of boots. *The pointed-toe boots look more authentic, the squared-off toes look more elegant, and the round-toed boots look like work boots.*

She searched for her size and tried on the right boot of each style; after she returned the pointed- and square-toed boots to their boxes, Wren stepped into the round-toed pair and walked to the front then returned to the boot aisle. After she put on her shoes and reboxed the boots, Wren selected a red bandana from a display then carried the box and the bandana to the counter before she strolled to the back corner.

Next, a camping chair. Wren picked out a red canvas chair then stared at the shelf.

What if Socorro stops by? She picked out a blue one then added them to her boots and bandana at the counter before she searched for the small electronics section that Sheridan had mentioned.

While she examined a combination air fryer and oven that was a little larger than what she originally had in mind, a bell jingled. *Sheridan has a bell on his door.*

Sheridan, Rascal, and the puppies hurried past her aisle as she studied the paperwork that was inside the oven.

"What are you doing here?" Socorro's voice was loud, and her tone was hard.

Wren raised her eyebrows. *Whoever that is, Socorro's not a fan.*

"Just saw your truck, sweet thing, and was surprised it's still running. Times must be hard if you can't afford one that's reliable. I'd be derelict in my duties as your long-lost husband if I didn't help you out with that; I will if you'll be nice to me," a man said.

Wren frowned. *What a sarcastic tone.*

"Get out of my store, Jeff," Sheridan roared.

When Rascal growled, Wren hurried toward the front.

The man's voice became shrill. "What are you doing with a vicious dog in your shop, Sheridan? Call him off."

Rascal growled even more menacingly then snarled, and the front bell jingled.

"Well done, Rascal; you saved me the trouble of pounding that smug look away from his face," Sheridan said as Wren reached the front.

He gave treats to Rascal and the puppies who posed next to Rascal in a puppy version of a threatening stance.

Sheridan praised the puppies while Socorro hugged Rascal. "Good boy."

After Wren and Socorro paid for their items, Sheridan helped carry their purchases out to their trucks.

"Thanks, honey." Socorro kissed Sheridan.

Ah ha! I was right about the hunky man at the hardware store.

"Aw shucks, ma'am." Sheridan smiled as he hugged Socorro. "It was nice to meet you, Wren."

"You too," Wren said.

After Sheridan went back inside, Wren asked, "Who was the man that Rascal wanted out of the store?"

Socorro snorted. "Jeff, my ex-husband; I thought he was still in California. I can't imagine why he'd come back here, but he can't leave Hidden Gulch, or Arizona, for that matter, soon enough to suit me. Follow me to the grocery store; I have my regular weekly shopping list, but I'll pick up only the necessities this time to cut my trip short. I don't want that lowlife to show up at the campground when I'm not there and get my guests all riled up. Will you be okay getting back to the campground by yourself?"

Wren raised her eyebrows, and Socorro's cheeks reddened.

"Sorry, I guess I'm more rattled than I realized; you and Rascal just drove here from Phoenix. That was a real goofy comment, wasn't it?"

Wren wrinkled her nose and sniffed in disdain. "Pretty much."

Socorro laughed. "I deserved that; let's get moving."

After Wren found all of the items on her list at the grocery store except for sweet tea, she checked the selection of premade teas that were refrigerated in the produce section. *No sweet tea. I'll check the aisle that has bottled water and sodas.*

While she searched for bottles of sweet tea in the section next to the bottles of water, a woman said, "I'm so glad I ran into you, Wren."

I don't think I'll ever get used to everyone knowing who I am. Wren rolled her eyes then turned toward the woman and smiled.

The gray-haired woman had inadvertently blocked the aisle when she stopped her shopping cart next to Wren's. "My friends and I have been worried about whether anyone has told you to carry a few bottles of water in your car. If you ever break down on the road between here and the campground, it's very important to have water for Rascal and maybe a few extra treats, so he doesn't become nervous."

"Thank you," Wren said.

When the woman remained next to her, Wren put six bottles of water into her cart.

The woman beamed as she continued pushing her cart past Wren.

"I think I'll give up on sweet tea and pick up some lemonade," Wren muttered and hurried to the dog food aisle for treats in case someone inspected her cart before she checked out with the cashier.

After Wren finished her grocery shopping, she rolled her cart out to her truck and dropped the bag of ice she'd bought into her new cooler.

While she loaded the items that needed refrigeration into the cooler, Rascal growled a soft, throaty growl. She glanced up and saw Socorro's truck, waiting for traffic to clear, so she could turn onto the road; then she saw the car two vehicles behind Socorro that had Rascal's attention: its lone occupant was a man with light brown, thinning hair with a balding circle on the back of his head, a thick neck, and wide shoulders. Wren tossed the rest of the grocery sacks into her truck then hopped in and pulled up behind the man's car. While Socorro waited for the traffic to clear, Wren took advantage of sitting in the line behind her and snapped a photo of the unknown car's license. After the car that was in front of her turned in the same direction that Socorro did, Wren followed them.

"So far, it looks like we're all going back to the campground, Rascal."

When Socorro signaled her turn and slowed, the car behind her slowed; after Socorro turned at the road that led to the office, the car resumed its speed.

Wren put on her turn signal and slowed to turn then furrowed her brow as she stared at the car. "Should I follow it, Rascal?"

When the car disappeared over the rise in the road, Wren completed her turn to the campground then headed to her camper.

After she carried the groceries inside and put them away, she narrowed her eyes as she stared out the window. "I'd say it was just a coincidence that a car was going past the campground, but you alerted to the driver." She sighed. "I'm confused; let's go for a walk, then we can sit outside and relax like we're camping on a normal vacation in Arizona."

Wren poured lemonade into a glass then carried her lemonade, a dry dishcloth, and Rascal's leash outside. She put the dishcloth over her glass while she pulled out the camp chair that she'd stored in the outside camper bin.

She set up her chair next to the picnic table where she'd set her lemonade. After Wren removed the cloth, she and Rascal watched the parade of trucks as they turned at the campground; Wren sipped her cool, refreshing drink then covered her glass after she put it back on the table close to her.

"I'll be right back."

Wren dashed into the trailer and grabbed her three-ring binder then returned to her chair.

"Reading is relaxing; I'll read the hints to see if there is anything I forgot; maybe I'll find something on the hot water heater."

After Wren quickly scanned the page, she said, "Nope; not a thing, but maybe I read too fast. I'll go slower next time."

Wren closed the binder and listened to a mockingbird as it rattled off nonstop one tune after another.

Wren smiled. "That poor guy sounds frantic, but maybe he's actually planning ahead for spring."

Wren sipped her cold drink and waved away the gnats that plagued her.

"Next time we go for a walk, Rascal, we need to see how other people keep away these persistent pests."

She lifted her glass for another sip, but two gnats were back-stroking in her lemonade. She poured out the lemonade and gnats on the ground then set her glass upside down on the table.

Socorro cruised along in her electric utility vehicle in the row next to Wren's. When Socorro stopped at a recently vacated spot and tossed the trash sack into her cargo area, she waved.

Socorro stopped her electric cart in front of Wren's camper; when Rascal trotted to the cart then politely sat, she gave him a treat. "I've been tidying up for our evening arrivals. Do you have plans for supper? Sheridan's brother from Sedona showed up unexpectedly at the hardware store, so I took out two batches of tamales from my freezer."

"I'm not sure I've ever eaten tamales, but I'm always willing to try new food, especially anything homemade; where's Sedona?"

"You'll love them; Sedona is about three hundred miles north of here."

"Can I help with anything?"

"You sure can; come over whenever you're ready, and I'll put you to work." Socorro sped away.

After Wren and Rascal went into the camper, Wren rinsed her glass then stared at the binder.

"Okay, water heater, it's you or me." She opened the binder and found the page with the information on how to troubleshoot the heater.

She read the first line. "This is embarrassing, Rascal; step one is to turn it on; step two is to wait up to thirty minutes to give the water time to heat."

After she flipped the switch for the water heater, she read the rest of the page then turned to the first page in the binder that had a picture of the control panel with all the switches labeled.

She read the details about all the control panel switches before she left the binder on the table and enjoyed her hot shower.

After Wren dressed, she and Rascal strolled to Socorro's house. "I'm glad I didn't send my report yet; there isn't a control panel for the bed, so I'm safe there."

Socorro met them at the door. "Good, you're just in time to help me decide on dessert. I have peach ice cream and fresh blueberries, but my pie crust skills are zilch. I have a great cobbler recipe unless you have that rare talent of making tender pie crusts."

"I don't at all." Wren chuckled.

"Care to tackle my cobbler recipe? I put a pork shoulder in my slow cooker early this morning; I had planned to freeze it, but I'll make pozole verde; I have everything ready to throw into my pozole verde except I have to roast the poblanos."

"Poblanos are a type of chile pepper, right? What is pozole verde?" Wren asked.

"It's a Mexican stew of pork, spices, chiles, and hominy. Verde means green, which means I'm using green chiles. It's really easy to make; I'll give you the recipe."

While Wren stirred the blueberries on the stove, Socorro said, "I learned how to make pozole from watching my abuela; she was a talented cook and loved to feed people. My mama said you could give Abuela five dollars, and she would prepare a feast for twenty people."

"My grandma was a great cook too, but my mom, not so much. Mom told me she was intimidated by her mother's skills in the kitchen. Dad told me not to be afraid to try something new because everyone starts as a beginner."

"Wise man. Where is your family?"

"Georgia."

"My family is scattered across Mexico, Arizona, and Texas."

While they worked and chatted, Rascal rose from his nap and trotted to the back door then quietly growled.

"What is it, Rascal?" Socorro asked.

When Rascal barked, Wren said, "We'll check."

After they were outside, Rascal's hackles rose as he alerted to the desert behind Socorro's house.

Wren spotted a rabbit ten yards away on its haunches as it stared at Rascal. "It's a jackrabbit; let's go inside."

The rabbit leapt into the brush and disappeared, but Rascal maintained his stance between Wren and the desert.

Wren opened the back door. "Come on, boy."

Rascal glanced over his shoulder at her then slowly padded into the house.

"What was it?" Socorro asked.

"I saw a rabbit, but there may have been a coyote or another predator stalking the rabbit because Rascal's hackles went up, and he didn't budge after the rabbit left until I made him come inside."

"Good boy, Rascal." Socorro gave Rascal a treat.

When Rascal grinned, Wren shook her head. "You two are bad influences on each other."

While the pozole simmered, and the cobbler cooled, Socorro's phone buzzed.

Socorro glanced at her phone. "Betsy needs me at the office. Want to go with me? You too, Rascal."

"Let's go." Wren picked up Rascal's leash. "It's just for show."

Rascal trotted alongside Wren while the three of them hurried to the office where a man and woman stood in front of a large RV.

"We're a week early, but we were so excited to see the campground we cut our trip in the Colorado Rockies short, so we could come here right away," the woman said.

The man sniffed then raised an eyebrow as he scanned the campground. "We don't have reservations, but from the looks of things, that doesn't seem to be a problem."

"The landscape is really authentic, isn't it?" The woman peered at the rocks at the side of the building then stared at the cactus and the dog bowl near the office door. "I'm sure your decorator had something in mind, but that cactus would give a more aesthetically balanced look if you moved it closer to the window, and the rocks should be distributed to give the illusion of pointing to the entrance; that dog thing is really an eyesore, isn't it?"

"Let's go inside and get you registered." Socorro led the couple into the building while Wren and Rascal waited near the door.

When the man and woman came out of the building, the woman whispered to her spouse, "Edrick, we were not supposed to say anything about her husband; he told us it was a surprise."

"I politely asked when she expected her husband, Audrey," he grumbled. "What was wrong with that?"

"That must be part of the surprise; honestly, you're hopeless." The couple climbed into their RV.

Socorro came out of the office and locked the building behind her.

"I told Betsy that she and Butch didn't need to stay late. I'll show our new arrivals to their site and meet you back at the house. Give the pozole a stir, would you?"

Wren watched as the bus-sized RV with its towed vehicle lumbered behind Socorro as she escorted them to their site. *They must be full-timers.*

After Socorro returned to her house, she joined Wren and Rascal in the kitchen. "I don't think they'll be here the entire two weeks because they're obviously supposed to meet with the owner of a campground somewhere to talk about buying it or going into partnership. The man wanted to know when my husband would be here; when I told them I didn't have a husband, the woman tried to shush him, and he laughed like I was joking."

"I know I said I'd help you, but don't ask me to pick up the cactus and move it. However, if you want me to toss them out over that dog comment, I'd love to be your bouncer." Wren grinned.

Socorro shook her head. "That was totally a shocker, wasn't it? They're lucky I'm immune to snide comments. She wanted to know if we allowed dogs inside the office. When I told her only our security dog, she informed me that Dobermans don't shed, which is why she hadn't broken out into a life-threatening rash. What a piece of work."

"There's dog hair all over the office, and Betsy just swept," Wren said.

"I know; it was hard not to laugh when she walked past one of our dust bunnies from dog hair, and it swirled like a tiny fairy dust devil. They definitely weren't our usual drop-in; our late arrivals normally are here much later at night; they pick a site and pay online or put their money in the envelope we provide and drop it in the slot."

"How do you keep people from sneaking in, staying overnight, then leaving before daylight?"

Socorro shrugged. "I suppose they could, and we've never had that happen in the fifteen years I've been here, but..."

"You wanted to be prepared," Wren said. "I saw the sign when we left the campground."

Here comes the real story of the warning sign.

Socorro's cheeks dimpled when she grinned. "I planned to put in spike strips, but the marshal told me someone's tires may not deflate quickly enough to keep them from driving away and crashing into someone else, so I told him I'd buy a fancy security system instead that takes photos of the driver and the license plate and sends them to his office; my warning sign states very clearly that the driver will be charged with defrauding an innkeeper. The marshal told me not to waste my money and refused to allow me to send photos by some new-fangled computer system to his office. He might have said overpriced and underperforming, so I'm interpreting what he really meant."

"His department's computer system probably isn't capable of processing photos," Wren said.

"Maybe, but he should have admitted it. He insisted I was seriously mistaken about the charges, and they didn't belong on the sign, but he didn't tell me to take it down."

I giggled. "I'm fairly certain the penalty for defrauding an innkeeper involves the stocks in the middle of the town square."

"Exactly." Socorro grinned.

Wren raised her eyebrows at the sound of a car engine followed by the crunch of tires on the sand. "A vehicle just parked in front of your house."

Chapter Three

Socorro smiled. "That better be Sheridan because I'm ready for a beer with tamales and pozole; if it's a trespasser, he's all yours."

Sheridan strode into the house. "Hi, honey, I'm not home!"

Socorro and Wren laughed.

Sheridan grinned as he stood in the doorway with a large grocery sack in his hand. "Hi, Wren. Sweetie, I brought extra beer. Cody will be here in a minute; how's a boy, Rascal?"

Socorro took the sack as Rascal wiggled to Sheridan and was rewarded with a massage of both ears.

When another car stopped at Socorro's house, Rascal gave a low growl.

"It's just Cody, Rascal." Sheridan stroked Rascal's back. "Socorro, he's just in time for a beer and your world-famous pozole."

"And tamales," Socorro said as her front door opened.

"Did I hear tamales?" a slender young man wearing tortoiseshell glasses strode into the kitchen with a small grocery sack in his hand. "Dump that loser, Socorro, and marry me."

"Did you bring one lone beer for all of us to split?" Socorro laughed. "Cody, this is my friend, Wren."

"I brought avocados; I'll make the guacamole. Hey, Wren, are you going to be the bridesmaid at our wedding?"

Cody knelt and stroked Rascal's neck as Rascal leaned against Sheridan.

"I was kind of holding out for flower girl." Wren smiled.

Socorro laughed. "Open four beers, honey, while we watch the smooth-talking guacamole master do his magic, then I'll dish up the pozole and pull out the tamales from the oven."

While they ate, Wren smiled as she listened to the banter and watched the frequent looks with growing smiles that Socorro and Sheridan exchanged.

When Socorro served the still-warm blueberry cobbler with the peach ice cream that slowly melted as they ate, Sheridan asked, "What brought you this way, Cody?"

"I represented the firm at a meeting in El Paso yesterday; the topic was how to recruit young lawyers, and I was their token young lawyer. It was a total waste of time because they don't want to recruit young lawyers; they want to be the young lawyers."

"Did you tell those well-established, middle-aged lawyers that their years of being the young ones were behind them?" Socorro asked.

"Not me, I'm a chicken. I'm sorry that you weren't there because I would have loved to have seen their reaction."

Sheridan cleared his throat. "Socorro, can I help with anything around the campground?"

Socorro glanced at Wren, who smiled.

"Sure, let's go for a ride to see if everyone's settled."

"Perfect." Sheridan rose from his seat. After Socorro left the room, he winked then followed her.

"Sheridan obviously wanted to talk to Socorro privately, so why didn't he say so? What on earth is going on?" Wren asked. "I am totally lost."

"Your flower girl comment was absolutely perfect; you'll have to decide on your outfit because my brother set this up. He knows how much Socorro loves drama, so that's what she got."

Wren laughed. "Won't Socorro be mad when she figures all this out?"

"She'll love it," Cody said.

"Tell me about you," Wren said.

"Sheridan told me you're a journalist; if I tell you about me, will I appear in your article?"

Wren shrugged to hide her smile. "Do you want to?"

"Depends on how dashing I appear; do I save the flower girl from the dragon?"

Wren rose to clear the table. "Sadly, I don't write fiction, but that sounds like a great story if I did."

While Cody wrapped then put the leftovers into the refrigerator, Wren ran hot water into the sink; she washed and rinsed the dishes before she submerged the slow cooker insert into the soapy water.

"How long have you known Socorro?" Cody asked as he dried the dishes.

"All day." Wren scrubbed and rinsed the ceramic insert and the rest of the pots.

"That's surprising because you two are definitely kindred spirits." Cody shook his head. "Another beer? One's my limit because I'm driving later."

"No, I'm fine."

After they sat at the table, Cody told her about his struggles with his life values and goals that conflicted with the day-to-day operations at a corporate law office. Wren talked about trying to establish her career as a journalist with a mother who was a highly regarded activist and politician and a father who was a successful lawyer.

Cody nodded. "A wise philosopher once said, 'If it's too hard to float upstream, grab an oar.'"

Wren laughed. "Exactly; that's how I feel sometimes. Who was the wise philosopher? You?"

Cody smiled, and his brown eyes twinkled as Sheridan and Socorro came into the house.

"Well, flower girl, we might have an opening for you, after all," Socorro said while Sheridan beamed.

Wren gasped as she threw up her hands to her face and raised her eyebrows. "Come on, y'all. Don't make me hold this pose."

Socorro laughed, and Sheridan blushed.

"You win; sorry, Cody, Sheridan and I are going to be married," Socorro said.

"No, I win," Cody said. "I'm gaining an intelligent, beautiful sister-in-law, and my brother is marrying up, so maybe he wins too."

"I'm the grand winner; I'm the flower girl," Wren said. "I'll share the grand winner title with you, Socorro, since you're going to be the bride."

After toasts with iced tea, Wren said, "I can't remember ever having a day that was this wonderful, but I'm still on east coast time, and I'm fading. Thank you for everything, Socorro."

As she and Rascal headed toward the door, Cody said, "I'll walk with you."

On the way, Cody said, "This was the most relaxed I've felt in ages."

"I haven't enjoyed being around people," Wren said. "Now, I think I was around the wrong people."

"What are your plans?"

"I'm here for a week or two, then I submit my article about the haunted campground in Arizona and go on to the next campground."

"Do you have enough information to write your article?" Cody asked.

"Not really."

"Good; then maybe I'll pop in this weekend for a status report."

Wren chuckled. "It wouldn't hurt for me to have a little accountability to keep me motivated."

Cody smiled then left.

After Wren and Rascal were inside the trailer, she locked the door.

"I am exhausted." Wren turned on the heat then hurried to get ready for bed before she collapsed; she fell asleep immediately.

Chapter Four

Wren woke an hour before daylight; while her coffee maker gurgled, she and Rascal went outside and were greeted by the shock of the crisp desert air.

Wren shivered while Rascal investigated the area by the bright moonlight. "Hurry up, Rascal; I forgot to put on my coat, and I'm freezing."

After they went inside the camper, Wren fed Rascal. While she sipped her coffee, she searched for the history of the Forgotten Oasis but didn't find anything, so she checked the hours of the local library.

"The library is open from ten until two, Tuesday through Saturday."

Wren read through her meager notes she had taken on her tablet. *I need to document the two stories from yesterday in more detail.* She turned on her laptop.

After an hour, she stretched and rose from the small dining table. "Let's watch the sun rise while we walk around the edge of the campground. I've got a great pair of binoculars; I'd like to scan the surrounding desert."

They began their walk next to Socorro's house. After a few yards, Rascal stopped and softly growled as he faced the desert.

Wren looked in the direction he was pointing and raised her binoculars. When she saw a flash in the field as the sun rose, she adjusted her binoculars.

"I thought I saw something, but I don't see it now." She didn't move or lower her field glasses as she waited then saw the flash again. "I can't tell what it is; it's most likely a piece of broken glass that's catching the sun just right."

They continued their walk until they reached the old structure; Wren stopped and gazed at the building while Rascal inspected the surrounding grounds for a rabbit.

"Whatcha looking at, girl?" Thomas asked.

"I was just wondering: are you still working at keeping the lady safe?"

"Course, I am; I ain't no slacker."

"Is she in danger?"

Thomas snorted. "Why would I need to keep her safe if she weren't? 'Bout the time I think that outlaw is gone, he comes back again."

"How can I help?" Wren squinted then shaded her eyes from the brightness of the rising sun with her forearm.

"Ain't never had no help before, much less from a girl. Don't go gettin' mad; I gotta think."

"I'll let you think then."

Wren whistled for Rascal.

As she turned toward her camper, Thomas said, "You whistle right good for a girl."

Wren rolled her eyes. "Thanks, Thomas."

"Don't mention it."

Believe me, I won't.

After they went into the camper, Wren said, "I think I'll go into town to soak up some local culture before the library opens. Do you want to stay in the camper or with Miss Betsy?"

Rascal stuck his nose in the door.

Wren chuckled as she dropped her tablet into her backpack. "Miss Betsy, it is. Let's go to the office to see how busy she is this morning."

When they strolled into the office, Betsy smiled and put down her micro cloth she was using to dust the shelves.

"There's my boy; good morning, Rascal. Are you planning a trip into town anytime soon, Wren? Can Rascal keep me company?"

"That's exactly why we're here; are you sure he won't be in the way?"

Betsy snorted. "Absolutely not; he'll keep me from talking to myself. Our old dog died a few weeks ago, and I miss having canine companionship while I work. One of my friends wants to give us a puppy, but we're not ready yet; does that make sense?"

"It sure does; I'm sorry to hear about your old dog."

"Thank you, not everyone understands."

Rascal leaned against Betsy.

"We do," Wren said.

Betsy brushed away a tear. "I meant to remind you about our break room; it originally had a TV and board games, but the television broke, and most of the pieces of our few remaining board games are missing."

Betsy smiled weakly as she led Wren to the room and pointed. "It has a large window for observing new arrivals, a good reading lamp next to a comfortable chair, and a round table with fairly comfortable chairs where people used to play board games and cards. Nobody uses it, so it could be your private office."

"Thank you; I'll probably take advantage of it." Wren hugged Rascal before she left the office.

Wren sighed as she strolled back to her camper for the pickup. *Rascal can add rescue dog to his resume.*

Wren drove past the hardware store then parked near a coffee shop in the first block of the two blocks of downtown.

She ordered a medium-sized coffee and a cranberry-orange scone.

After the elderly man behind the counter rung up the sale then handed Wren her change, he said, "Second cup is free; come up to the counter and wave, and we'll give you a fresh cup." The man pointed. "You'll be more comfortable on that side."

Wren took her breakfast to one of the two round tables that was where the man had pointed. All four tables had four wooden chairs around them. A long, tall table stood parallel with the walls in the middle of the room; it had tall bar stools with black vinyl backs and seats on both sides of the table. *If I were going to be here very long, I'd opt for the soft seats.*

Wren watched as young mothers pushed in large strollers with tiny, sleeping babies, ordered a fancy cold coffee then left; earnest young men stood in a group, tossed down their coffee, and picked up their second cup then left; an older couple beelined to a table and set up their laptops as the man behind the counter spoke to someone in the kitchen; when the couple approached the register, the man handed them their coffee and cinnamon rolls.

Wren smiled as she glanced toward the register. *Thanks to the cashier, I didn't accidently sit at their table.*

The cashier glanced at Wren and winked as he returned her smile.

A large man with a badly sunburned face and arms came into the shop and bought a coffee then stood at the high table in the middle of the room close to Wren.

Wren pulled out her tablet and noticed the man scowled as he stared at her. She scrolled through her notes then twisted slightly in her seat and snapped a photo of the man with her tablet.

Wren furrowed her brow at the tablet as she set it on the table but watched the sunburned man in her periphery as he scanned the area around her. "Where's your dog?"

Everybody knows about Rascal. Wren narrowed her eyes. *He almost sounds like the man in the hardware store.*

When Wren tapped her tablet for the next page and didn't respond, he took a step closer to her and growled, "I asked you a question; you too good to talk to me? You better tell her to watch out."

Wren met his gaze with a glare. The older man at the table across the room rose from his chair as a young man in a khaki law enforcement uniform strode into the coffee shop; the large man left his coffee on the table and hurried out, and the older man resumed his seat while the older woman smiled and patted his hand.

Wren's eyes widened at the marshal's badge on the young man's shirt. *The marshal's much younger than I imagined when Socorro told me about her sign; he's not much older than me.*

The elderly man had a large coffee and a cinnamon roll waiting on the counter; when the marshal paid his bill, the man nodded toward Wren.

Wren felt her cheeks warm. *I wonder if Cody can get me out on bail.*

The marshal stopped at her table and smiled. "May I join you, Miss Weaver?"

"Please do and call me Wren."

"I'm Justin." They shook hands, and he sat next to Wren, facing the front door. "We're a small town, Wren; how's your story going?"

Is he softening me up? "Not as smoothly as I expected, but I'm just getting started."

"Do you have a Georgia carry permit?"

Wren raised her eyebrows and peered at him.

"Thought so; that's good. What's your plan for today?"

"I'm going to the library when they open; I'm hoping to find a book that talks about the early years of the Forgotten Oasis."

"Did you know one rumor has it that the original name of the saloon was Forbidden Oasis?"

"Nobody told me that."

"It's probably one of those things that everybody knows, isn't it?" Marshal chuckled. "Have you seen the structure at the back of the campground?"

The marshal peered at her face as she slowly nodded.

"You've seen him, haven't you?" the marshal asked.

Wren raised her eyebrows.

"No matter; not many have." He pushed back his chair.

"Have you?" Wren asked.

"I asked you first. Are you going to write about him?"

"I need more coffee; excuse me," Wren said.

"Keep your seat; I'll get it."

After the marshal set her fresh cup on the table, Wren said, "Yes; please sit."

"I've seen him, but that's all," the marshal said.

"I don't plan to write about him. His name is Thomas; he was a stagecoach guard. A man gave him a silver dollar to make sure the lady was safe. I don't know who the original lady was, but I think he's guarding Socorro."

"That makes so much sense to me; I wonder why you can hear him, and I can't."

"I don't know, but he's very annoying."

The marshal chuckled. "This is a very strange conversation that no one will ever hear from me, but I can tell you everyone knows about the Flower Girl."

Wren choked on her coffee.

"Bad timing; I'm so sorry," he said.

Wren caught her breath and glanced around the room at everyone who stared at her.

"I'm fine; my coffee just went down the wrong way," she said loudly.

Everyone sighed and resumed their conversations.

Wren smiled. "It was an impulsive comment that worked perfectly into Sheridan's scheme."

"Sheridan's a good man." The marshal shook his head. "I have an older sister who is just as headstrong as Socorro; Sheridan has a life of adventure ahead of him."

"Socorro told me the story about her warning sign."

He chuckled. "I don't think she realizes she was a marketing genius when she put that up. People in town tell me they see her sign all over social media."

"Are you from here?" Wren asked.

"No, I grew up in Flagstaff; I was a deputy in Maricopa County before I came here."

Wren nodded as she bit her lip. *I'll have to look up Maricopa County.*

"Phoenix is in Maricopa County." He chuckled. "I thought Flagstaff was a big city, but it's nothing like Phoenix; when an old friend of my dad told me he was retiring as marshal here, and Hidden Gulch was having a hard time finding anyone who was willing to come to a small town in the middle of the desert, I was happy to apply for the marshal's job with his blessing. What about you? Have you lived in Georgia all your life?"

Wren cocked her head as she peered at him. *How did he know where I'm from?*

"Everybody knows you're from Georgia, but your accent gives you away too."

"I don't hear my accent, but I guess nobody hears their own." Wren smiled. "This is the farthest I've ever been away from my hometown; I'm really excited about traveling and seeing more states."

"It's always good to broaden our horizons." The marshal rose. "Let me know if our friend Thomas needs my help. Good luck with your article; I think you'll find the library particularly helpful with the history of the area."

Before Wren finished her second cup of coffee, an elderly woman stopped at her table. "My friends and I were just talking about our marshal; we all agreed he's a nice young man and good-looking too."

The woman glanced around the shop then leaned close to Wren and whispered, "He's single."

Wren smiled as the woman left holding onto the arm of an elderly man.

I wonder if the marshal realized what a stir he caused when he sat at my table.

Wren slipped her tablet back into her backpack and rose; all heads in the room turned to watch her as she headed toward the door. *Don't trip.* She resisted the urge to wave as she strolled to her pickup.

When she pulled into the library parking lot, Wren rolled her eyes. *I could have walked here from the coffee shop except it's already too hot for much of a stroll.*

She went inside and was surprised at the buzz of conversations. *Sounds like everyone in town who wasn't in the coffee shop is here.*

"Excuse our noise," a frail woman with pale skin and wispy hair said as she moved a book from the front desk to a cart. "Today is book club day, and some of our discussions become quite heated although we don't allow fisticuffs. How can I help you with your research, Wren?"

Wren smiled. *Everybody knows, just like the marshal said.*

"Do you have any non-fiction books about the area around 1820?"

"I have two; one is better written than the other, but the second one has more facts. I also have a Western novel that was written by a local author in 1845. You might enjoy it because the author put in quite a bit of research to make the story as historically accurate as possible and based the novel on the stories told to her by the old-timers."

"That sounds interesting," Wren said.

"It's a little hard for some to read because of the out-of-date language, but others enjoy being immersed in the time period."

"Where will I find them?" Wren glanced toward the rows of books.

"You won't," the librarian smiled. "I pulled them for you first thing this morning and have all three right here. I've already checked them out to you. I also pulled together a folder for you with maps and other documents. We house all the original courthouse documents that are more than ten years old; I selected several that might be of interest and checked them out to you too."

The librarian put three books and a thick folder on the desk.

"I can't wait to read them; I just hope I don't get a speeding ticket on my way back to the campground."

The librarian grinned. "The marshal might stop you, but I don't think he'll give you a ticket."

Wren's cheeks burned as she put the three books and the folder into her backpack; she bit her lip to hold back the spreading warmth but was unsuccessful.

"Thank you."

"You're most welcome; keep them as long as you like and come back if you have any questions because not all the details of any time period are put in writing."

The librarian side-glanced the nearest book aisle then pulled out two books from the book return box and spoke loudly. "These are exactly like the books you mentioned, and they just came in."

Wren casually scanned the book aisle where two women tittered as they peeked around the corner.

"Nosy nellies," the librarian mumbled.

Wren raised her eyebrows as she stared at the two books. *Romance?*

The librarian smiled then continued speaking clearly enough for the onlookers to hear. "You're surprised a small-town library has them, aren't you? We take care of our readers. Enjoy!"

"I sure am; thank you."

As she headed toward the door, Wren held the two books against her chest, so anyone could see the titles and the covers that shouted, 'spicy romance novel.'

When she opened the door, the sunburned man quickly climbed into a car and sped away.

Did he follow me here? That's not the car that followed Socorro yesterday.

She returned to the desk. "These books are perfect; I found a new one that is similar."

Wren pulled up the photo of the sunburned man. "Do you have this?"

"That's Jeff Reed," the librarian whispered as she shook her head. "Be careful."

She furrowed her brow then tapped her pen on the desk. "I'll see if I can order it for you."

"Thanks, you're the best." Wren hurried to her truck.

She put the two romance books on the passenger's seat with her backpack on top of them then headed toward the campground.

Wren stopped at the office. Rascal opened his eyes then grinned and yipped.

Betsy carried out a box of holding tank chemicals from the storeroom. "Hey, Wren. Did you find what you needed?"

"I think so; the lady at the library had it ready for me."

Betsy chuckled. "I'm not surprised; everybody knows you and Rascal are here, but Miranda would have been busy setting aside material to help you with your research for your article about our haunted campground. People ask me all the time if I've ever seen a ghost around here; I hate to disappoint them, but I haven't."

Wren smiled at Betsy's wistful sigh.

"Ready to go?" Wren asked; Rascal trotted to the door.

After Wren set her backpack and romance books on the dining table, she and Rascal toured the campground then stopped at the dog park. While Rascal investigated every inch of the grounds, Wren watched a small dust devil dance on the desert. Rascal trotted to the gate, and the dust devil disappeared. "Time for me to go to work."

After they were inside, Wren refilled Rascal's water bowl. "I'll read the more factual book first and take notes as reference when I read the other two."

She pulled out the books and her tablet from her backpack and sat on the small sofa to read and take notes.

After two hours, she stretched. "I owe Charlie Hogue my feedback on the trailer."

After she typed the email on her computer, she read over what she'd written. "I told him about the bed and the oven. I like all the electrical outlets, so I can plug in all my electronics, and the camper was easy to pull and set up, and we like the size."

She sent the email. "Let's take a break, then I'll have lunch later."

They reversed their earlier walk: first the perimeter, then past the rows of RVs.

"We have the smallest camper here, but I haven't seen any families; did you notice, Rascal?" She smiled. "I feel like an experienced camper because we know how to travel light."

Rascal grinned.

Wren giggled. "I'm ignoring the whole water heater incident."

When they returned to their camper, Wren read and took notes until Rascal whined.

Wren's eyes widened when she glanced at the clock. "It's past lunchtime. I'll make a quick sandwich."

While Wren pulled out the fixings for her lunch from the refrigerator, she said, "After I eat, we'll take a short walk before it gets much hotter. Maybe I'll accept Betsy's offer to work in my new private office while you guard her. It wouldn't hurt either one of us to have a little change of scenery."

Wren ate her sandwich then checked her email. *I have an email from Charlie.*

She narrowed her eyes as she read.

"Rascal, Charlie said his editor found a few typos in my email and corrected them then asked Charlie to return the edited email to me, so I wouldn't make the same mistakes again. Can you believe the nerve of that chump?"

She slammed her laptop shut. "I sent an informational email, not a document to be published, and why was the editor even reading it? I'd love to have a few choice words with that arrogant snoop...let's go for a walk before I get any hotter. I'll reply to Charlie later, maybe tomorrow."

Wren dropped her book and her tablet into her backpack, then the two of them headed toward the dog park.

As they neared the dog park, a small dog that was inside the fence spotted Rascal and began snarling and barking. Wren whispered, "I was so irate, I forgot your leash. Let's go to the office and see Betsy; you can get a treat, and I'll buy some ice cream to cool me down."

When they walked into the cool campground office, Betsy hurried around the desk with a treat in her hand. As Rascal sat, she gave it to him. "Are you going to stay a while? I cleaned your office."

"We thought we would if we won't be in the way. I need ice cream."

"The ice cream truck comes by here every Wednesday and Saturday mornings, so we have excellent choices. My favorite is the chocolate and peanut covered vanilla ice cream bar."

Wren paid for her ice cream bar then carried it and her backpack into the game room. While she ate her ice cream and read, the campground phone rang.

"It's a wonderful day at our Forgotten Oasis Campground, how can I help you?" Betsy asked then listened.

Wren glanced at Betsy.

"Why don't you ask her yourself?" Betsy asked.

She looked at Wren and rolled her eyes. "If I don't forget, I'll mention it to her if I see her. Why can't I just give her..."

Betsy stared at the phone. "He hung up on me." She shook her head. "You won't believe who just called."

"My obnoxious editor?" Wren asked.

"What? No, but I want to hear about your editor. It was Sheridan; he said Cody wanted Sheridan to ask me to ask you if it would be okay if I gave Sheridan your phone number. I assume for Cody; those two must be twelve years old." Betsy giggled. "Sheridan was really embarrassed; he couldn't get off the phone fast enough after he delivered the message."

Wren smiled. "Do you have Cody's number? Why don't I get you out of the middle and send him a text?"

"I might." Betsy pulled out her phone and frowned. "No, I don't have it, but I'll steal your idea. I'll send Sheridan a text and offer to get him out of the middle of this. He'll be happy to send me Cody's number."

Immediately after Betsy sent a text, her phone chimed, and she chuckled. "This is wonderful; Sheridan says he owes me. Ready for Cody's number?"

Wren picked up her phone. "Go."

After Wren tapped in the number, she tapped a text. "How does this sound?"

Wren read the text aloud. "'Betsy suggested I text you, so you'd have my number.'"

"That doesn't sound at all like you," Betsy said.

"You're right." Wren erased the first text then added another. "Is this better? 'Why did you want my number? Wren.'"

Betsy laughed. "Perfect; send it."

After she sent the text, Wren grinned. "Maybe he's in a meeting."

"We can certainly hope, can't we?"

Socorro came into the building while the two of them were still chuckling. "I'm sure you two are up to no good. Clue me in."

Betsy told her about Sheridan's call and Wren's text.

Socorro laughed. "I can't wait to hear how Cody responds."

"Where have you been?" Betsy asked. "You've been gone longer that you usually are."

"I had a meeting with my lawyer, the county assessor, and a general contractor to discuss an offer I received to go with a nationwide franchise. We decided against it. I'm not sure we're really ready to deal with the stress of construction, more sites, and hiring extra people. I think we're fine as we are."

"The county assessor? What was she doing there? That took you most of the morning and half of the afternoon to figure that out?" Betsy narrowed her eyes.

"Sure; the general contractor bought lunch."

A crew cab truck pulling a long fifth wheel trailer stopped in front of the building; two dogs stood at the half-lowered window in the back while the short, spry, gray-haired woman hopped out of the truck and headed toward the office, and the tall, gray-haired driver strode around the truck to join her.

Betsy hurried to the door to greet the new arrivals; Rascal followed Wren and Socorro to the game room.

"Where were you, really?" Wren asked.

Chapter Five

Socorro rolled her eyes. "What makes you so smart? Sheridan and I applied for our marriage license before he had to open the hardware store, then I scooted to Tucson to find a wedding dress."

"What did you get?"

Socorro snorted. "Mostly irritated; everything was too frilly and too much cleavage for me. I looked like a dance hall girl except none of them were red with red feathers: that might have been okay, but I'd have to wear a T-shirt under any of those dresses. I stopped at a western wear store on a whim and found the perfect shirt, a long, suede skirt, and new boots; the shirt has pearl buttons and lace trim, which makes it kind of frilly, but it doesn't have the cleavage issue, so I like it."

"Sounds perfect; when's the wedding?"

"We're planning on Saturday, ten days from today, but we don't know what time yet. Sheridan wants Cody here to be his best man, which reminds me, we have to find something for the flower girl to wear."

Wren's eyes widened. "I'm not in the wedding; I was just giving Cody a smarty-mouth answer."

"I know, but everybody in Hidden Gulch knows you're the flower girl," Socorro said.

"I don't get it," Wren said.

"Betsy should be my matron of honor, but she won't leave the office unattended. We could put up our overnight sign for people to pick their own site and leave their money, but she would want to stay close. I don't really know anybody except Sheridan, Cody, Betsy, my lawyer, and you."

"So, you're getting married at your haunted campground. Does that mean I'm standing in for the saloon keeper?"

"Will you be the flower girl if I say yes?"

Wren sighed. "I'll be the flower girl but no red feathers."

She examined Socorro's face. "Is the wedding ceremony going to be near the old building in back?"

"How did you know?" Socorro asked.

"I don't know, but it's the right thing to do. Who else will be here? A preacher?"

"I'm going to talk to the Catholic priest from town; Sheridan will invite the marshal and a few other of his friends."

"The marshal? Why would Justin be here?"

"Sheridan, Justin's father, and our recently retired marshal are old Army buddies in spite of the differences in their ages. Don't ask Sheridan about his Army days because he has stories, or better yet, do ask him, and you'll be here for months." Socorro smirked as she headed toward the door. "We'll go to Tucson to find you a flower girl dress or shirt."

"I don't think I really need anything special."

"What? It's my wedding; my flower girl has to wear something special."

Wren exhaled. "When can I see your wedding shirt and skirt?"

"Why don't you come for supper? Don't tell me you have other plans; I have lots of leftovers. After we eat tonight, I'll freeze the rest."

"Sounds good."

Socorro paused at the doorway. "What have you been doing all day?"

"Diving into history." Wren turned to her book and tablet.

"Better you than me." Socorro waved.

"The hardest part about research is getting back into it," Wren mumbled.

"Socorro, Butch went into town to get some supplies. The electrical went out on site number 42, and we'll be close to capacity this weekend," Betsy said.

"I'll swing out that way then pick up any trash," Socorro hurried out the back door.

Wren's phone buzzed a text. Wren picked up her phone and read.

"Fifth."

Wren laughed, and Betsy hustled into the room.

"Did we hear back from Cody?"

"We sure did." She handed her phone to Betsy.

Betsy stared at the phone. "I don't get it."

"He's a lawyer, and he pleaded the fifth amendment; you know, the right to remain silent, so he won't incriminate himself."

"Okay, that's funny, right?"

"It's absolutely hilarious except he's busted because it took him so long to think of something to say."

"Maybe he was in a meeting."

"Nope; we got him, Betsy."

"Ah. Are we going to reply?"

"Maybe, but we'll wait a while, but not as long as he did, to build the suspense."

"We like him, right? This is fun." Betsy smiled as she returned to the desk to answer the phone.

"It's a glorious day at our Forgotten Oasis Campground; how can I help you?" Betsy asked then listened.

"No, he isn't. I'm sorry, but I don't have any idea where he is. Ms. Socorro is out of the office; if you'll leave your number, she'll return your call."

Betsy's voice cracked. "You don't understand; I have no way to know."

Wren rose from the table at the sound of rising panic in Betsy's voice. When she neared the desk, Betsy's eyes pleaded with her.

"Perhaps our assistant manager can help you."

Betsy put the phone on mute then whispered, "There's a man on the phone looking for Jeff; it's hard for me to understand him because his voice is muffled, but he's very insistent and got me flustered."

"I'll talk to him."

Betsy handed the phone to Wren.

"How can we help you?" Wren asked after she took the phone off mute.

"I'm Jeff's business partner. We planned to meet on Saturday at the campground, but I have a higher bidder and need to talk to Jeff right away before he accepts any deposits on a sale."

Wren raised her eyebrows. *In spite of that muffling, I can tell he has a southern accent; sounds like Virginia to me.* "We haven't seen him; does he know how to reach you? If we see him before Saturday, we can certainly tell him..."

"Do you have any idea where he might be?" the man asked.

"Our lone hotel and the few restaurants in Hidden Gulch might be a little meager for his tastes; most of the visitors to our area stay in Tucson if they aren't interested in camping or our quaint accommodations in town."

"He could be in Tucson, but I'll check with the hotel in town first. Thanks for your help; I appreciate it." The man hung up.

"That was awesome; how did you come up with all that?" Betsy asked.

"I wrote an article for a hotel chain on customer service and interviewed a lot of people and listened to a lot of desk clerk war stories. That guy was actually fairly pleasant, but he did sound a little stressed. I learned the trick is to be on their side without being condescending and never tell them what to do. Does that make sense?"

"I suppose, but it certainly isn't intuitive. The man's call didn't make any sense at all to me because Jeff never showed any signs of having any business or entrepreneur skills when he was married to Socorro. After the divorce, Socorro bought the campground with money she saved from waiting tables and her cleaning business and money her family gave her; as far as I know,

Jeff has never set foot on her campground, and I certainly don't see why he would."

"Has anyone approached Socorro before about selling the campground?"

Betsy snorted. "She gets offers in the mail all the time, but they're the trawling bottom feeders who are trying to find property for a super cheap price. I suppose they must occasionally hook desperate owners who are so ready to sell that they let their property go at a price that's a fraction of what it's worth. I certainly can't imagine why anyone would drive here for a cold call unless they're fanatics for old saloons."

Wren smiled. "You just gave me an idea for a text to Cody."

She tapped her phone then showed it to Betsy.

Betsy frowned. "Is that a question? 'Sour mash?' I don't get it."

Wren waited then giggled when Betsy snort-laughed.

After Betsy wiped her eyes, she said, "Saloon is what sent you on the path to a fifth of sour mash whiskey, isn't it? Send it. The entire string of texts is positively alive with twists of words and their meanings."

After she sent her text, Wren hurried back to the table and the factual book.

As she sat, her phone buzzed a text; Wren's eyes widened as she read it and returned to the desk.

"You're right about twists, Betsy, read this."

Wren put the phone on the counter, and Betsy read aloud. "Shyster yields to Wordmaster. Dinner Friday night?" The campground phone rang.

"Bad timing, phone," Betsy grumbled then answered cheerfully, "It's a fantabulous day at our Forgotten Oasis Campground, how can I help you?"

Betsy glanced at Wren and smirked. "Got it; Friday and Saturday nights. See you on Friday."

After Betsy disconnected, she reached down to scratch one of Rascal's ears as she giggled. "Rascal, you'll never guess. Cody has a reservation for one of our four camping cabins for Friday and Saturday nights, and I'm absolutely sworn to secrecy not to tell Wren, so I don't think you can either."

Wren laughed, and Betsy beamed.

Wren tapped on her phone then sent her text. "I told him 'absolutely' because you are absolutely sworn to secrecy. You don't know how tempting it was to add your place or mine, but I restrained myself. Maybe now we can all get some work done."

Betsy rolled her eyes. "I suppose, but it was still fun."

"I thought so too." Wren smiled as she returned to her reading and notes.

She was almost three quarters of the way through the book when Betsy tapped on the doorway.

"Wren, Socorro called and told me to remind you to come to her house in an hour. You've been so heads down that you must not have heard the phone ring."

"I guess I didn't." Wren moaned as she rose. "I'm stiff; I need a long walk. Thanks for everything, Betsy."

"You're most welcome; I enjoyed the afternoon."

Wren dropped her tablet and the book into her backpack. "Ready to go, Rascal?"

On the way to her camper, Wren said, "It's really hot, let's take our walk later when it's cooler."

The hot wind carried Thomas's faint voice from the back of the campground. "Hey, girl. You can help."

Wren and Rascal hurried to the old structure.

"Didn't know if you'd hear me," Thomas paced on the façade. "The library lady is hurt; I can't help her, but you can."

"Is she at the library?"

"Yes, and go fast. The man is setting a fire."

This doesn't make sense. "What man?"

"Just go, girl!" Thomas cried out.

The panic in his voice startled her; she raced back to her truck, and she and Rascal jumped inside.

As she sped toward Hidden Gulch, she said, "I don't know if I should call anyone until I get there to see what's wrong."

She slammed on her brakes when she arrived at the library and raced to the door. *Locked.* She sniffed then coughed. *I smell smoke.*

Rascal raced to the far corner of the building and barked at the fingers of dark smoke that seeped out of the eaves. Wren pulled her multitool out of her backpack and smashed a window, then while she dialed nine-one-one, she used her backpack to clear the glass away from the sill.

"Fire at the library," she said when the dispatcher answered.

"Fire department and the marshal are on the way, Wren," the dispatcher said as Wren dropped her phone back into her backpack.

Wren coughed then tied her bandana over her nose and mouth and climbed inside. The smoke burned her eyes, but she didn't see any flames.

As she headed toward the far side of the library, she heard the crackle of flames.

"Where are you?" she shouted.

"Here; I'm here." Miranda's voice was weak.

Wren dropped to her hands and knees to crawl through the smoke then found the old woman, who had pulled up her shirt over her nose. She had a gash that was bleeding freely on the side of her head.

"Cross your arms on your chest; I'm going to get you out," Wren said.

The old woman was suddenly racked by a round of coughing, but she crossed her arms. Wren grabbed her under her arms then crawled backward toward the door while the sounds of sirens mixed with the growing crackle of the fire.

Rascal barked from outside the window then appeared at Wren's side as she dragged the lightweight, frail woman. Before she reached the front door, Wren was overcome by coughing and collapsed on the floor. Rascal tugged on the leg of her jeans until she pushed herself up to her knees and crawled the rest of the way to the door while she held onto Miranda.

When Wren reached the front door, she went up on one knee and unlocked the deadbolt, then she and Rascal pulled the old woman away from the building.

Miranda suffered another round of coughing then peered at Wren. "Thomas sent you, didn't he?" Her voice was raspy.

"Yes, ma'am, he did."

"He's a good boy."

A fire truck and the marshal pulled up; the marshal raced to Wren while a firefighter leapt off the truck and pulled a hose line.

"Are you okay, Wren?"

Wren nodded as a man, who had run from across the street to the fire truck, pulled out oxygen and a first aid bag from a compartment then knelt next to the librarian and applied an oxygen mask to her face.

"An ambulance is on the way." Justin helped Wren to her feet. "Is there anyone else in there?"

"I don't know; I shouted when I went inside." Wren coughed. "Miranda answered me; I didn't hear anyone else."

"Let's get away from the smoke." He picked her up and carried her to his car as a deputy pulled up next to him.

"Bring Rascal here then give him some oxygen."

"Got it," the deputy said.

After he lowered Wren onto the passenger's seat, Justin popped open his cruiser's trunk then removed his small oxygen tank and removed Wren's bandana from her face before he applied the oxygen mask.

"Do you know what Miranda was doing here so late?"

Wren shook her head.

"Did you just drive by and see..." Justin peered at Wren's face as she stared at him. "Thomas?"

She nodded.

The ambulance arrived, and the crew rushed to scoop up Miranda onto their cot then immediately left with their siren blaring.

Wren took in a deep breath then exhaled slowly and ended with a slight cough.

Justin furrowed his brow. "I'll take you to the hospital."

Wren shook her head. "My throat's just a little raw. My lungs are fine; I stayed low and wasn't in there all that long."

While the chief from the fire department strolled to the marshal's cruiser, Wren glanced at the driver's visor that the marshal had left pulled down. She gazed at the small photo of a smiling young woman with bright blue eyes and long red hair. *He taped her photo on the top left corner, so he could see it when he flipped down his visor. I don't think anyone in town knows about her.*

"We've knocked down the fire and searched the building," the chief said. "We didn't find anyone else, and the fire was isolated to the one section in the corner of the library where the old town records are stored. The fire marshal will be here in the morning to investigate."

Just the old town records? I'll look at what Miranda gave me.

Wren inhaled then exhaled; Rascal trotted to her and licked her hand.

Wren smiled then removed her mask. "Rascal tried to pull both of us out when I was overcome by a coughing fit."

"Good boy, Rascal." Justin rubbed Rascal's face.

The deputy joined them. "I think Rascal's fine; he wanted to check on Wren. Is there anything else for me here, Marshal?"

"No, I'll take care of the report."

After the deputy left, Justin said, "When you're ready, I'll take you and Rascal back to the campground."

"I'm fine; I'll take my truck."

The marshal snorted. "I'll follow you."

"Without lights and sirens," Wren said.

The marshal's mouth quivered as he helped her out of his cruiser. "I'll think about it."

When Wren turned at the campground, she glanced in her rear-view mirror and laughed. "The marshal just flipped on his red lights, Rascal."

The marshal turned off his flashing lights when Wren parked at her camper then grinned and waved as he turned to leave.

Wren laughed as she grabbed her backpack and returned his wave.

"Let's walk out to see Thomas, Rascal, then it's time for us to go to Socorro's."

When they reached the old saloon, Wren frowned as she scanned the structure. *No Thomas.*

"Thomas?"

"Whatcha want?" Thomas appeared near the peak of the roof.

"We got to the library in time. I think the librarian will be okay; she asked me if you sent me. I told her you did."

"That's good; me and her is old friends. The man didn't get the papers he was lookin' for."

"That's good news." Wren furrowed her brow. "Do I have them."

"I don't know; do you?" Thomas chortled then disappeared.

"You're very annoying sometimes, Thomas," Wren fumed as she stomped toward Socorro's house with Rascal at her side.

"I know, but at least I don't ask any dumb questions like a girl."

"Boys stink," Wren mumbled.

"Do not."

When they reached Socorro's house, Wren inhaled then exhaled. "Didn't cough; that's good, but I'll bet I smell like smoke. I didn't think about that."

Wren opened the door. "Hey, Socorro; Rascal and I just got back from town. Do I have time for a shower?"

"Go right ahead," Socorro called from the kitchen. "I haven't started warming up anything yet. I'll wait until you get here, so take your time."

"Thanks."

Wren and Rascal hurried back to her trailer. "The door is open." She frowned. "It must have blown open while we were gone, but I wonder if there's a problem with the latch."

When they went inside, Rascal sniffed around then flopped down on the cool floor while Wren checked to make sure nothing was missing.

She frowned. "My laptop is open. I always turn it off and close it. I was in a hurry, though."

Wren locked the front door then turned on her water heater. "I could walk to the campground shower, but I'm too tired for more traipsing around." She pulled out her tablet and the book from her backpack and wrote notes as she read two more pages.

After she lined up her shower soap, shampoo, and towel, she turned on the water in the small shower. When the water temperature suited her, she quickly stripped then hopped in.

After she scrubbed, shampooed, and rinsed, she turned off the water, dried, and dressed.

After she brushed her light brown hair with its reddish streaks, she grabbed her backpack and made sure the camper door was securely locked before she and Rascal headed back to Socorro's house. "I'll bet my hair's dry by the time we get to Socorro's."

Rascal raced ahead then waited in the shade on the porch as Wren approached the house.

When she went into the kitchen, Socorro put the tamales in the oven and the pozole on the burner to heat up.

"You smell good, Wren. I'm not sure I noticed before how much red you have in your hair."

Wren smiled. "Mom said I got Dad's light brown hair and her red hair that she always wanted."

Socorro chuckled. "I wanted sandy brown hair when I was in high school because my hair has always been so dark. When a classmate with light brown hair told me she hated her hair because it was too mousey, I realized we all tend to think someone else has it better than we do."

"I didn't like my green eyes because nobody ever got my eye color right; they'd say I had hazel or brown eyes. I got into a fight with a boy on the playground when I was six because he said I had cat's eyes; Dad still jokes about his black-eyed daughter."

"Thanks for the warning about the cat's eyes. What did the boy mean by that?"

"I didn't know, but I didn't like it." Wren giggled. "I had only one black eye; he had two."

"I'm not a bit surprised. Tell me about your boyfriend."

Wren scowled. "My most recent so-called boyfriend is an asinine jerk. I met my no longer best friend our freshman year of college in a journalism class. I majored in English literature, and he was a journalism major. We were absolutely inseparable and planned to start our new careers together in Atlanta, but that all changed the second half of our senior year when he met Ashley."

Socorro stopped stirring the pozole and gazed at Wren. "Uh oh. We don't like Ashley, do we?"

"Not one bit. She was everything I wasn't: a bubbly extrovert, popular, tall blonde who was a political science major, debate club champion, and stellar athlete who excelled at tennis and golf. Mr. Blake Patterson fell all over himself because Ashley offered to open doors for him in the New York City publishing world. He had an uncle who was a publisher, but I don't think he was in New York. All Blake could talk about was Ashley and how she could help his career because her parents had connections. I quit returning his texts the last two months before we graduated, and he never noticed."

"Never noticed? We don't like shallow Blake either, do we?"

"No, we don't."

Socorro opened the oven then lightly tapped the tamales. "Not quite warm enough yet. I'll give them another five minutes." Socorro opened two beers and handed one to Wren.

"Here's to jerks: may they always get what they deserve," Socorro said.

"Absolutely." Wren tapped Socorro's bottle with hers. "Tell me how you and Sheridan got together."

Socorro laughed as she pulled out the tamales and dished up their pozole. After she set their plates and bowls on the table, she said, "I'll tell you after we eat while we enjoy leftover cobbler and ice cream."

While they ate, Wren asked, "Which version of the haunted campground do you consider the most authentic?"

"If you put them all together, the one common thread they seem to have is that at one time, this was the site of the original settlement. I firmly believe our old structure on the back of the property is what's left of a fine establishment, Forgotten Oasis hotel, saloon, or comfort station for weary gentlemen."

Wren giggled. "That last one is priceless."

"Thank you, I made it up myself. I think it was a saloon that may have been multipurpose because it was quite large and a two-story structure. I don't think we've heard the most authentic version yet, though. I think the Saloon Lady is authentic, but I'm not certain she's the source of the haunted campground. If we had to declare a ghost, she would be the most convenient and the easiest to build a good story around. What do you think?"

"I like it; it gives us a basis for a good travel story. If I move forward with it, will you be able to handle the increased traffic it might bring? An article in a travel magazine would be like free advertising for you, and you may suddenly find more visitors wanting to come here."

"I hadn't thought about that. Maybe I was a little hasty in shutting everyone down on the idea of expansion."

Wren shrugged. "The flip side is what if the article flops, and not one extra visitor shows up?"

Socorro rolled her eyes. "Flip and flop: did you do that on purpose?"

"No, but I have to write that down, so I can work it into the article somehow."

After they began eating cobbler and ice cream, Socorro's phone buzzed a text. "Just a second; I need to check my phone."

Socorro returned. "It was the marshal with a message I'm supposed to relay. I think you owe me a story because he said he had more on the librarian for you. Is that code or something?"

Chapter Six

"Rascal and I went into town to pick up a few things..."

"I thought you didn't write fiction; but whatever, go ahead." Socorro sipped her beer. "Ugh, my beer got warm. Did you know that technically, we're inside the Hidden Gulch town limits? Someone had grandiose plans at one time. Would you like some iced tea? I know you're from Georgia, so I'm warning you this is not sweet tea, but I'll give you some sugar, and you can sweeten it yourself."

Wren cringed. *Granules of sugar settling to the bottom of a glass of cold brown liquid like sand at the bottom of a murky lake? Not for me.*

"Ice water would be good; my beer's warm too. So, anyway, we went past the library..."

"There are no stores for you to buy anything that are close to the library; your fictional story needs more research." Socorro glanced at Wren's face as Wren glowered.

"Sorry for the interruption; go ahead." Socorro put two fingers over her lips.

"We went past the library and saw smoke."

Wren continued with breaking the window, finding Miranda, and pulling her out of the burning library.

"The fact that you are an actual lifesaving hero was not interesting enough to tell me when you came into the house?" Socorro leaned close to Wren and sniffed. "You smell like smokey flowers."

"Really? So, what did the marshal say?"

"Miranda is in ICU, but her doctor said she'll be fine. The hospital probably plans to keep her for a few days for observation because of her age, but if you ask me, they'll kick her out tomorrow because she will refuse to be a model patient."

Wren exhaled. "Thank you; so, where were we?"

"I owe you my Sheridan story. One of the clients I had when I was still married was the owner of the campground. The owner hated Arizona and told me he couldn't spend another summer here and was going to sell the campground. I had been paying all the household bills and buying all the groceries because Jeff was always broke, but I still managed to save a little money. I was shopping in the hardware store for a specific cleaning product, and Sheridan and I got into a conversation. He'd been my sounding board for a while, so I mentioned buying the campground to him."

"Did he say, heck no, let's get married?" Wren asked.

Socorro burst out laughing. "We were good friends; no, he didn't. You want to hear this? Never mind, I think I might like your version better: you go ahead."

Rascal growled and trotted to the front door.

"Just a second; I need to see what Rascal's disturbed about." Wren pulled out her flashlight from her backpack then slung her backpack onto her shoulder.

When Wren opened the door, Rascal raced outside then disappeared as he headed toward the campground office.

"Socorro, can I use your golf cart? I need to follow Rascal; something's wrong."

"I'll drive." Socorro ran outside with Wren; the two of them hopped into Socorro's utility vehicle, and Socorro raced to the campground office.

"What now?" Socorro asked.

Rascal barked.

"That sounds like he's behind my house. Do we go back?" Socorro asked.

"Go to the road. I think he's on the property next to your house."

Socorro sped along the side of the road past the edge of her property.

Rascal barked again, and Wren pointed into the brush. "We need to go there."

As Socorro maneuvered her vehicle over the rough terrain and brush, Wren whistled for Rascal then frowned as an engine started not far from them on the road; she listened as a car drove toward town.

"Did you hear that?"

"Hear what?" Socorro asked.

"I thought I heard an engine..."

"Sound does strange things in the desert. It might have been someone at the campground," Socorro said.

Rascal barked another time; Socorro headed toward her property, then Rascal yipped as they joined him where he waited in the brush before they reached Socorro's fence.

Socorro stopped, and Wren hopped out with her flashlight. While Socorro weaved through the underbrush and cactus to return to the road, Rascal led Wren close to the fence behind Socorro's house, where she found a man on the ground.

"Call nine-one-one, Socorro," Wren called out. "We have a badly injured man here."

Wren held her flashlight to look closer at the man who lay face down in a pool of blood in the brush with a depression in the back of his skull and a knife in his neck.

His skin was white, devoid of all color in spite of his badly sunburned skin on his arms. *Jeff.*

She watched for any sign that he was breathing. *He's dead.*

"Text the marshal; we have a DB."

"I told him you said we had a DB; he's on his way," Socorro said after she sent the text. "What's a DB?"

"Dead body," Wren said.

"It's not Sheridan, right?"

Wren heard the panic in Socorro's voice. "It is not Sheridan, and I think I might be in trouble with the marshal."

"Oh. You were supposed to rest or something, weren't you? Do we know who the DB is?" Socorro asked.

"I'm not sure how to answer," Wren said.

"Tell me," Socorro growled.

"I think it might be Jeff."

"That makes no sense; what's Jeff doing out here, besides getting himself dead?"

"Bad timing? I don't know, but we wouldn't be here if Rascal hadn't alerted then led us here."

"Did we scare off a killer? Is that the engine you heard? Is it okay if I hyperventilate?"

"No, you aren't allowed to hyperventilate, and who knows about the rest of it."

"Should I stay here on the side of the road to flag down the marshal?" Socorro asked.

"That might be a good idea."

"Are you going to stay with...DB?"

"I might as well, so the marshal doesn't have to search the area."

After Socorro left, Wren sat on the ground next to Jeff, and Rascal faced away as he guarded her. She looked more closely at the knife in the man's neck. *Is that a chef's knife?*

Her breathing became shallow and more rapid as she examined the depression in his skull then trained her light around his body.

She focused her light on a large rock near the body. *Blood and...organic matter. It's almost as big as the rocks on the side of the building at the office.*

Wren felt her stomach gurgle then roil; she turned away from the body as she heaved.

When she heard the distant siren as it headed her way, her breathing slowed. *The marshal will be here soon, and he'll take over.* She exhaled.

Wren listened as Socorro tried to tell the marshal what they found.

He interrupted her. "Where's Wren?" he growled.

"That's my cue, Jeff. I have to stand up, so they can find us," Wren said.

When Socorro and Justin roared up in Socorro's campground vehicle, Wren waved. "Here."

Socorro stopped; the marshal hopped out of the vehicle and joined Wren. After he glanced at Jeff's body, he called out, "Stay where you are, Socorro."

In a softer voice, he said, "Wren, give me a rundown."

Wren told him about Rascal growling, running outside the campground, and finding Jeff's body.

"Is that it?" Justin narrowed his eyes; even in the moonlight, Wren saw his kindness.

She added hearing a vehicle leave. "I'm not sure which way it went; Socorro told me sometimes determining the direction of a sound isn't easy in the desert."

"Go with Socorro back to the campground; let me know if you think of anything else."

"I will." Wren trudged to Socorro and the utility vehicle, and Rascal followed her.

On the way back to the campground, Socorro asked, "Was it really Jeff?"

"Yes," Wren said. *I need to tell Justin why I knew it was Jeff.*

Wren added, "Can you send me the marshal's cell phone number? I'm supposed to let him know if I remember anything else."

"Sure. Have you remembered something?"

I don't want to scare her.

"I just don't want the marshal to think I held back from telling him if I do."

"Makes sense." Socorro sent the number before she took Wren to her camper where Rascal had run ahead to wait for her.

After Wren and Rascal went inside, Wren sent the marshal a text. "There's more. Call me."

She stared at her phone. "Rascal, can you believe that I said call me? I might have discovered the advantage of a phone call: a conversation can cover all the bases."

Wren put on her pajamas. "I'm not going anywhere; I might as well be comfortable."

She finished reading the book and taking notes while she waited for the marshal to call her.

When she answered her ringing phone, the marshal asked, "What do you have?"

"I forgot to tell you that I guessed it was Jeff when I saw him in the coffee shop." She told him about taking the photo of Jeff.

Justin asked, "Why did you take his picture? Didn't he know that's what you were doing?"

"He stared at me like he was angry with me about something, but I'd never seen him before, so I held my tablet like I was scrolling and snapped it. I thought I recognized his voice, but I wanted to be sure, so I showed his picture to Miranda, and she told me."

"Is that it?"

"He asked me where my dog was then told me to tell her to watch out. He stepped toward me then hurried out of the coffee shop when you came inside."

"He said to tell her to watch out, not you watch out?"

"Yes."

The marshal exhaled. "What else?"

She told him about the car that followed Socorro from the grocery store to the campground. "I didn't recognize the driver, but I snapped a picture of the license plate."

"Text those two photos to me. Is there anything else?"

"That's all I can think of."

"Thanks; don't go anywhere else tonight, okay?" The marshal hung up.

Wren picked up her second book. After she read the first ten pages, she smiled. "This is much easier to read; it's definitely more colorful in portraying the culture of the 1800s, but I'm glad I read that facts-only book first because this one skirts around a few of the details that might not meet the approval of our current culture."

She flipped to the copyright page. "Interesting; this was written only fifteen years ago, so that explains the modern slant."

Chapter Seven

After Wren scrambled an egg for Rascal, she scrambled one for herself while her slice of bread toasted in her combination oven and air fryer.

"I'll have to watch the bread more carefully next time," she grumbled as she buttered her burnt toast.

While she ate, her phone rang. "Who is calling so early?"

She picked up her phone when she saw the call was from Socorro.

"Are you coming to the office today to work?" Socorro spoke so rapidly that Wren had trouble processing what she had said.

Wren furrowed her brow. *No good morning?*

"I thought I might later."

"Come now; Betsy's nervous about being alone, and I have to go into town." Socorro hung up.

After Wren quickly dressed and shook her boots upside down, she added the book she'd started reading, her tablet, and her laptop to the two books and the folder that were still in her backpack. When she and Rascal arrived at the office, Socorro's car was already gone.

"Oh good, you're here," Betsy said as Wren and Rascal hurried inside.

Wren inhaled an earthy aroma with an herbaceous, slightly sweet scent. "Smells good in here; is that sagebrush?"

"There's a candle shop in Hidden Gulch, and I couldn't resist; I feel like I've brought the outdoors into the office."

"I love it; it goes with the rustic, old west décor."

Betsy giggled. "It's actually a casual interior design inspired by old cast-offs and hand-me-downs. Socorro and I went on a scavenger spree after she bought the campground. We even ditched the old metal registration desk after we rescued the old bar from a woman who was completely remodeling her kitchen to more modern cabinets and planned to throw out all her cabinets; Sheridan helped us install the cabinets in our storage room after I sanded and stained them."

"That must have been a lot of work."

"Lots of elbow grease, but the price was right. Socorro offered to pay, but the woman told her she should pay Socorro to haul it away."

Wren rubbed the registration desk with her fingertips. "I love the feel, and it's developed a beautiful patina."

"It has definitely improved with age." Betsy cleared her throat. "Thanks for coming to the office so quickly; I hate to be a baby, but Jeff being murdered practically in our backyard spooked me."

Tears slid down her cheeks. "But worse is that Sheridan was called in for questioning; Socorro went to open the hardware store for him. Cody called a Tucson lawyer who is a friend of his to represent Sheridan; Cody gave Sheridan strict orders not to say anything until his lawyer arrives." Betsy sobbed. "This is such a mess."

"Can you show me enough that I could cover for you, so you can take a break?"

Betsy straightened her back and held up her head. "I need to pull myself together. We don't want our guests to see a blubbering woman behind the desk."

Betsy rushed to the restroom then returned a few minutes later. "I splashed some water on my face. Are my eyes red?"

"Not at all; what can I do?"

"I'd appreciate it if you could work here until Socorro returns. She's certain Sheridan will be in his store later this morning."

"I can do that, but feel free to put me to work if I can help."

While she set up her laptop at the table in the game room, Wren mumbled, "I might be looking for a new job anyway; working at a campground would be fine."

I won't respond to Charlie's email until after I'm not so angry at him and his editor.

She jotted down a few notes she'd meant to include the night before then resumed reading the second book where she had marked her page. It wasn't long until the background noise of the campground phone and people coming in to browse and chat with Betsy became soothing white noise.

"Wren?"

Wren was so engrossed in the book that she jumped.

Betsy stood in the doorway. "I'm sorry; I didn't mean to startle you. I made a fresh pot of coffee; would you care for some?"

Wren rolled her shoulders then rose from her seat. "I was deep into that book, wasn't I? I'm almost at the end, but I do need to take a break."

"You've been heads down for a couple of hours."

"The book I've been reading is an excellent source for my article. I have enough background to write a first draft, but I want to finish the book first." Wren smiled as she followed Betsy to the store's coffee station.

"I'm like that too," Betsy said. "Butch watches his shows at night, and I read."

"If I throw together a first draft, would you be interested in reading it?"

"I'd love to." Betsy beamed.

"I appreciate it. It won't be polished, but I'd like to be sure I don't have any glaring missteps that would be obvious to anyone from Arizona, which reminds me: You know that thing about 'everybody knows'? In Georgia, everybody knows we have hurricanes and tornados, but newcomers aren't even aware how severe our storms can be. Is there something everybody in Arizona knows about the weather that I need to know too?"

"Has anyone explained haboobs to you?" Betsy asked while she checked online reservations.

Wren furrowed her brow as she sipped her coffee. *Is this a riddle?* "A what?"

"A haboob: it's a dust storm on steroids caused by the wind from a weather front."

"At home, we get strong gusts of wind when a weather front moves in; is it like that?"

"Same principle." Betsy turned away from the computer screen to focus on Wren. "If you see a wall of dust coming at you, pull off the road and away from the shoulder as far as you can, turn off your lights, and don't put your foot on the brake; you don't want another driver to see your rear lights because they will think you're on the road, follow your lights, and slam into you."

"Thanks for the tip; the marshal told me there are things that the locals know and don't realize a newcomer wouldn't. He called it 'everybody knows'."

"That's it exactly."

Wren refilled their cups then returned to reading. *So far, I've learned to drink extra water, shake out scorpions from my shoes, and avoid haboobs.* "We're not in Georgia anymore, are we, Rascal?"

She jotted down more notes as she read the last thirty pages. After she opened her laptop, her fingers flew on the keyboard as she typed the article she had composed in her head.

She leaned back and exhaled as she scanned what she'd written. *It's not a bad first draft.*

"I heard you sigh," Betsy said. "How about a break?"

Wren strolled into the office and chuckled at Rascal, who had made himself comfortable in front of the desk.

"The first paragraph needs some work, and the ending falls flat, but I have a semblance of a first draft. If you can deal with rough..."

"I'll read it for the newsy stuff," Betsy said.

Wren put her article on a thumb drive then copied it. Betsy popped the drive into her computer.

Betsy smiled as she read; when she finished, she said, "You have to dump the entire thing and spend another week here."

Wren's eyes widened, then Betsy giggled.

"You had me going for a minute there."

"I couldn't resist; the only thing I found was when you mentioned the office manager, you left out a few critical details. You forgot to describe her as lithe, graceful, stunningly beautiful, mysterious, and kind."

Wren laughed. "I'll keep that in mind; modest too, right?"

"Of course." Betsy grinned. "Seriously, you've got a great first draft. The only suggestion I have is for you to look at the first three paragraphs on your second page. They may be stronger if you change their order for a better flow. You'll see what I mean when you look at it again. Whatever you do is great, though, because your article pulled me right in, and in fact, I feel like I should make a reservation to check out that place."

"That's exactly what I was going for."

"Ready for lunch? We keep the fixings for sandwiches in our refrigerator. I'll make us sandwiches, and we can share an apple."

"Is it time for lunch already? The morning went really fast; have you heard from Socorro?"

"Keep an eye out and holler if anyone drives up." Betsy went into the kitchen; after a few minutes she returned with two sandwiches, an apple, and her tumbler of cold water. "I forgot to tell you we keep a pitcher of cold water in the refrigerator. Help yourself; I'll take our lunch to the game room."

"I'll carry my sandwich; I have papers and notes spread out all over the table that I need to pick up, so we can eat." Wren hurried to the game room with her sandwich and quickly collected her papers and dropped them into her backpack then closed her laptop before she picked up her RV cup and hurried to the kitchen.

When Betsy sat at the table with her lunch, Rascal flopped down next to her.

While Wren refilled her large plastic cup, the office door opened.

When Audrey came inside, she gasped. "What is that horrible odor? You need to tell your pest control service to spray in the evening, not in the middle of the day to drive out your precious few guests; it's absolutely ghastly in here. Our service uses only organic, natural solutions, and I've never had a problem with any of their products. Edrick, I can feel the poison on my skin; I have to leave immediately." She wheeled around and slammed the door as she rushed out.

Betsy's face was fiery red as she left the game room and strolled to the desk with her head down while she quietly counted to ten.

After she was behind the desk, she raised her eyebrows. "What can we do for you, Mr. Foster?"

"I need to talk to Mrs. Reed immediately." He crossed his arms and glowered.

Wren strolled past the desk then turned to watch him when she reached the game room doorway.

Betsy smiled; Wren shuddered. *I didn't know Betsy had a wicked smile.*

"I don't believe we have a Mrs. Reed here, but I will certainly check." Betsy tapped on her computer.

"The owner's wife; don't be a dolt," he roared.

"Oh, do you mean Ms. Mendez? She isn't here, but I'll give her your message as soon as she returns."

Betsy picked up a pen from the desk them peered at him. "What is your concern you'd like to discuss?"

"None of your business," he growled as he stomped out of the office.

"He didn't slam the door; I guess he didn't want to compete with the missus." Wren strode to the desk and held out her fist.

Betsy giggled as they fist-bumped.

"You were awesome, Betsy. I was ready to shoot him in the back of his knee if he made one threatening move toward you which definitely would have been an unfortunate, accidental, self-inflicted wound."

"I did think he was a little clumsy with your gun when he asked to hold it." Betsy giggled.

"I don't think we'll see either of them for a while; we can eat our lunch in peace," Wren said.

While they ate, Wren asked, "How did you and Butch meet?"

"I was the CPA for his father's manufacturing business. Butch was being groomed to take over, but he hated the corporate world and all the entrapments of money and the jockeying for power by all the others who were his father's inner circle. We quietly agreed to meet at one of the blue-collar bars for a beer every Friday while the rest of the executives went to a fancy bar for fancy cocktails. The first time we met at the bar, he introduced himself as Butch to the man who sat next to him. I liked it and always called him Butch away from the office." She giggled. "I've all but forgotten what his birth name is."

"How did he break away?"

"He invited his father to have a beer with us; I expected his father to blow a gasket when Butch told him how he felt, but his father said he'd been worried because he knew Butch was unhappy. Butch's cousin also worked there and was a natural for the business, so his cousin replaced him as vice president. Unfortunately, I had already given notice and had left the company, so I missed the drama of the other company officers, but his dad told me at our wedding it was a doozy, and he wished he'd filmed it before he cleaned house and fired the lot of them."

"That is so awesome; what a wonderful man. How did you happen to come here?"

The phone rang. "A story for another time." Betsy hurried to the desk.

Wren returned to her laptop to work on her opening sentence for the article and to find the best title.

When her phone rang, she exhaled. *I'm not sure I'm ready to talk to Charlie.*

Before she answered, she mumbled, "Be like Betsy."

"Hey, Charlie; how are you?"

"I think I must have accidently deleted your email when you responded. Did you have a chance to read over the editor's comments and recommendations?"

"Not really, but I'm certain there is an opportunity for me to delve into his thinking processes."

"Good; how's the article coming?"

"Still in rough draft, but I'll have a more polished version next week. Do I send it directly to you, or do you want me to send it to the editor?" Wren held her breath in anticipation. *Ready to hand off the reins, Charlie?*

"Send it to me; I'd like to read it first. Do you have anything more for me on the camper?"

"I actually do; I'll get that to you by tomorrow morning."

"That's great; the CEO already has designers studying ways to address how to make the bed. He told me one of them argued it wasn't a big deal, so he asked the designer if he'd ever made a bed. Poor schmuck proclaimed that his wife took care of all that. The CEO sent the designer and his wife on an all-expenses paid, five-day camping trip at a high-end RV resort. The CEO gave the designer's wife his cell phone number and asked her to call him after the trip with her feedback. I bet him she'll also mention the oven, and he told me no bet." Charlie chuckled. "So, is the campground haunted?"

Wren copied Betsy's wicked smile. "You'll have the article next week."

"You writers."

After Charlie hung up, Wren smiled. *That was fun.*

"Who was that?" Betsy asked. "I'm being nosy."

Wren cleared off the table to throw away the trash. "It was my publisher. Where can I wash the dishes?"

"I'll take care of them; are you procrastinating?"

"Absolutely, which has obviously become my favorite word this week."

Betsy giggled as the phone rang. "Oh, good; it's Socorro."

After she hung up, Betsy said, "She'll be here in a half hour. Sheridan has been released."

"Cleared?" Wren asked.

Betsy shrugged. "She didn't say, and I wasn't about to ask. We can grill her when she gets here. While you're avoiding writing, come talk to me while I take care of our plates."

"This is another one of the appliances we hauled away." Betsy opened the dishwasher and loaded the plates on the lower rack.

"Y'all are really high-class here."

"We are, aren't we?" Betsy fluffed her hair.

After Socorro returned, Wren packed up her laptop and papers before Socorro rushed inside.

"What a morning. Sheridan's still what they call a person of interest, but the lawyer that Cody found is a keeper because he pointed out to the head investigator that their case was so flimsy, it wouldn't get past a district attorney, and Sheridan is a long-time resident and a pillar of the community."

"Good news." Betsy cleared her throat. "Socorro, I have a message for you."

"I'll see you later; I have to write," Wren said.

"Stay inside this afternoon, Wren; we're under a heat advisory," Socorro said.

As Wren and Rascal walked back to the camper, Audrey stepped out of her RV and screamed, "Your dog is loose!"

Wren looked at Rascal who was by her side and continued walking.

"Didn't you hear me? All aggressive, vicious dogs have to be on a leash; you'll be kicked out of the campground with no refund before the end of the day if you violate the rules!" Audrey screeched as Wren ignored her and maintained her steady pace to her camper.

Wren shook her head. "Rascal, I couldn't think of one thing to say that would pass the Betsy test. Audrey is so lucky that today isn't my 'Be like Socorro' day."

After they were inside the camper, Wren plugged in her laptop. "I didn't realize how hot it was outside until we came into the camper. The heat is really deceptive."

She stared at her laptop. "Maybe the novel will motivate me to shift to tension for my opening of the article."

She kicked off her boots and stretched out on her sofa with the book. After she read the first five chapters, Wren put her receipt from the grocery store into the book where she had stopped and stretched. *The writing style from 1845 was a little difficult to read at first, but it didn't take me long to become immersed in the wild west.*

Wren returned to her laptop and wrote four different versions of the first part of her article but saved each one in a document she named 'Forbidden Oasis Cuts' before she deleted the version and wrote a new one.

Wren put her head on her desk and moaned. "I need to do something else to take my mind off worrying about how mad the editor's going to make me. Let's go for a short walk, Rascal."

She put on her ball cap and sunglasses; when they stepped outside, the intense dry heat took away Wren's breath, and Rascal whined.

"It's hotter than it was, and it's too hot for your feet, isn't it?" Wren opened the camper door, and Rascal leapt inside then turned and stared at her.

"I'll just walk one row."

After she closed the door, she trudged along with her head down; when she reached the end of the row, she looked back at her trailer. *This was a bad idea. I still have to go back.*

She peered at the next row. *There are fewer sites and not as many RVs; I'll take a short cut through the empty sites back to my camper.*

Wren squinted from the bright sun in spite of her sunglasses. *My feet are burning through my boots. I should have gone to the pool.*

As she neared the Fosters' site, she heard Audrey's shrill voice from inside. "What do you mean raise our offer? We agreed on a price, and I'm not budging; I've poured enough of my money into you and your harebrained schemes."

"Your money?" Edrick roared. "It's my money; your family was headed straight to the poor house before I took over, which is right where we'd be if I let you make any decisions."

"You're a simpering joke..."

Wren exhaled when she was finally out of earshot.

At least there are no other campers close to them that have to listen to their arguments.

By the time she reached her trailer, her heart was racing from the heat. She hurried in, snatched up her water bottle, and guzzled it down then refilled it and drank half of it. Wren soaked a washcloth in water from the tap. *This is tepid, but I'm burning up.* She wiped down her face and neck before she put the washcloth and her refilled water bottle in the refrigerator.

"That's better." she sank down onto the sofa. After she had cooled a bit, she took a shower then sat at her computer and wrote a fifth version of the introduction to her article and promptly cut it.

"I just wrote two paragraphs about how miserably hot afternoons are in Arizona." Wren snickered. "That's a definite deal-breaker, isn't it, Rascal? Should I submit it to see whether our illustrious editor realizes how bad it is?"

She sighed. "I definitely need to straighten up my attitude when it comes to the editor."

When she opened her computer, she rolled her eyes. "An email from Charlie, and its subject is 'Any feedback yet?'"

She opened the email and snickered. "There's nothing else. Do I tell Charlie that would have been the perfect text?"

She pulled out her water bottle from the refrigerator. *I did promise him feedback.* She responded to his email with her observations about wind blowing open the door after she'd locked it, and the failure of the lock bolt because it was so short. "Should I purposely put in a typo, Rascal?"

Rascal raised one eyebrow then went back to sleep.

"You're right; I add typos and punctuation errors just fine without any effort at all as it is." She clicked send then quickly closed her email. *I'll see an error if I leave it open.*

She opened her refrigerator then the freezer. "I need to start a grocery list, Rascal. The quart of lemonade I got from the grocery store deli was okay, but I want real lemonade like Mom and I used to make when I was a kid. Grandma made hers from scratch, but Mom and I used frozen. Mom told me the lemons were frozen, so it counted as homemade. I tried to see the tiny lemons when she coaxed the frozen cylinder of lemonade from the cans, but I never did." Wren smiled at the memory then rolled her eyes at Rascal who snorted in his sleep.

"How can you nap? I'm too wired." She opened her laptop and stared at the wallpaper of the week that her system selected for her.

She checked the weather. "Here's a flash: it's hot. I wonder if there's a maximum for the number of days a person can complain about the heat in Arizona without being a curmudgeon? I'll check."

After her search led to more links, Wren read them and followed the next link then the next. After she read the article about the temperature of the core of the earth, Wren closed the article. "That was interesting but totally useless."

She idly typed 'Edrick Foster' in her search bar, but her laptop helped her out and changed it to Eric Foster.

Her eyes widened as she read an article about talented chefs to watch: "Edrick's is a fine-dining restaurant in Washington DC. Chef Edrick is widely known as being temperamental, but the cuisine and service benefits from his meticulous focus on perfection."

She read more articles. *Chef Edrick's name is Eric Foster.*

"This is so interesting," she mumbled as she picked up her phone and sent a text to Betsy. "Call when you can."

When her phone immediately rang, Wren answered. "It's nothing urgent."

"You said when I can; I can." Betsy giggled.

"Literalist. Are you sure you weren't an editor in your previous life, not a CPA?"

"Not answering because you're getting peevish. What's going on?"

"I am not peevish; I just wondered if there was any more information about the chef's knife."

"You mean the one that Jeff stuck into his own neck? Not that I've heard, but I'm on it." Betsy hung up.

Wren blinked. "Okay, then."

Rascal rose from his nap and leaned against Wren.

"I wish I could go outside without being in danger of heat stroke, Rascal. I suddenly feel like Thomas wants to tell me something."

Rascal trotted to the door and put his nose on the frame.

Wren removed her water bottle from the refrigerator and put on her ball cap and sunglasses before she picked up her backpack and slipped her phone into the back pocket of her jeans.

"Okay, I'm ready. If it's too hot for either of us, we turn back."

She opened the door, and Rascal trotted outside and did his business then quickly rushed into the camper.

Wren closed the door. *He may be the smart one.*

Chapter Eight

When she reached the old structure, she scanned the area then stood in the shade of the old building. *I'm loving this; it feels ten degrees cooler in the shade.*

"Hey, girl. You figured out what the shade is for," Thomas said.

He took off his hat and rubbed his forehead with the back of his forearm. "Heat'll getcha; whatcha here for?"

"I don't know; just felt like I should come see you."

"Maybe you are pretty smart, for a girl."

Wren glared at him. "It's hot out here, Thomas, even in the shade."

"Smart to ask about that knife; did you know the killer did the lady a favor?"

"How is that?" Wren asked.

"He was going to steal her place; read up on it, girl."

"In the papers the librarian gave me?" she asked.

"What else you got to read?" Thomas sneered.

Wren rolled her eyes then turned away. "Girl stuff."

"I knew it; it'll rot your brain, and you won't be smart no more."

Wren nodded as she walked away. "It happens."

"You is funnin' me, aincha, girl?"

Wren turned back and smiled. "Yes, I am."

Thomas laughed. "I take it back; you'll always be smart."

"Thanks, Thomas," Wren said quietly as she hurried to her camper.

"Don't mention it." The words drifted to her.

She smiled. *We're even.*

On her way back, she received a text from Betsy. "Call any old time."

As soon as she was in the camper, she called Betsy. "Is it time?"

"Sure is. Why did you ask about the knife?"

"I'm not sure." *Except now I am because Thomas said I was smart.*

"The chef's knife was a knock-off that you could buy in any big box store."

"Really? So, someone was trying to frame a chef?"

"That would be my take; can you cook?" Betsy asked.

Wren giggled. "Not as good as you."

"Couldn't be me. There's no way I'd buy a cheap anything except I'm always open for a bargain. I do have a question, though. How did you know it was a chef's knife when you saw it?"

"I have an alibi: I wrote an article about a Cajun chef last year. I know my knives."

"You win; I must be the murderer." Betsy giggled.

"Now that we've solved Jeff's murder, I do have a question. Is the rock that was on the side of the building still there?" Wren asked.

"Just a sec."

When Betsy returned, she said, "The rock's still there. Why?"

"I forgot to check earlier; it was a loose end."

Betsy's voice became serious and quiet. "I'm worried, Wren; I can't help but feel like Socorro's in danger."

"She has people watching her back," Wren said.

"That's a fact," Betsy said.

After they hung up, Wren shuddered. *I'm not sure I convinced Betsy or myself because I've had that same feeling.*

She rubbed her forehead then exhaled. *I'd like to get a draft to Betsy before the end of the day; I'll buckle down.*

She wrote another version for the beginning of her article. "It's not what I wanted, but it's getting close, Rascal."

When Wren saved her latest version in her cut folder, she stared at her screen then smiled. "I must have unconsciously named the folder 'Forbidden Oasis' because the marshal told me that was the saloon's original name. I need to check on that, but for now, that's exactly how I will open the story."

After she wrote two and a half pages, Wren reread what she had written then jumped to the end of the article and massaged it to work with the beginning. She texted Betsy. "I have a rough draft ready."

Betsy replied, "Send it to the campground email; will read tonight."

Rascal whined and nosed the door. "The sand is hot, isn't it? If we had an awning, we'd have a little shade; I'm going to add that to the next suggestion that I send to Charlie."

After they went outside, Rascal ran behind the camper and did his business then rushed back to join Wren.

When they went inside, Wren said, "Let's go into town and talk to Sheridan; he might have a suggestion for us. Wait here while I start the engine, so the inside of the truck will be a little cooler than a pizza oven when we leave."

After she started the truck, Wren lowered the windows and turned on the air conditioning. When Wren could touch the steering wheel without burning her hands, she invited Rascal to join her.

Wren headed into town with all the windows lowered but after half a mile raised them. "The wind's as hot as the air; we're better off with the air conditioner. It won't be long until it kicks in."

She searched for a shady spot to park, but the few that existed were taken, so she parked as close as she could to the hardware store's front door.

When she and Rascal went into the store, Sheridan and the puppies rushed out from the back.

Wren giggled when the puppies rushed her then sat politely in a row after Rascal gave a low growl that sounded like a dad clearing his throat.

"Sure am glad to see you; I've had a steady stream of people wander in not as casual as they thought, so they could be around in case I confessed out of remorse. You don't know how much I wanted to say if I confessed, it would be because I was bragging." Sheridan rolled his eyes. "What brought you here on this scorcher of a day?"

"The camper doesn't have an awning, and the truck was as hot as all get out. I need a portable awning or something at the campground, so Rascal and I can be outside for a short while without me getting heat stroke or him burning his paws, and I need to do something about my steering wheel. I thought maybe gloves."

"The pickup is easy: I have dash screens, which will make a huge difference, and if you drape a towel over your steering wheel, your hands won't be burned to a crisp. I can order portable awnings, but they have to be attached to the camper. Doesn't sound all that portable, does it?"

Sheridan showed Wren several dash solar screens.

She read the labels. "I think this pair would work for me."

"I agree; as far as..."

The bell on the door jingled.

"Excuse me, Wren; I won't be long. I have a couple of possibilities for shade for you and Rascal."

Wren examined the shades one more time then furrowed her brow when Sheridan said, "Go to the back."

Who is he talking to? As Wren carried her screens to the counter, Rascal led the puppies to the back. After she reached the counter, she realized a man stood near the front door, and Sheridan's arms were crossed. She set down the screens then remained at the counter with her back to the man while she listened.

"We weren't supposed to meet until next week, but he told me he was already here, so I showed up early and have been looking for him," a man said. "I've asked a couple of people, but I haven't found anyone who knows him. I thought that was odd because I was certain he told me he was from here. We haven't been partners all that long, and I don't know him very well; I might have misunderstood him."

"Nope, don't have any idea," Sheridan said. "Did you check in with the marshal?"

"I didn't think of that; a small-town marshal is supposed to know everything, am I right?" The man's chuckle was hollow. "Well, my partner told me he always stays at one of the high-end hotels, and Tucson has one, so that's probably where he is. Thanks for your time."

The man held out his hand; Sheridan paused before he shook it.

After the man left, Wren asked, "What was all that about?"

"You don't want to know," Sheridan growled.

Wren raised her eyebrows.

"Sorry; he was trying too hard as far as I was concerned. He told me he was looking for Jeff; he seemed really shifty to me, but I might be prejudiced." Sheridan's chuckle was hollow. "Any partner of Jeff's would not be an acquaintance, much less a friend, of mine."

"He was Jeff's partner?"

Sheridan exhaled. "That's what he said. Let me show you what I have in mind for shade for you and Rascal."

While Sheridan headed toward the opposite side of the store, he whistled, and Rascal and the puppies trotted out to him. "Good boy, Rascal, thanks for taking the puppies to the back."

Sheridan stopped and pulled out dog treats from his shirt pocket. After he gave one to Rascal, he broke two in half and gave a piece to each puppy after the three of them sat for their treats the same way Rascal did for his.

Sheridan stopped in front of the camping equipment then pointed to a canopy tent. "It comes with metal stakes, but I think you'd be better off if you use canopy sandbags. It's supposed to be a one-person set-up; I'll show you some tricks, so you don't have to ask for help unless you want to. It's big enough for you and Rascal, and lightweight enough for you to handle.

"That looks perfect."

"Give me a few minutes; I'll make sure I have the sandbags."

While Wren examined the electric flashlights that doubled as lanterns, her phone buzzed a text from the marshal.

"I have a few more questions for my report. Are you coming into town anytime soon?" Wren hurried to the back storage room doorway.

"Sheridan, I just got a text from the marshal; he has some follow up questions."

"If you're going to his office, just leave my puppy-sitter with me, and we'll be fine."

"Thanks; I'll tell him I'm in town."

After Wren returned his text, the marshal replied, "Meet me in my office in ten minutes. I'm on my way there. Chocolate or vanilla milkshake?"

Easy answer. "Chocolate."

She chuckled. *Profiling me?*

"What's funny?" Sheridan asked.

"You were right about meeting in his office. He asked me whether I prefer a chocolate or vanilla milkshake; evidently the inquisition has already started," she said.

Sheridan laughed. "You're probably right. We'll have everything ready for you when you get back. My part-time clerk will be here in half an hour; I'll meet you at the campground to help you put it up."

"Thanks."

As she headed to the door, Sheridan said, "Wren."

She turned and tilted her head as she met his gaze.

"If you're still at the marshal's office when I'm ready to leave, Rascal and I will go to the campground, if that's okay with you."

Rascal gave her his best pleading look.

"That's fine; Rascal loves Betsy."

As she parked next to the marshal's cruiser, Wren examined the small, sturdy, wooden building that belonged on an Old West movie set but housed the modern-day marshal's and the dispatcher's offices and a two-cell jail.

When she entered, a deputy, who sat at a desk behind a counter that was reminiscent of a honky-tonk bar, pointed. "That way to the marshal's office, Wren."

"Thank you." She sneaked a glance behind her to see if there was an old piano in the corner. *I must be getting Old West fever.*

She strolled along the short hallway to the office with a marshal's badge painted on the opaque glass window in the door. Wren smirked. *Eye height for someone who is taller than me.*

As she raised her hand to knock, the deputy called out, "Just go on in; he's expecting you, and your ice cream is melting."

When she went inside, Justin handed her a large chocolate milkshake. "Have a seat. How's your day been?"

Was that a social or a law enforcement question? Wren furrowed her brow as she sat in the visitor's chair across from his desk.

I'll go with social. "I completed a first draft; I'll probably send it to the publisher in the morning."

Wren slurped up milkshake through her straw until it was clogged then lifted out her straw and ate the thick chocolate ice cream.

Justin scooped off the whipped cream from the top of his vanilla milkshake with his straw. After he'd eaten the whipped cream, he spooned up bites of creamy milkshake until it melted enough to slurp through the straw without clogging.

Wren finished her milkshake. "That was good."

"Glad you liked it. What were you doing in town? Where's Rascal?"

"I don't have an awning on my camper, and the sand's too hot for Rascal, so we went to see Sheridan."

"Did you get a canopy tent?"

"Exactly, how did you know?"

When he smiled, Wren noticed that one side of his mouth was a shade higher than the other, and his hazel eyes crinkled.

He has a very disarming smile.

"Sheridan called and asked to borrow a couple of small sandbags until he could get in the canopy sandbags for you. Yours will be in on Tuesday, in case you wondered."

So, why did you ask if you knew?

Justin sighed. "That was bad, wasn't it? I'm better at interrogating criminals than I am at small talk."

"Good thing." Wren cringed. *I didn't mean to say that out loud.*

"Can you go through what you remember before you found Jeff Reed's body?"

Wren began with Rascal barking behind Socorro's house then leaving the yard and the campground. "Socorro offered to drive when I asked to borrow her golf cart, and Rascal met us on the road. I followed him into the heavier brush, and that's when I heard a car drive away."

"How do you know it was a car, not a pickup?"

Wren tilted her head as she peered at him. "The engine sounded like a car engine, not a truck engine."

Justin narrowed his eyes. "You can tell the difference between a car and a truck by the engine sound?"

Wren smiled. "I've written articles about stock car drivers and street races. I can even tell the difference between the automotive brands and between the types of engines. Stock car drivers are really particular; did you know that? I can hear the differences in an old diesel, a new diesel, and a gasoline truck, but there's actually a subtle difference in the smell of the exhaust. I wrote an article for an oil refinery, and they were kind enough to educate me. I research everything before I submit a final draft."

Justin shook his head. "Are all writers as thorough as you are?"

"Everybody's different. The hardest part for anyone who wants the details to be right is accepting 'good enough' in place of the perfection they'd rather submit. Magazine deadlines aren't flexible, so when one looms, no editor or publisher in the world accepts any excuse for a delay. I've picked up assignments that were three days from the deadline because the original writer couldn't deliver. Can you imagine how insanc that sounds to so many authors?"

"How did you do the research and get a first draft to a final in three days?"

"No sleep; it was the only way, and I had a beta reader who had the amazing skill of ferreting out what I meant to say in my foggy, sleep-deprived brain and shoot it back to me quickly enough that I got the final to the editor before my deadline. The rest of the scramble was on them."

"Sounds nerve wracking, but it was exciting in its own way, wasn't it?"

"It really was, but I'm enjoying a slower pace. Two weeks is like a gift."

"You're almost at the end of your first week, have you sent in your first draft?"

Wren stared at him. "No."

"It's done, isn't it? Why haven't you sent it?"

Wren narrowed her eyes. "I'm mentally distraught by the trauma of finding a dead body."

"Sure; tell me later." Justin rolled his eyes and put their trash into the empty sack still on his desk.

Wren exhaled. "I'm struggling with a nagging thought I'm missing something, but I don't know what. Whenever I'm stuck, it's best for me to let my manuscript rest for a bit."

"I think that's smart. Tell me about the fire; this is just between you and me."

Wren stared at her hands. "I had a feeling that Thomas had something to tell me. When I rushed out to talk to him, he said a man was hurting the library lady; he was in such a panic that he asked me to help, which for him was huge."

Justin raised his eyebrows. "Why?"

"I'm a girl."

Justin guffawed. When he regained his composure, he said, "Poor Thomas."

Wren snorted. "He's annoying."

Justin cleared his throat as he picked up a pen and tapped on a blank notepad.

"Do you know the story behind how Forbidden Oasis became Forgotten Oasis?" Wren asked.

Justin smiled. "A preacher from back east showed up in Hidden Gulch with his young wife. After a particularly fiery sermon about the demons in tequila, the saloonkeeper decided to take down the sign over the entrance before he became the subject of another sermon."

"Did he change the name then?"

"No, because the story continues with the saloonkeeper running off with the preacher's wife; the preacher hunted them down and shot them both. The next saloonkeeper decided Forbidden Oasis was bad luck because of the demons, so he named it Forgotten Oasis."

"I love this story. A scandal is a perfect way to capture the readers' attention; I'll update my draft and work this in."

"Where do you go after you leave Hidden Gulch?" Justin asked.

"East is all I know; I'm traveling across the country and camping at different haunted campgrounds for the travel magazine."

"What will you do after that?"

"I don't know; Charlie, the publisher, took me on as staff for the magazine, but I think that may be just for the haunted campground series."

Justin raised his eyebrows. "Doesn't that make you nervous?"

"Why should it? I've been a freelancer since I graduated from college; I've become accustomed to setting aside a little money from each assignment, so I'll have a cushion to tide me over between jobs."

"You're braver than I am, but don't tell Thomas; I want to keep my tough marshal image."

Wren giggled as she rose. "You got it."

Justin gazed at her then stuck out his hand, and they shook. "Thanks for coming in."

She smiled. "Thanks for the milkshake."

After she started her truck, Wren pulled out her phone from her backpack, so she could send a text to Sheridan.

Her eyes widened when she saw the time. *I was in Justin's office for an hour for a ten-minute interview.*

She texted Sheridan. "Leaving Marshal's office."

He replied, "We're at the campground."

When she was halfway to the campground, Wren tapped the steering wheel in thought. *What about the red-haired beauty with the blue eyes?*

"Get over yourself. It wasn't like it was a coffee date with milkshakes. He has a brilliant interrogation style. You probably told him far more than you know."

Wren clenched her jaw. *That's it: he's a skilled law enforcement officer with a subtly effective technique for interviewing witnesses.*

After Wren reached the campground, she stopped at the office.

Rascal greeted her with kisses when she went in; she hugged him.

Betsy smiled. "Sheridan is waiting for you with your canopy at your site. Rascal and I knew you'd stop here first."

"Thank you; we'll see you later."

Wren drove past the Fosters' site. *Their car's gone; maybe they've gone to Tucson.*

After Wren and Rascal reached their site, Sheridan asked, "Ready to put up the canopy?"

"I'm ready to learn." Wren unlocked the camper door, and Rascal jumped from the ground and over the steps to go inside.

After the two of them put up the canopy, Wren said, "I had my doubts about it being cooler, but this is not bad at all."

Sheridan showed her how to put the stakes in the ground as deep as possible, so she could use them as an addition to the weights.

After he rigged the sandbags to anchor the tent legs, he pulled out an outdoor mat from his pickup bed.

"This is the same size as your canopy. It will keep Rascal from collecting a ton of sand in his fur then depositing it inside the camper."

"That's great; I have to sweep every time we go inside."

After they rolled out the mat and put Wren's two camp chairs in the shade, Sheridan said, "I'll see you later; Socorro must have been running errands because I haven't seen or heard from her in a while. She's probably back at the house now."

Wren opened the camper door and coaxed Rascal outside. "Come on, Rascal; you might like being outside now that we have some shade."

Rascal dashed for the mat and flopped down under the canopy. Wren went inside and grabbed the 1845 fiction book to read while she sat outside.

When Rascal whined, she looked up from her book; he had one front paw up as he aimed his nose toward the camper door.

Wren chuckled as she stuck her bookmark into her book and closed it. "Where did you learn that? You're right, though; I'm hot too."

After they were inside, Wren glanced at her phone that she had left on the counter. *A new text?*

The text from Cody had arrived twenty minutes earlier. "You doing okay?"

She replied, "No, I melted."

"Come to Sedona; it's cool."

Wren raised her eyebrows then smiled. "I'll call his bluff."

She sent her text. "I'll think about it; I might surprise you."

Wren pulled out her water bottle and the jug of cool water for Rascal from the refrigerator and filled his bowl. After she picked up her book, she pulled off her boots before she relaxed on the sofa with her feet up.

She was deep into the story when her phone rang.

Chapter Nine

Must be an emergency; it's Betsy. She held onto her book as she answered.

"What are you up to? I just got a frantic call from Cody. Are you thinking about going to Sedona for the weekend?"

Wren giggled. "I'll be right there. Don't go anywhere."

"Where would I go?" Betsy hung up.

Wren reluctantly closed her book with her bookmark inside before she turned her boots upside down to shake them. "I'm going to see Betsy. Do you want to go? I'm going to walk."

Rascal stared at her then slowly rose to his feet and trudged to the door.

"That was painful to watch." Wren put on her boots, hat, and sunglasses and slipped her phone into her back pocket.

When she opened the door, Rascal raced toward the office as she followed him at a much slower pace.

Wren frowned when the wind whistled; it sounded like Thomas calling her.

She shook her head. *I'm still spooked from finding Jeff Reed.*

She opened the office door, and Rascal grinned. "Fine, you won the race."

"You owe me details, Missy," Betsy growled, but the twinkle in her eyes gave away the mirth she was trying to hide.

Wren opened her phone and the texts from Cody. "Here; read."

Betsy laughed so loud that Rascal howled an accompaniment.

"This is absolutely, wickedly priceless. You definitely caught him off guard. What's our next step?" Betsy rubbed her hands together.

"I don't know, but it has to be good because you used our favorite word; this is a hard one to top, isn't it? What did he say when he called?"

"I'm supposed to snoop and ask prying questions to see if you are making plans to go to Sedona." Betsy furrowed her brow. "Like are you packing your long johns and a warm coat for a little drive. You have to help me make a list of questions to ask."

"I could casually ask you if I can go to Sedona without driving through Phoenix."

"That's a good one; we'll just be casual. Where are you eating dinner Saturday night? Wait a minute, I need to write all these down. I especially like the part in your text where you said you might surprise him. That was brilliant."

While Betsy wrote, Sheridan rushed into the office. "Have you seen or heard from Socorro lately?"

Betsy frowned. "Now that you mention it, we haven't seen her since right after lunch; for some reason, I must have thought she had gone back into town and has been with you."

"No, and her car is at her house. I'm calling the marshal."

"I'll text her," Betsy said.

"Okay, but I've texted her at least ten times and haven't heard anything from her."

"I'm going to take a stroll around the campground," Wren said. "Maybe she's fallen or something."

"I'll text Butch to look for her," Betsy said.

Before she left, Wren sent Cody a quick text then showed it to Betsy. "Decided to stay here."

"Good," Betsy said. "It's nice to let him off the hook. There's no reason to go into any details because we actually don't have any."

"Thanks; he's fun to joke with, but I didn't want to leave him dangling. Rascal, you can stay here if you like; it's cooling down a little outside, but I'm sure the sand is still hot."

Rascal followed her to the door, and the two of them beelined to the old saloon.

Thomas stood on the peak of the old building with his arms crossed. "It's about time you got here, girl. That man took the lady."

"When was that?"

"While you was in the marshal's office. You were so long, I was afeared you was going to go to jail."

"Where did he take her?" Wren held her breath.

"I don't rightly know; I'll go find her, but first, an old friend needs me." Thomas disappeared.

Thank goodness Justin knows Thomas, so I can tell him that Socorro's been kidnapped and about what time.

Wren hurried back to the office, and Rascal stayed by her side.

When she went inside, Betsy said, "Sheridan has gone to Socorro's house to see if he can find anything. The marshal will be here soon."

Wren nodded then stepped outside to watch for him; Rascal went with her.

She pulled out her phone and sent Justin a text. "Thomas said a man took her while I was at your office. He doesn't know where."

Justin replied, "3 min."

When Justin pulled up in his cruiser, he said, "We can talk after I talk to Sheridan. Are you going to be here or at your trailer?"

"We'll have more privacy at my camper; I'll wait for you there."

Wren went into the office. "The marshal will talk to Sheridan, then he'll want to talk to you and me, most likely separately. Will you be okay here by yourself?"

"I'll be fine; after Butch makes his rounds, he told me he'd stay in the office to guard me."

"Talk to you later."

Betsy nodded then sat on the stool for the counter.

I've never seen Betsy sit on the stool; she always pushes it out of her way.

"Are you sure you'll be okay?"

Betsy teared up as she nodded.

Rascal left with Wren, so she ran to the trailer with him by her side. "Let's go inside; I'll make a batch of sweet tea."

After the tea steeped, she removed the tea bags then measured and stirred in the sugar. She dipped in a spoon for a taste. "Perfect; at least I won't have to worry about anyone drinking up my sweet tea."

She frowned at her gallon jug of sweet tea. "I should make some unsweet tea, so I'll have some for the marshal."

She boiled the water then dropped the tea bags into the hot water and set her timer.

While she waited, she peered at the unadulterated tea. "You don't know how bad I want to add just two tablespoons of sugar."

A knock on her door interrupted her as she moved the half gallon jug of unsweet tea out of the sink and to the counter.

"Come on in."

The marshal opened the door. "Don't do that; we don't know anything about the kidnapper."

Wren pointed to Rascal. "His tail was wagging like crazy."

"Would you like some iced tea?" She pointed to the half-gallon jug. "This is unsweet."

Justin squinted at the jug of tea. "Is that something special? What makes it unsweet?"

"No sugar." Wren filled two glasses with ice and poured tea for him then poured sweet tea for herself.

"Isn't that just tea?" he asked.

"Not in the south; if you order tea, you'll get sweet tea."

As they sat at the dining table, Justin said, "Tell me what Thomas said."

"He told me a man took the lady. Thomas has been keeping an eye on Socorro. I asked him when, and he told me while I was at your office. When I asked where, he said he didn't know, but he'd find her. I don't know how."

"Why did you ask Thomas?"

"After I got back from your office, I parked next to my camper. On my way to the campground office, the wind whistled, and it sounded a lot like Thomas calling me. I ignored it, but when Sheridan arrived a few minutes later and asked if we'd seen Socorro, I rushed to the saloon because I felt like he wanted to tell me something important."

"You told me Thomas had a silver coin that a man gave him to watch the lady."

"Right, and I always thought it was the saloon lady from the 1800s, but I realized that Socorro owns the saloon now, so she's the saloon lady."

"He's still looking after the saloon lady," Justin said quietly. "He's definitely faithful to his job, isn't he? Sheridan wants you to stay at Socorro's house until we find her."

Wren shook her head. "I've got Rascal; I'll be fine."

After Justin left, Wren paced then exhaled. "I need to do something besides worry."

She sat at her desk and added the story of the Forbidden Oasis Saloon, the saloon lady, and the church ladies of Hidden Gulch as her opening. When Wren finished reviewing and editing her article, she read it aloud as a final revision before she attached it to an email to Charlie then read the email to Rascal.

"Attached is the first article for On the Haunted Campground Trail: The Forgotten Oasis Campground, Hidden Gulch, Arizona; I will be happy to address any clarity issues or gaps in content you may find." She peered at Rascal. "What do you think? Good enough?"

Rascal gazed at her with his adoring eyes, and she cooed to him as she hugged him. "You're a good boy."

She sent her email then closed her laptop and tapped her fingers on the table while she went over the last time she saw Socorro. "I wish there was something I could do to find Socorro."

She rose from the table and poured a large glass of sweet tea before she sat on her one-person sofa with the 1845 book and read.

She was so deep into the story that when her phone rang, she glanced around. "I wonder what that is?"

I was lost in the 1800s. She shook her head then answered.

"I just got a call from Miss Miranda's niece, Francine," Betsy said. "After the doctors said they could do nothing more for Miss Miranda, the librarian insisted on going home, but first, she wanted her niece to bring her out here to talk to you. Francine offered to convey any message to her aunt's faithful friends and followers, but Miss Miranda insisted she had to talk to Wren while she could. I think Francine had more to tell me, but she broke down." Betsy cleared her throat. "I told her I didn't know if you could leave anytime soon."

Wren exhaled. "I'm really torn; if I go into town, would you let me know the second you hear anything?"

"You know I will."

"It must be something important; I suppose it would be something to do besides worry."

"I understand that; I don't know what I'd do if I didn't have the responsibility of keeping the ship afloat."

"The good ship Campground Forgotten Oasis?"

"That's it exactly. I'll text you the address. Are you a landmark person or a street person?"

"That's easy: streets, one hundred percent."

"I'll add the directions by street names. Don't judge me if I add in a couple landmarks, though." Betsy cleared her throat. "Do you want me to go with you? I could ask Butch to watch the desk for me; he'd do it if it was to help you."

"Thanks for the offer, but I'll have Rascal with me. I know Butch isn't crazy about working the desk, so we'll save that for an emergency."

After they hung up, Wren said, "Ready for a road trip? Miss Miranda wants to see us."

Rascal stood at the door while Wren read the directions from Betsy before she grabbed her backpack and keys. She slowly cruised by the old saloon with her window down. *Still no sign of Thomas.*

She parked in front of the address that Betsy had sent her; her eyes widened at the size of the sprawling log home and the huge, oversized yard.

Wren peered at her phone to doublecheck the address. "This is the right house; I expected to see a modest cottage with a small hanging basket of flowers on the compact front porch."

Before they reached the front door, an overweight, middle-aged woman with unnaturally dark brown hair hurried out of the house; her eyes were red-rimmed, and her cheeks were streaked by tears. "I'm Miranda's niece, Francine, Wren;

I'm sorry to run off the second you arrive, but the hospital called. One of the housekeepers found items in a drawer in Aunt Miranda's room. If you prefer, you can wait out here, except it's too hot." She furrowed her brow. "The foyer's cool; you can wait there if you like; I'll be back soon."

As she unlocked her car, the woman sobbed. "I can't believe we missed the most important items of all."

Wren opened the door; Rascal followed her inside. After she sat on the chair near the door, Rascal stared at the hallway and whined.

"Wren? I'm in here." Miranda's voice was strong and clear.

Wren and Rascal headed down the hallway until they came to a large room on the right. Wren's eyes widened at the ceiling-to-floor bookcases that lined three of the walls. The large windows on the outside wall overlooked a patio that had colorful pots of different types of cactus.

"I love your home, Miranda." Wren gazed at all the books; when she saw the three library ladders that were attached to railings near the ceiling, she smiled.

Miranda sat in a yellow, black, and red overstuffed chair with her feet propped up on a small, brownish-copper ottoman. "Thank you; I'm not supposed to climb the ladders anymore, but if I'm smart enough not to fall, who is going to know?" Miranda's eyes twinkled as she pointed to a bright green love seat.

After Wren sat on the comfortable sofa, Rascal lay at her feet.

Miranda continued, "I bought the house forty-five years ago when I first came to Hidden Gulch to live. My husband and I drove through here once not long after we were married, and he told me this was a perfect place to raise children." She chuckled at the memory. "After he was gone, I felt drawn to settle down here. The house was a bed and breakfast, but the owner was burned out from ten years of all the peopling, as she called the constant attention required by a houseful of paying guests. I was a young widow with two small boys and a lump sum from my husband's life insurance; I thought a bed and breakfast was my best bet for income for my small family. While the children and I scoured yard sales for furnishings to give the home the Old West feel that it deserved, my parents-in-law retired, sold their house in Kansas, moved in with us, and my father-in-law paid the utility bills and property taxes. My mother-in-law was thrilled to take over the cooking and household chores when the library board asked me to fill the position of librarian temporarily while they searched for a replacement after the abrupt, scandalous departure of the librarian and the fire chief; but that's a different story for another time." Melinda smiled.

"I'd love to hear it," Wren said.

"Better yet, I've written a collection of short stories that I will never publish based on the events in Hidden Gulch over the past forty-five years, including the oral history from relatives of the original settlers." She pointed to the box of papers at her feet. "Take the box to your truck now, so you don't forget it; you might want to use some of the stories as ideas when you make the shift to writing fiction."

"I don't ever plan to write fiction, but I love to read; thank you." Wren picked up the box. "I'll be happy to return them to you after I read them." She hurried to put the box on the passenger's floorboard while Rascal waited for her on the porch.

When Wren and Rascal returned to the room of books, Wren glanced around. "Have you been collecting books all your life?"

"Not until after I began bringing home the excess donated books because the idea of following the library's policy to destroy them horrified me; my father-in-law built the shelves and installed the library ladders, so I could reach all the books. I'm always fascinated by how small incidents shape our lives, aren't you? Did you bring the folder I gave you?"

"I did." Wren flipped open her backpack and pulled out the folder. "I've kept it in my backpack with me, but I'm not sure why."

"Ah, you have good instincts; bring the folder here and pull this footstool closer, so we can go over the documents together."

After Wren was in position, Miranda said, "Let's start with the copy of the legal document and the hand-drawn map."

Wren pulled out the legal document and the map; Miranda pointed to a section on the document. "This is a copy of the original deed. The town fathers took out a loan on the property to raise money for a railroad scheme that collapsed; the loan went into default, of course, and the property became part of the bank's inventory. You can read about it in the short stories. What you care about is that the deed to the property included the entirety of the original town of Hidden Gulch and the surrounding undeveloped area as defined by an authenticated private land claim. The outer edges of the property were marked by surveyor's rods fifty years after the claim was filed and authenticated; twenty years after that, a young man who was studying to be a surveyor found most of the surveyor's rods and recorded the coordinates." Minerva pointed to a separate sheet that listed the eight coordinates and nothing else.

"The next section of the deed describes the details for the claim as being a circle with a radius of five hundred varga from the northwest edge of the blacksmith's shop; a varga was a Spanish measurement that was about thirty-three inches, so five hundred varga is about four hundred fifty yards. The BLM has the plat that defines the location of the blacksmith's shop, which was very close to the saloon."

"I can't even imagine nine football fields laid end-to-end with the saloon in the middle." Wren exhaled then peered at the legalese. "So, what does that mean?"

"Perfect lead-in question; let's look at the map." Miranda pulled out a yellow, wooden pencil from her hair.

Wren blinked. *Where did that come from? There wasn't a pencil in her hair a second ago.*

After Wren unfolded then spread out the map, Miss Miranda drew an imaginary circle with the eraser end of her pencil.

"This circle is the original town of Hidden Gulch: the campground, Socorro's house, and the saloon."

She drew a much larger circle with her pencil that included the smaller circle. "This is what the deed referred to as the undeveloped area. Let's look at the property that Socorro bought."

Miranda shifted a paper with her eraser then pointed to the paper that was under it. "There it is."

Wren pulled it out, and her eyes widened as she read the deed. "This says Socorro bought the campground and surrounding undeveloped property including all mineral rights." Wren furrowed her brow. "Everyone who has reviewed the deeds when the property changed hands from one owner to the next must have assumed the old saloon defined the edge of the property."

Miranda nodded. "However, you would have seen the difference after you studied the documents and the map; I wanted to save you some time. Thomas said you'd be here, so I waited. Now, I can rest. Why don't you wait in your truck for my niece? Then I won't have to listen to her drama."

Wren smiled. "Thank you for everything; I'll do that."

As Wren and Rascal headed to the door, Miranda said, "You really need to ask Justin about that photo."

Wren frowned. *How did she know it's been bothering me? Am I that obvious?*

After Wren started her truck and opened the door for Rascal, he jumped inside as Francine pulled into the driveway. "Stay in the truck while I talk to Francine, then we can go."

Wren waited for Miranda's niece in the yard near the front porch.

Francine hugged Wren. "Thank goodness they hadn't disappeared. She wanted to be at home, so I helped her sit in her favorite chair in the book room. She told me to be sure to give you these."

Francine gave Wren a coin and a silver pen. "Her father gave her the coin when she graduated from college. He told her that as long as she had the silver coin and kindness in her heart, she would never be poor; her husband, my uncle, gave her the silver pen as a wedding gift because she was so fascinated by stories and history and was always writing in her journal, her notebook, and even the backs of envelopes. She told me she wanted you to have them; the last thing she said to me before she passed was to promise I'd tell you that the key is silver."

Wren stared at Francine then the house. "Before she passed?"

Tears flowed freely down Francine's cheeks. "She smiled when she said your name then took her last breath."

"She died in her chair?"

"Not long before you got here; I think she was grateful to you for pulling her out of the fire and giving her a few extra days to put things in order. I'm glad you're here, so I can give you the silver coin and pen."

A large, black vehicle backed into the driveway. "If you'll excuse me..." Francine rushed to the vehicle.

Wren stumbled to her truck. *She waited for me.*

Chapter Ten

Wren stared at the box of stories on the passenger's seat. *She gave me her coin, pen, and stories; where do I find the silver key?*

She slowly pulled away from Miranda's house and headed to the campground. When she parked next to her camper, Wren rubbed her forehead. *Miranda said Thomas told her I'd be there. Thomas said an old friend needed him, and Miranda told me that she and Thomas went way back.*

She carried the small box into the camper and was suddenly overcome by grief. Her tears flowed and almost blinded her as she set the box next to her comfortable chair; after she collapsed onto her chair, Wren cried until she had no tears left.

Wren sniffled then splashed cold water on her face. "Let's walk to the office and tell Betsy."

Wren kicked the rocks and sand as she walked. *Tell Betsy what? That Miranda died before I got there, but she waited for me?*

When Wren and Rascal went inside, Betsy glanced up then rushed to give Wren a quick hug. "I'm so sorry, Wren; Miranda passed, didn't she?"

Wren nodded. "Her niece gave me a silver coin and a pen that Miranda had left me."

"Is there anything I can do for you?"

"No, but thanks for the offer; Rascal and I wanted you to know."

When Wren headed toward the door, Betsy said, "The marshal called here for you; I told him you weren't in the office, and he should call your phone if he wanted to talk to you. I had the distinct impression he was checking up on your whereabouts."

Wren smiled. "Thanks, Betsy; you didn't tell him we were in Cahoots, did you?"

Betsy laughed. "In Cahoots; that's hilarious."

After Wren left the office, she said, "Let's check the saloon, Rascal; Thomas might be back."

When they reached the saloon, Thomas was swinging his feet while he sat on the false front. "The library lady was glad she waited for you."

"Is she gone now?" Wren asked.

He tapped his temple with his index finger as he rose. "You're right thick in the head sometimes for a smart girl; her job was done, so she's gone."

"When's your job done, Thomas?"

"You're slowing me down with your jabbering, girl. I gotta find the saloon lady."

Definitely infuriating.

As the hot wind picked up, Wren watched a small dust devil dance on the desert behind the campground then disappear as quickly as it had appeared.

"Things appear then quickly disappear around here, don't they, Rascal? Let's look at those maps again."

Wren poured a glass of tea and sipped while she studied the map. "There are eight coordinates listed: there must be eight rods. I have an idea."

She pulled out the magnifying glass the forensic science technician with a specialty in entomology had given her when she wrote the article about the advances of forensic research and the revealing details found in soil and insects at a crime scene. Wren smiled. *Nobody loves bugs like an entomologist.*

After she spread out the map, she narrowed her eyes then found a black dot near the road that led to the current town of Hidden Gulch. *That must be where the easement starts.*

She examined the map along the road on the other side of the campground and found another dot. *Someone must have marked the map with the location of the surveyor's rods using the young surveyor's coordinates. I could find all of them with my phone.*

Rascal whined. "It is suppertime, isn't it?"

Wren fed Rascal then opened her refrigerator then closed it. *I don't really feel like eating now; maybe later.*

After Rascal thoroughly cleaned his food bowl, they went for a walk that, as usual, ended up at the saloon. *No Thomas.*

When Rascal walked past the Fosters' RV, she raised an eyebrow. *I would have expected them back by now.* She shrugged.

"The office closes in half an hour; let's see if Betsy has heard anything."

Rascal trotted ahead then turned to glance at Wren. "I'll meet you inside."

He grinned then raced away toward the office. When Wren went past the restrooms and laundry, she sighed. *My laundry's starting to back up.*

Betsy smiled when Wren joined her and Rascal inside the building. "How are you doing?" Betsy asked.

"I'm a little sad, but I'm okay."

"Did you happen to notice whether the Fosters were back?" Betsy asked then answered the phone.

"I really can't say; I'm sorry you'll have to call them directly because we aren't equipped to take messages."

After she hung up, Betsy said, "The same man has been calling all afternoon for Audrey Foster; his voice sounded familiar, but I talk to so many people during the day, everyone sounds alike."

"That's strange, isn't it? I didn't see their car; there aren't any lights on, but it's probably too early for that."

"It depends on how tinted their windows are."

"They have their curtains that cover the windshield closed like all the other RVs do, but I just realized most of the others have had at least one interior light on all day."

"They certainly didn't seem like the RV type of people to me; I won't be surprised if we get a call from them saying that a tow truck will be picking up their RV. I think they left for Tucson or Phoenix to fly home."

When Betsy answered the phone and took a reservation, Wren and Rascal headed toward the door.

Betsy completed her call. "Before you go, I was wondering about your article."

"I sent it this morning; normally, I would have received an email of acknowledgement, but I haven't heard anything from Charlie. I'll follow up first thing tomorrow if I don't hear anything tonight."

"So far, he hasn't been the ideal employer, has he?"

"He started off strong: one of his friends, who is a pilot, flew Rascal and me from Atlanta to Phoenix in his private jet. That was huge because I wouldn't have flown even if Rascal could ride in a crate in the air conditioned, pressurized pet cargo hold; we would have driven across country and would be arriving next week sometime, which is assuming Charlie had even hired me after I told him Rascal and I don't fly, and we'd get here when we get here."

"I guess he deserves a huge pass," Betsy said. "You stay right here at the Forgotten Oasis while our favorite publisher, Charlie, goes to the beach or whatever he has planned for the weekend. We'll even send him bon voyage flowers if he'd like to take a two-week cruise."

Wren smiled. "You put it all in perspective; thanks; the deadline was his, not mine."

"And there you go; what are your plans for supper?"

"I plan to celebrate by catching up on my reading. I have snacks, the fixings for a sandwich, and a pepperoni pizza in the freezer. I have options."

Before Wren opened the door, she said, "Maybe I won't follow up tomorrow after all; you've convinced me that Charlie deserves a weekend off."

The office phone rang; before she answered, Betsy said, "Hold off for one minute before you leave, Wren."

"You are? Okay, it will be ready when you get here." Betsy snorted. "Of course, not."

After she hung up, she said, "That was Cody, Rascal. Can you believe that he's on the road and will be here tonight? He wants to surprise Wren, so we'll keep this quiet, won't we?"

Betsy smirked as she glanced at Wren. "Oh, you're still here? See you in the morning unless one of us hears anything about Socorro."

After they left the office, Wren said, "I feel like I'm stalking Thomas, Rascal; let's check the saloon one more time then see if we can find those surveyor's rods before dark."

When they reached the old structure, Wren examined the peak and both sides of the false front. "Are you here, Thomas?"

She sighed. *Even the wind is still.*

Wren and Rascal hurried to the camper. She put fresh water in Rascal's bowl; while he drank his fill, she put two bottles of water into her backpack and slathered on sunscreen. After she stuck her light jacket into her backpack, she picked up the map and coordinates.

"I'm ready now."

After they walked past the fence behind Socorro's house, they continued along the road toward town until Wren said, "We should start here; I'll check our coordinates."

Wren opened her gps app to check their location then rolled her eyes. "I'd forgotten I'd left it on the street view; according to the gps, we're standing in front of the abandoned snake tourist trap. I guess the person who added the coordinates was not an actual surveyor." She sighed. "It was a good idea in theory; guess we're doing this the old-fashioned way, Rascal. After we find the first one, we'll at least have an idea of what the surveyor used as a marker."

After half an hour, Wren said, "Let's just say we're close and head into the brush; we need to walk along the curve of a circle, and I have no idea how we'll maintain a slight curve without a reference point."

Rascal grinned.

"This is not the best idea I've ever had; let's just walk a ways into the brush and watch for another surveyor's rod then turn toward the fence and head home."

The farther they walked from the road, the thicker the brush became. Wren shuddered. *I forgot about snakes.*

Wren focused on her feet with each step; she paused and hovered her foot before she touched it to the ground in case a snake decided to suddenly jump into her path. "This is going slow, Rascal." She glanced around. "Rascal?"

Rascal barked. *He's not very close.*

She put on her lightweight jacket to protect her arms then pushed through the brush as quickly as she could.

Rascal's barking became more insistent.

"I'm hurrying."

When she reached him, he stood next to a hole that was a little over three feet across. She stood on the edge and peered into the dark. "That must be deep."

"Ain't you the clever one; what took you so long?" Thomas said from deep inside the hole. "I need some help down here; I been holding onto the saloon lady to keep her from sliding down farther into this old mine shaft, but now I'm slipping."

Wren shined her flashlight into the hole and caught a glimpse of Thomas's battered hat.

"I can't get her to be still; she keeps trying to climb out, but every time she moves, she slides deeper."

"Maybe she can't hear you."

"You may not be smart, but you talk good. I think she's listening. Grab my rope, would you? I dropped it. Maybe you could toss down one end, so she won't slide down no more."

I'm going to find a ghost's rope and hang onto one end while I toss the other end down into a hole; Thomas is right: I'm not very smart.

"Do you see the rope, Rascal?"

While Rascal sniffed around the hole, Wren searched too until Rascal pointed and growled.

Wren peered into the grass. "Good boy, Rascal, you found the rope."

She squinted at the rope. *That looks like a snake.*

She kicked a little dirt on it, and it slid away.

"We can't find it, Thomas; maybe it slipped into the hole," Wren said.

"Call for help on that newfangled thing you talk into but stay close to the hole. She's worn out, but I'm sure she's listening to you because she kind of perks up when you say stuff."

Wren called Justin. When he answered, she said, "I think I found Socorro in a deep hole. I'm in the brush maybe two hundred or so yards west of the campground, and I'm guessing a hundred yards from the road. I'm staying close to the hole, so Socorro can hear me; I'll shout when I hear you getting close."

"Got it; on my way."

"I called the marshal; he's on his way."

"Just keep talking to her." Wren realized Thomas was standing next to her.

"I need to find my rope." He disappeared.

Wren heard a light scraping sound then falling gravel.

"Stay real still; the marshal's on his way, and he'll bring help."

Rascal whined.

Of course.

"Rascal, go to the road then bring the marshal here. Good boy."

After Rascal dashed away through the brush, Wren watched a small, completely black snake across from her as it slithered away from the hole and deeper into the brush. *If I lived in Arizona, I'd know what kind of snake that was. I'm just happy it didn't come my way.*

Wren heard a siren not far away; when the wail stopped on the road near where she was, she smiled. "That was for our benefit, saloon lady; Rascal will show the marshal where we are."

When Rascal burst through the brush with the marshal close behind him, Wren felt light-headed. She reeled as she tried to rise to her feet, and the marshal caught her before she tumbled into the hole.

"I'm okay," she mumbled.

"Sure you are; your face is really flushed. Do you have any water?"

She nodded. "In my backpack."

Justin helped her sit on the ground then pulled out a bottle of water while Rascal licked Wren's face. After Justin opened the bottle, he handed it to her, and she took a long drink then poured a little water into her palm and patted her cheeks.

"A trench rescue team is gathering in Phoenix," he said.

"That's not what we need." Wren drank more water as she stroked Rascal's back. "Do you have a rope or two?"

"Sure, I have two ropes; wait a minute, why?"

"I wrote an article about cavers and attended three weeks of training in vertical caving before they'd let me follow them for the article. If you'll lower me with a rope, you're strong enough to help me come back up while I hold Socorro in a rescue bearhug. Maybe I can walk up the shaft wall, so you'll have a little leverage as you pull. The second rope can be my safety rope."

"Three weeks doesn't sound like much."

"It's more than an hour of lecture, which is what only a few trench rescue classes include."

"What happens if I drop you?"

Wren peered over her sunglasses at him. "Then I'll fall and be really mad at you."

Justin laughed. "I asked for that, didn't I? I'll get the ropes, but I'm calling for backup."

"We don't have time," Wren growled.

"It won't take that long for Butch to get here. He can hold onto me while I go down to get Socorro," Justin said.

Rascal followed Justin as he hurried toward his cruiser.

When Justin returned with the ropes, Wren said, "You can't go down; your shoulders are too wide, and you'll make the sides fall in on her."

"I'd feel a whole lot better if we had professionals here."

"I love the extra length of this rope." Wren made herself a makeshift harness then stepped into it. "I'm a professional journalist. We're covered."

Butch crashed through the brush in the campground UTV with Rascal leading him.

"I'm ready," Butch said. "What are we doing?"

"I'm convinced Socorro is in the hole that is most likely a mine shaft. I'm going down; I'll wrap a rope around her and hold onto her while you and the marshal pull us up," Wren said.

Butch's eyes widened. "Is she serious, Marshal?"

"That's what she wants to do. I want to wait for the Phoenix rescue team."

"Which will turn into a recovery team because they won't have all their equipment and rigging in place before morning," Wren said.

"You're being too cynical," Justin growled.

"Oh, really? When do you think they'll get here?" Wren rose to her feet and crossed her arms while she jutted out her jaw. *He's as irritating as Thomas; why have I not seen that before now?*

"Wait a sec," Butch said. "We can use the winch on the UTV; it won't be as dramatic, but it will save my back."

Wren furrowed her brow. "Can we set up a triangle or rigging, so we can drop the line down and pull straight up?"

"I like the way you think, Wren. Give me two shakes, and I'll have it done." Butch handed Wren a headlamp. "So, how are we going to lift out Socorro?"

"I'll fasten my seat harness to a rope and take down a second rope with me; when I reach Socorro, I'll put the safety rope around her, and hang onto her while you pull us up."

"We can do something like that." Butch pulled out equipment and began working on the rigging.

"Okay; we'll go with the plan, except I'll go down then bring Socorro up," Justin said.

Butch paused as he stared at Justin then met Wren's gaze and smiled as he returned to his work.

Wren snorted. "Have you seen your shoulders? You won't fit."

Justin growled, "I'll scrunch them and cross my arms."

Wren rolled her eyes as she helped Butch set up the rigging. "For the sake of argument, which you seem absolutely determined to continue, how would you hold onto her and bring her up with your scrunched up shoulders?"

"I'd figure it out." Justin's tone was cold.

"And delay getting Socorro the help she needs? Nice." Wren dumped out her backpack onto the ground before she hooked the backpack to the safety rope then her harness and the safety rope to the lowering rope; she tugged on all the attachment points then straddled the hole and nodded. "Ready."

"What do you think you're doing?" Justin growled.

Rascal whined as Butch slowly lowered her.

"Don't mean to rush you, but if you're done yelling at her, Marshal, I'd appreciate it if you'd stand by the rigging to monitor her descent," Butch said.

Wren smirked then turned on her head lamp; as she went deeper, the walls around her narrowed, and she kept her light trained on the hole below her.

"No way could he have pulled in his broad shoulders with those rippling muscles to get through this," Wren muttered. *Rippling muscles? Where did that come from?*

She narrowed her eyes as a shape emerged in the shadows below her.

"Slower," Wren shouted.

"Slower," Justin repeated.

As she grew closer, she saw someone on a narrow ledge.

"Socorro?" Wren whispered. "Don't move."

Chapter Eleven

Socorro moaned. "My face hurts; I knew you'd come get me."

After she was next to Socorro, Wren shouted, "I found her. Stop."

"Stop," Justin said.

"Socorro, I brought a backpack. Do you think you could slip it on backwards? I'll fasten the chest strap across your back, then Butch can pull you out."

"I can't move because I'll slide down the wall and into the dark." Socorro's voice quivered.

"She's okay and talking to me." Wren called out to Justin while she snapped the chest strap to the backpack then loosened the strap as far as she could.

"I'll slip the chest strap over your head while you put on the backpack backwards with one arm then hold the backpack to your chest."

Socorro moaned in pain as she raised her arm to go through the strap. When she had the backpack against her chest with one arm, Socorro sighed in relief. "Doesn't hurt as much to breathe."

"Good; I'll bearhug you with my arms and legs, then you can hang onto me while you put your other arm through the backpack strap."

"You can't hold me; I'll slide and fall."

"I already had this fight with the marshal, and he lost. I'm stronger than you think; you might slide a little, but that will just be from the slack in the rope; maybe I can do something about that too."

When Wren wrapped her arms and legs around Socorro, Socorro's voice shook. "Don't let me fall."

"You know I won't," Wren said.

Socorro groaned as she lifted her other arm then sobbed as she lowered it, "Can't see the strap."

"Do your best; we'll be fine." Wren tightened her hold onto Socorro with her arms and legs.

"Take out the slack in the ropes," Wren shouted. "We're almost ready to come up."

After Wren felt her rope tighten, she checked Socorro's rope.

While her heart pounded, Wren said as calmly as she could, "Wrap your arm around me then put your other arm through the shoulder strap. Slow your breathing and take your time."

"Breathe slow; take my time," Socorro muttered. "Can't see; hard to breathe."

"You're close; keep going."

"I'm right here, honey." Sheridan's voice boomed down from the top of the hole.

"Good," Socorro whispered.

When the sand loosened under Socorro's feet and slid into the abyss, Socorro screamed.

Wren quietly hummed to soothe Socorro and herself then said, "We're doing great; take a slow breath in then blow it out." Wren breathed slowly in then out.

Socorro copied Wren's breathing then grunted. "There; I got my arm through the strap."

"Perfect, now clasp your hands together behind me and don't let go."

"I won't." Socorro moaned as she moved her arms. "Everything hurts."

"Ready," Wren shouted. "Bring us up."

The winch creaked as Wren and Socorro slowly ascended. When they were halfway out of the hole, Sheridan snatched them away from the mineshaft.

Justin steadied Wren while Sheridan pried loose Socorro's fingers and pulled her away from Wren.

When Wren tried to stand, her legs collapsed; Rascal yelped. Justin immediately grabbed her; when she uncontrollably shivered, he wrapped his arms around her. "I gotcha, Wren."

Her teeth chattered. "I was terrified that I wasn't holding Socorro tight enough."

"How about you, sweetie?" Sheridan asked.

"I was afraid to let go of Wren; I didn't want her to fall." Socorro moaned as she wrapped her arms around Sheridan's neck. "My ribs are sore."

Sheridan examined her face then growled, "Your eyes are swollen shut, and you have dried blood on your lip under your nose. Who was it?"

"Ambulance is on the way, Sheridan," Butch said.

"Don't know." Tears spilled out through the slits of Socorro's swollen eyes and rolled down her battered face.

Her breathing was ragged as she tried to talk. "I didn't see him before he hit me in the face with his fist; all I saw were his fists."

"It's okay, honey; you don't have to say anything." Sheridan stroked her hair away from her face with his fingertips.

"He asked me where it was then hit me again and again when I said I didn't know. I was in a hot shed then I was on a cold ledge in the dark," Socorro gasped as she spoke.

"Shhh, shhh." Sheridan swayed from side to side to comfort her.

"When I moved, part of the ledge dropped away," Socorro sobbed.

"Let's meet the ambulance at the road, Butch," Sheridan said.

"I'll come back for you and my equipment, Wren." Butch unhooked the winch from the ropes then helped Sheridan remove Wren's backpack from Socorro.

When Socorro cried out as Butch slipped away the backpack that she held tightly across her chest, Sheridan said, "Grab something; we took away her splint."

Butch quickly folded his cotton work jacket, and Sheridan placed it against Socorro's chest. "Wrap your arms around the jacket, honey."

Socorro's rapid, shallow breathing slowed. "Much better. Thanks."

After Butch left with Sheridan and Socorro, Justin said, "Butch picked up all your things from your backpack that you dumped out, Wren."

"I think I can stand now; I must have worn out my leg muscles by holding on so tightly to Socorro."

"We can wait until Butch returns," Justin said.

Wren inhaled in preparation of delivering her scathing argument but raised her eyebrows at the light woodsy aroma mixed with sweat. *He smells good.*

"I'm fine." She unconsciously tapped his shoulder twice.

The marshal chuckled. "Did you just tap out like a high school wrestler? Does that mean I win?"

Wren pressed her lips tightly together, but her giggle escaped. "Not at all; you cheated and made me laugh."

Justin smirked as Rascal returned with Butch following him.

When Butch parked next to them, Justin helped Wren into the passenger's seat, then the two men disassembled the rigging and loaded the pieces into the cargo bed of the UTV.

Justin returned Wren's items to her backpack.

"If you scoot over a bit, Wren, I can catch a ride back to my cruiser."

When Wren sighed, Justin said, "I'll scrunch my shoulders."

As he sat on the seat next to her, Wren dramatically flinched to emphasize her displeasure at being inconvenienced while she slid closer to the driver's seat. *I will not smile.*

Butch hopped into the driver's seat. "Hang on; it's bumpy."

Justin put his arm around Wren to steady her; she leaned against him when they hit the first bump, so she wouldn't jostle Butch, and Justin pulled her closer.

After they reached his cruiser, Justin said, "I'll meet you at Wren's camper, Butch, to make sure she's settled before I leave. You want a ride, Rascal?" Justin opened the back door of his cruiser, and Rascal leapt inside.

On the way to her camper, Butch said, "Betsy wants to check on you. I told her you'd text her after you were settled."

As they went past the row of the Fosters' site, Wren's eyes widened. "The Fosters' RV is gone. When did they leave?"

"I'm not really sure. A tow truck showed up not long before I got the call from the marshal to come help. The driver showed Betsy a bunch of paperwork, then I showed him and his helper where the Fosters' RV was. I stuck around and watched. I've never seen such a slick operation: they dumped the holding tanks, disconnected the RV from the utilities, and left in less than fifteen minutes of the time they arrived at the office. I commended the driver for their skills, and he told me they typically pick up repossessions. He said the only way they knew how to pick up an RV these days was by the old-fashioned grab and run method." Butch chuckled.

When Butch stopped at her camper, Justin stood near the door with his arms crossed. "I thought you had better sense than to leave your door unlocked. "

"What are you talking about?" Wren shouted.

Butch sped away.

"Your unlocked door," Justin growled.

Wren narrowed her eyes and spoke in her chilliest tone. "I locked it before I left; where's Rascal?"

"He's inside; I gave him fresh water."

"I locked it," she grumbled as she hurried into the camper.

Justin followed her inside. "It was unlocked when I got here; before I leave, check to see if anything is missing."

Wren carefully examined all the drawers, shelves, and the closet. "Nothing is missing."

"You're sure?"

Wren glared at him. "If you'll excuse me, I'm sure you have other things to do."

Justin slammed the door behind him when he left.

Wren poured a large glass of tea and gulped it down while she pulled each item out of her backpack then brushed off the sand into her trashcan.

She groaned when she took her backpack outside. "It's still hot. I thought the heat might have taken a break by now, but it's still brutal."

While she shook out the sand from her backpack, her phone rang. She rushed inside and answered.

"Hey, it's Cody. I'm on my way to the hospital; I'm going to stay in a cabin at the campground and should be there in a couple of hours. If you don't mind eating late, I'm picking up something for my supper; I thought maybe you could join me."

"I hate to put you to the trouble. Wouldn't you rather spend a little time with Sheridan at the hospital?"

"I'd just be in his way; I'll let you know when I'm in town."

After they hung up, Wren slipped her phone into her back pocket. "Let's go to the saloon to tell Thomas we found Socorro."

When she opened the door, Rascal slowly rose to his feet as the heat rushed inside full force.

"Why don't you stay here? You did a lot of running; I won't be long."

Rascal flopped down and grinned.

Wren smiled as she strolled to the saloon. *It's too hot to hurry.*

When she reached the saloon, Thomas was on the porch in the shade. "You got the saloon lady outta that mineshaft; you did good, girl. What are you doing here? It's too hot to be running around this time of day."

"Do you know who attacked her?"

"Heck, yeah. It was one of them smooth-talking, bad-tempered outlaws from out of town."

"Why did he attack her?"

"He wants that paper he was looking for when the library lady caught him. He started the fire out of spite when he couldn't find it."

"Do I have it?"

"Not yet, girl, because you haven't gone to get it." Thomas chuckled as he disappeared.

"Where do I go?" Wren asked.

When Thomas didn't answer, she crossed her arms and stared at the saloon. *It's too hot to stand in the sun.*

She trudged back to her camper with her head down while she was deep in thought.

"Wren?" Betsy pulled alongside her in the golf cart.

Wren jerked.

"I'm sorry, Wren, climb in, and I'll give you a ride; I didn't mean to startle you. I was on my way to invite you to the office for a chat, then I spotted you. It's too hot to be wandering around."

Wren nodded.

"Where's Rascal?" Betsy glanced around.

"He took me up on my offer for him to stay in the camper where it's cool."

"Good." Betsy sped to the office.

When they went inside, Betsy hurried to answer the ringing phone. "Oops, I forgot to take it with me."

"It's a marvelous day at our Forgotten Oasis Campground, how can I help you?" Betsy asked then listened.

"Thanks, Sheridan; I appreciate it, and I'll let Wren know."

After she disconnected, she said, "Socorro has a concussion and bruised ribs, but nothing broken. She has an abrasion on her back from being dragged across the sand. Sheridan thinks she was attacked somewhere on the property, so he asked if we'd check her house to see if anything was missing. He thinks I will be able to tell, and he's right. Socorro was meticulous about putting things back where they belonged."

Betsy grabbed two bottles of water out of the refrigerator then handed one to Wren. "I'm not good about drinking enough water. I'll bet you aren't either."

Wren drained her bottle on the way to Socorro's.

"Socorro never locked her house during the day," Betsy said after she parked. "She said it was too much of a hassle."

When they went inside, Betsy pointed to the open file cabinet drawer. "Air conditioning seems to be working just fine;

thanks for coming with me to check. A new arrival will be here any minute, so let's head to the office."

After they were outside, Betsy and Wren hopped into the golf cart, and Betsy sped away then stopped in the shade of a large RV and sent a text.

"Why did we leave?"

"I asked Butch to meet us at Socorro's house. The open file cabinet drawer spooked me."

When Butch waved from Socorro's, Betsy left the shade and parked in front of the house.

"Sheridan wants me to see if anything is missing, but the top file cabinet drawer was open, so we left."

Butch pulled a baseball bat out of the back of the golf cart then went inside. Several minutes later, he came out. "The coast is clear; let me know if you need me."

Betsy frowned as she went through the drawer. "Socorro's recipe file is missing."

Wren hurried to the kitchen. "There's a folder on the counter with paper inside it."

Betsy joined her and flipped through the file then frowned. "Her recipe for barbeque chicken wings is missing."

Wren went through the papers one at a time then handed a sheet to Betsy. "Is this it?"

Betsy glanced at the paper and sighed. "Yes, but I still feel like something's wrong."

Wren stared at the back door. "When you said that Socorro didn't lock her door during the day, did that include the back door?"

"No, the back door was locked most of the time because she rarely used it."

The campground phone rang. "It's a perfect day for a dip in our sparkling pool at the Forgotten Oasis Campground, how can I help you?"

Betsy listened then raised her eyebrows as she replied, "Give me one second, and I'll check our schedule. Please hold."

Betsy sighed. "I have to go to the office."

"Go on, I'll lock up."

"Thanks. I'll talk to you later."

After Betsy left, Wren opened the unlocked back door then stepped outside and stared at the ground. "Are those drag marks, or is Betsy's case of nerves catching?"

Wren went back inside. *I don't see any sign of a scuffle, but Socorro had dried blood on her face and mouth around her nose.*

Wren opened the kitchen trash can. When she smelled the distinct iron odor of blood, she pushed aside the coffee filter filled with wet coffee grounds, junk mail, and other papers then stared at the blood-soaked hand towel that had been shoved down into the trash. She rushed out of the house and sat down on the porch with her head between her knees until the waves of nausea passed.

She pulled out her phone and called the marshal.

Chapter Twelve

Justin immediately answered his phone. "Are you okay, Wren?"

"No, I found a blood-soaked towel in Socorro's kitchen trash. I think she was attacked and beaten in her kitchen."

"Where are you?"

"On her front porch."

"Go to your camper; I'll be there in ten minutes."

Wren stumbled to her camper then went inside and sat on the floor with Rascal while she sobbed.

After her tears slowed, she rose from the floor and blew her nose then splashed water on her face.

When a car stopped at her camper, she peered out then opened the door for the marshal.

"Why don't you have a seat while you fill me in," Justin said.

After they sat at the small dinette, Wren said, "The amount of blood on the towel shouldn't have shocked me, but it was such a graphic reminder of how brutal the attack on Socorro must have been. Sheridan asked Betsy to check the house, and Betsy wanted me to go with her."

After Wren recounted the events beginning with going with Betsy to check Socorro's house, Justin said, "I'll let the investigators know Socorro was probably attacked in her home, and I'll check the back of the house before I leave. Anything else?"

She shook her head. "I probably should have taken a breath or two before I called you, so you didn't have to come all the way out here. I could have told you everything over the phone."

Justin rose. "Don't worry about it; it's my job."

Wren nodded. *It's his job.*

After he left, Wren angrily brushed away a stray tear. "The marshal is a polite, brilliant law enforcement officer who is highly skilled at encouraging people to trust him. I think I've read a little too much into his protective approach that is strictly professional, Rascal."

Wren poured a glass of tea then sat on the sofa next to the box. *I need to quit thinking about just myself; reading Miranda's stories is a good place to start.*

She smiled as she read the first story. "This story is fun; Miranda had a great sense of humor."

After a half hour of reading, Wren stretched then sniffed. "I need a shower, and it wouldn't hurt to sweep the floor and straighten up a bit before Cody gets here. I think I'll spoil myself and take a shower in a space that's larger than a matchbox."

Wren collected the stories she'd read and put them under the stories she hadn't read yet. After she wiped down the small counter, she swept then took the rug outside and shook it out while Rascal investigated their campsite. When Wren opened the camper door, Rascal dashed inside.

After she spread out Rascal's colorful rug, Wren put her hands on her hips while she inspected the living and dining space. "What do you think, Rascal? I think it's good enough."

Wren hurried to gather her shower gear, towel, and clean clothes and put them into her shower bag with the smiling unicorn that she'd had since she was six.

She glanced around the room when she went inside. *Doesn't look like anyone's been in here today. Most people must prefer to shower in their own RVs.*

She hung up her shower bag next to a shower stall then pulled back the curtain to turn on the water. Her eyes widened at the woman's purse that was on the built-in shower seat. *I'll bet someone's been looking for this since yesterday; I'll take it to the office first thing in the morning.*

She picked up the purse and hung it on the hook near the sinks then turned on the shower. After Wren undressed, she climbed in and closed the shower curtain then sighed with delight as the warm shower spray soaked her. She lathered up then slowly turned to rinse in the warm, soothing sheets of water before she shampooed and rinsed her hair. She enjoyed the refreshing spray then reluctantly turned off the water and vigorously dried herself. When her hair was towel-dry, she dressed then carefully combed out the tangles. After Wren put her bath gear and dirty clothes into her shower bag, she stuck the purse on top. *I'll take this to Betsy in the morning.*

As she strolled back, she ran her fingers through her hair and chuckled. *I've fought my curls my entire life; who knew I just needed to come to Arizona?*

After she was inside her camper, Wren set the purse under the bathroom sink and hung up her towel and bath gear to dry in the shower stall before she dropped her clothes into her small laundry basket.

She stared at the empty drawer where she had kept her carefully folded clean clothes. "I have only one acceptable choice, Rascal. I have to do laundry first thing in the morning or wear dirty clothes. I've always thought it was a good idea to pack light for my long weekend trips, but I need to change my thinking because there may not always be a convenient laundry."

After Wren brushed her dry hair, she picked up her phone and smiled. "Cody sent a text forty-five minutes ago saying he'll be here in an hour. I guess I was loving that shower far longer than I realized. We may see him any minute. Let's sit outside while we wait for him unless it's buggy like it always is at home, then we'll wait inside."

While she sat in her camp chair, Wren inhaled the tantalizing aroma of grilling meat and listened to the conversations and laughter at the camp sites around her. A dog barked, and Rascal answered while a third dog howled; the entire dog population at the campground soon joined in with barks, yips, and howls.

When the canine bark fest died down, Wren chuckled. "I didn't know there were so many dogs at the campground."

When Wren's phone rang, she narrowed her eyes. "Would it be rude if I let Charlie's call roll over to voice mail?"

Rascal growled.

Wren rolled her eyes then answered.

"Am I calling too late?" Charlie asked. "I have trouble with the time zones sometimes. It's only seven thirty here."

"I'm fine," Wren said. *I'm pretty sure I was supposed to say some reassuring phony something. Phone calls annihilate my brain.*

"I just wanted to let you know I read your article. It's good, Wren; your voice and personality are so alive in your articles. You have a knack for making a story feel real; I felt like I should pack, make a reservation, and be at the campground first thing tomorrow in case the Saloon Lady needs me." Charlie chuckled.

Why do I feel like another shoe is about to drop? Let's get to the editor, Charlie.

"Our editor has a few points that he feels will make your story much stronger. I'll send them to you by email, then we can have a conference call in the morning at your convenience. What time shall we say?"

Never. "I'll have to review the comments before I can really say; I'm sure your editor will want to discuss the impact of any substantive changes on the publish date that will result from his desire to put his fingerprints on my work."

"You're absolutely right; I agree with you completely," Charlie said.

"Did you even hear what I said?" Wren asked. *Oops; I said that aloud.*

"Of course, I did. So, what do you suggest?"

Fire the buttinsky editor. "I can't say until I've had a chance to review and digest the editor's complaints; I'll be happy to respond to any legitimate issues in a day or so."

"Sounds reasonable to me; just between us, he's a bit of a prima donna."

Wren chuckled. "Are you playing both sides of the fence, Charlie?"

"It's my job as the publisher," Charlie said. "Just do me a favor and don't quit or maim him. That's all I ask."

"I might promise one and not the other; I'll have to let you know."

"If it comes down to a choice, don't quit." Charlie hung up.

Wren stared at her phone then smirked. "I'm a nice person, Rascal. I let Charlie have the last word."

Charlie just ruined all the great benefits of my amazing shower. I have to tell Justin what Charlie said; he'll help me put it into perspective.

Wren rose from her chair. "Let's go inside, Rascal."

As she put away her camp chair, Wren frowned. *Did I say I'd tell Justin? I meant to say Cody. Charlie and his annoying editor are befuddling my head. Maybe I'll just tell Betsy.*

After they were inside, Wren snorted. *Maybe I should tell Thomas, except he'd say something insulting.*

Wren's thoughts were interrupted by a tap on the door. When she opened it, Cody grinned and held up two large, white sacks. "Are you starving? I am. Take the food. I have Sheridan's favorite beer and a bottle of Socorro's favorite wine in my car, so you'll have a choice."

Wren put the sacks on the table and pulled out paper plates while Cody came inside with beer and wine.

"Which shall I open first?" he asked.

"It depends; what's for supper?" Wren asked.

"Excellent question, milady. We're dining on green chile cheeseburgers with Swiss cheese and fries." Cody set down the bottle of wine then held up a hand in mock modesty. "I know, typical gourmet food; hope you don't mind."

"Beer and cheeseburgers go together. I always thought New Mexico was the land of the green chile."

"True, but chile laughs at the arbitrary state borders." Cody grinned.

After he put the beer on the table, Cody said, "I stopped to talk to Sheridan. Socorro still can't have any visitors except for Sheridan, so I didn't keep him very long. Socorro claims she's going home tomorrow, but she doesn't realize how strong her painkillers are. You probably know she has bruised ribs and a mild concussion. The hospital plans to keep her under observation for at least three more days."

"I can't tell you how refreshing it is to hear good news; Socorro's going to be just fine if she's already planning to leave." Wren tore open the sacks while Cody moved the wine to the counter and opened two beers before he put the rest in the refrigerator.

"Sheridan warned the head nurse that Socorro will try to bribe her way out."

While they ate, Cody asked, "What about you? What trouble did you get into?"

Wren rolled her eyes. "It's not exactly dinner conversation. Tell me about your day."

"I can't really talk about my day because it's an active case in the judicial system, but if I did, I'd tell you about a lazy public defender, a brilliant criminal, and a disengaged judge who is obviously daydreaming about his next vacation somewhere on a South Pacific island. It's a little scary that the only person in the entire courtroom who is paying attention to me is the defendant: he's taking notes. I'll bet anything that he's enrolled in an online school and will be sitting for the bar within a year."

"Have you always wanted to be a lawyer?"

While they ate and talked about career paths, Cody's phone rang.

"It's work; I'll take it outside," Cody said.

After Cody stepped out, Wren raised her eyebrows. *Both of us are hyper focused on our work.*

Wren wrapped up the half of her cheeseburger that was left and put it into the refrigerator.

Rascal stared at her.

She shrugged. "I lost my appetite. If I decide not to eat it for breakfast, it's yours."

Rascal leaned against her, and she rubbed his ears then giggled when he slid to the floor. After she threw away her fries, she wrapped up Cody's and put them into the refrigerator.

She sat on the sofa, and Rascal hopped up to join her. While she absentmindedly stroked his back, she read the next story in Miranda's box.

"This isn't one of Miranda's usual stories, Rascal. The first and last parts are a complete story if you put them together, but the middle part is very disjointed like it's not related at all. I might be too tired to read."

Wren set it aside. "I'll read it in the morning."

Wren went to the window and peeked through the blinds. Cody was waving his arm in emphasis while he talked on the phone.

She returned to the sofa and pulled out the next story. As she read, her eyelids became heavy, and she leaned back onto the sofa arm for support while she put up her feet.

Wren woke sometime during the night with the light blanket from her bed covering her. She locked the door then stumbled to bed, dragging her blanket behind her.

Chapter Thirteen

Wren woke when Rascal whined. She pulled her sheet and blanket over her head then opened one eye and groaned, "It's already daylight, Rascal. I must have fallen asleep while I waited for Cody to finish his call."

She stumbled to the kitchen to make coffee then stared in a groggy daze at the coffee maker until it sputtered while it heated the water; she shook off her morning fog. She sighed while she dressed. *This is the last of my clean clothes. I won't have anything clean to wear tomorrow if I don't wash clothes today.*

While she poured her first cup of the day, Wren glanced at the table. "Is that a note?" She picked up the slip of paper from a small notepad then sat at the table while she sipped her coffee and read.

"It's an apology from Cody for being so long on the phone. I think he should apologize for answering it in the first place," she grumbled. "He wants me to text him; I'll need more coffee first, then maybe I won't be so cranky."

After she poured her second cup, she sent Cody a text: "Got your note."

She furrowed her brow as she read his reply. "Open your door."

Cody sat at her picnic table. "That was about the lamest note I've ever written in my life. I apologize for taking the call in the first place: that was my first mistake; the second mistake was thinking I wouldn't be long, which only compounded the first one. I'm filling in for Sheridan at the hardware store today, but I wanted to talk to you before I left for the day."

"Do you have time for coffee?"

Cody grinned. "Sure do; thanks."

While Wren poured his coffee, he asked, "What are your plans for today? Need any hardware?"

Wren snickered. "That wasn't quite as lame as your note."

"At least you didn't take away my coffee; that's a good sign, right?"

Cody drained his coffee cup. "The store doesn't open for another hour, but I haven't worked there in a year, so I need the extra time to learn where everything is on the shelves now and the prices. Nobody wants to hear, 'it used to be here.' Drop by if you have a chance."

"I might." Wren smiled.

"You could follow me into town and pick up some breakfast burritos at the food truck that comes to the gas station every Friday and Saturday if you'd like to have breakfast in a hardware store with an annoying lawyer."

Rascal trotted to the door.

"You have Rascal's approval; evidently that's the best offer we've had all day."

"That's great; Sheridan keeps a coffee maker and coffee in the back; I'll provide hot coffee."

"I've got a couple of things to do, then we'll pick up the burritos before we come to the hardware store."

Rascal whined.

"Will the puppies be there?" Wren asked.

"Sure will; Sheridan's neighbor took care of them last night; Sheridan will pick them up then drop them off at the hardware store." Cody whistled as he headed out the door.

After he left, Wren frowned. "I might duplicate Cody's mistake of underestimating how long something will take, Rascal, because I thought I'd walk up to the office to give Betsy the purse; that would never happen, would it? I'll take it to her after we get back from breakfast. I don't think she's in the office this early, anyway, but I'll take it along with us, so we can drop it off when we get back."

Wren quickly made her bed. "Okay, let's go."

When she passed the office on her way out, she smiled. "Betsy's not there, so I don't feel so guilty."

When she parked at the gas station, Wren stared at the long line at the food truck. "I hope they don't run out before I get to the front of the line. I'll leave the engine running, Rascal. I can't believe how hot it is already."

Wren found the end of the line while more people lined up behind her; she listened to the surrounding conversations while she waited.

"That hole Socorro fell into must have been dug by an armadillo. They're notorious for digging deep where it's cool," one man said.

"I don't know about that; how big a hole can they dig?" a man asked.

"It probably wasn't wide enough for even a small person to fall into, but I'll bet a coyote tried to dig it out. Armadillos can dig fast and deep, so the hole would have been pretty narrow not too far down because coyotes aren't likely to jump into a hole unless they see their dinner."

"Armadillos always have a second exit; I'll bet that coyote went hungry."

"You're probably right."

The man who stood behind her said, "Excuse me, are you Wren?"

Wren raised her eyebrows at his southern drawl. *He's Jeff Reed's partner.*

She turned, and her heart pounded while she smiled at the man who had light brown, thinning hair, a thick neck, and wide shoulders. *He reminds me of the man who followed Socorro from the grocery store.*

"Sure am; you are?"

The man held out his hand. "Rick."

They shook. *Firm handshake.*

Rick casually scanned the people in front of them and the newcomers behind them then met Wren's eyes. *He doesn't miss much.*

"How's your article coming along?" he asked. "Or are you tired of complete strangers asking you about your writing?"

The twinkle in his eyes and his disarming smile were flawless. *He's good, but so am I.*

She returned his smile. "Not at all; very few people really want to know; usually after I say fine, they tell me about a book that they've always been told they should write. I love hearing their stories."

"Have you ever thought about writing fiction?"

She chuckled. "I would never get through page one of chapter one because I'm driven to research every tiny detail before I write; I'll always be an avid reader, though. What about you? What do you do?"

"I'm kind of like you; I spend most of my time doing research." He smiled. "You're next up."

Wren turned and was surprised no one was between her and the order window; the young woman handed her a large white sack. "Wren, Mr. Cody called in the order for you."

"How much do I owe you?" Wren asked.

"He paid for it too." She smiled.

Wren put two dollars in the tip jar at the window then hurried to her truck.

"I made a new friend, Rascal. He's as sneaky as Cody who ordered and paid for the burritos. I wonder what Cody would have done if I had decided to be a no show? Although, he really roped us in with breakfast burritos and puppies, didn't he?" Wren giggled.

After she parked in front of the hardware store, Cody met them before they reached the door. "Come on in; the coffee's ready, and I think the puppies heard me tell Sheridan that you and Rascal were having breakfast with us because they've been hovering around the front of the store since they arrived."

When Wren and Rascal were inside, the three puppies rushed to greet them. Rascal yipped, and the puppies lined up then followed him to the back.

Cody chuckled. "Sheridan told me Rascal was training the pups, but it was still amazing to watch him in action."

As they strolled to the back of the store, Wren said, "That was sneaky calling in our order and paying for it."

"I prefer to think of it as clever," Cody said.

While they ate, Wren asked, "How's Socorro?"

"Terrible, according to Sheridan, but I think he was talking about her attitude. He wants her to stay in the hospital a few more days, but she announced she's expecting to be released today. Sheridan may fold if she'll agree to stay at his house, but I'm positive he will end up moving to her house. I asked him once why he always argues with her because she always wins. He told me he was wearing her down."

Wren laughed. "Poor Sheridan."

"Don't feel too sorry for him; he loves every minute."

"You're right. He gets this funny look in his eye right before he pokes at Socorro and sets her off."

Cody grinned. "You've noticed that? Not many people do. You have excellent observation skills."

Wren stared at him then frowned at her coffee. "Thanks."

"Did I say something wrong?"

Wren sighed as she met his gaze. "I've always prided myself on being the invisible observer; I'm not used to being, you know..."

"Talked to like an actual person?"

Her mouth quivered as she tried to hold back her smile. "Something like that; did you know your style that goes directly to the point is rare and refreshing?"

"That sounds too much like a genteel sparkling wine; I'd rather be thought of as an ancient, frontier whiskey: raw and slightly dangerous."

Wren giggled. "My apologies: your style is rough and unbridled."

"Thanks; you are a mysterious wraith."

"That's exactly how I see myself."

Cody picked up their trash and put it into the white sack. "I have to open in fifteen minutes. I'd rather put a sign on the door."

"What would it say?" Wren asked.

Cody paused and furrowed his brow; the deepening dimples on his cheeks spoiled his attempt to maintain a serious demeanor. "It's national play hooky day."

Cody grinned when Wren laughed.

While Wren followed Cody to the front of the store, he asked, "What are your plans for today?"

"I have a lot of reading to catch up on, but my number one task is laundry."

"You live a glamorous life."

Wren sniffed. "I know."

When she reached the door, she asked, "Are you going with me, Rascal?"

Rascal and the puppies trotted to join her.

"Stay, puppies," Wren said.

When the puppies lowered their heads and sat, Cody chuckled. "They never listen to Sheridan or me."

"I can't take full credit: Rascal gave them a look."

After Wren and Rascal were in the pickup, she said, "I can't think of anything we need in town; we can stop by the office and give Betsy the purse."

When they were not quite halfway to the campground, Wren's phone buzzed a text from Betsy. "Where are you? Call me ASAP."

Wren pulled onto the shoulder and called.

Betsy was out of breath when she picked up before the first ring completed; her voice was panicky. "Where are you?"

"I'm almost halfway to the campground from town."

"Turn around and speed like crazy back to town. The campground's going to get hit by a haboob in less than five minutes. Do you see it?"

Wren peered at the horizon. "It looks like a dark brown haze in front of me."

"Text me when you get into town, so I'll know you're safe. I'm running from RV to RV to warn our guests to stay inside their RVs and off the road or come to the office, and we'll have a dust storm party."

Wren turned around in the middle of the road and sped toward town. She was not quite within sight of the town when she saw a car ahead of her that was stopped on the opposite side of the road. After she pulled onto the shoulder across from it and parked, she ran to see if she could help.

A man lay on the ground as he jacked up the front of the car on the passenger's side.

"Sir, are you okay?" Wren asked.

"Dang rental car blew a tire, Wren," he said.

"Rick, we need to get back to town immediately; there's a huge dust storm headed our way. Get in; you can take care of your car after the storm clears."

"Dust storms aren't that big a deal. It won't take me long to change the tire."

"Just get in my truck, and we can argue on the way." Wren's voice was hard.

She headed toward her pickup. "I'm leaving; who's your next of kin?"

Rick snatched his duffel bag out of the trunk and strode to the pickup behind Wren who raced back to hop into the driver's seat. After Rick climbed into the passenger's seat, he said, "I forgot to put on my four-way flashers. I'll be right back."

Wren slammed her foot on the accelerator and peeled out toward town before Rick could open the door.

Wren hissed, "That's the worst thing you could do; someone trying to drive through the storm will follow the lights and slam into the car."

Rick fastened his seatbelt. "Tell me about the dust storm."

"I'm driving; look up Arizona dust storms on your phone."

Rick shrugged then pulled out his phone. "A haboob? Is that what's headed toward us? Thanks for stopping; I would have done exactly the wrong thing. I didn't even have time to take it off the jack and move it farther off the road, did I?"

"Nope."

"Where are we going?" he asked.

"The marshal's office." Wren side-glanced Rick. "Is that a problem?"

Rick's face darkened. "I hate to be an inconvenience, but I suppose not."

Wren glanced at her phone. *I missed a text from the marshal.* She picked it up and read it. "Where are you?"

She called him; when he answered, she said, "I'll be at your office in three minutes."

"Good. Park in front of the door; double park if you have to."

"Leave your duffel bag in the truck or take it in," Wren said as she slammed on the brakes in front of the door and jumped out. While she opened the back door for Rascal, Justin rushed out to grab her backpack; Rick picked up his duffel bag and followed Wren, Rascal, and Justin into the building.

"You're hitchhiking these days, Rick?" Justin asked.

Rick chuckled. "More like kidnapped by an avenging angel. I had a flat tire, and Wren told me to get in her truck or tell her who my next of kin was."

"She did you a favor; let's go into my office." Justin put his arm around Wren when the wind suddenly roared and the blowing sand scratched against the windows; as they headed down the hall, he asked quietly, "Are you okay?"

Strictly professional. "I'm fine."

When they walked into Justin's office, Rick frowned. "That wind is fierce, isn't it? Do you have an office I can use, Justin? I have information for the investigating team, and I should let them know I've been delayed by a dangerous storm."

"Sure, I'll show you."

Rick followed Justin out of the office.

"I hate the wind, Rascal," she whispered.

Rascal put his head on her knee, and she hugged him. "Thank you."

When Justin returned, Wren asked, "How long have you known Rick?"

Justin stared at her then picked up his phone. "When did we last do a video check?"

He nodded. "Sounds like a good idea to me. Let it run about thirty minutes; that gives me some time to do some tests."

He chuckled as he glanced at Wren. "I doubt it, but it's an option."

After he hung up, he said, "Sorry, administrative things sometimes fall through the cracks here." He furrowed his brow. "So, what was it you asked me?"

She raised her eyebrows. *Why is he playing the role of a bumbling marshal?*

She shrugged. "I've forgotten."

As she peered at him, Justin turned toward the window then stood in front of it while he examined the thick curtain of sand as it obscured everything outside.

Rascal yawned.

"Can I interest you in any coffee?" Justin asked.

Wren rolled her eyes. *Are you asking me or Rascal?* She joined him at the window. *What are we looking at?*

"Thanks, but I don't think so; how long have you known Rick?"

Justin stared at her. "Did you know you have a tenacious streak?"

"Yes, now it's your turn to answer my question."

Justin chuckled. "I created my own trap; I've known him for two days. He's with the FBI; someone at the Phoenix office called our office on Monday to let us know he'd be in the area. He's been interviewing a few of our oldtimers, but I'm not certain what his focus is since his questions sound random to me; I get phone calls immediately after he talks with one of our residents, but I haven't heard any particular focus for his questions. He must have planned to return to Phoenix today, which is why you found him on your way back to town. Why?"

She told him about Rick calling the campground office and telling Betsy he was Jeff's partner.

"That's really odd; I hadn't heard that the FBI had stepped in to assist in the investigation of Jeff's death. You said the voice was muffled; could it have been someone who was trying to sound like Rick?"

"No; I don't have any clue about the differences between northeastern and midwestern accents, but I know southern accents: each state and even each region is unique. I have something else."

Wren told him about Rick following Socorro then continuing past the campground earlier in the week.

Justin began pacing. "That's the license plate you sent me? It was stolen off a car in Tucson sometime in the past two weeks, but didn't you say you didn't recognize the man who followed Socorro? How can you be certain it was Rick?"

Wren sat down as he continued to pace. "I'm getting dizzy watching you; can you change directions?"

Justin stood at the edge of his desk and crossed his arms while he scowled.

Wren continued, "I didn't recognize the man because the first time I saw Rick was earlier this morning; he got behind me in the line at the food truck and struck up a conversation. I recognized his voice when he spoke then when I turned around, I realized he was the man who followed Socorro."

"This is a lot to digest," Justin said.

"Tell me about it; I think this is the last point, at least so far: Rick's car with the flat tire was a different vehicle, but I didn't think to check the license plate."

Justin began pacing again.

That must be how he concentrates while he's thinking. Wren gazed at his narrowed eyes and the intense look of concentration on his face. *I do my best thinking when I quit trying to think; that must be why he paces.*

She smiled. *He's definitely what they call easy on the eyes.*

Justin suddenly stopped and met her gaze then raised his eyebrows. "What? Did you think of something else?"

Wren felt her cheeks grow warm; she cleared her throat. "No, I was just lost in thought." *Which is definitely the understatement of the century.*

Chapter Fourteen

Justin picked up his phone. "Pat, go to the interrogation room in about ten minutes and tell Rick that you have ordered a rental for him, courtesy of the county, and it will be here in forty-five minutes."

Justin nodded and smiled while he listened.

"You got it; I'm going to check his car. I'll text you when I get close." He glanced at Wren. "Tell him she's in the ladies' room or that a friend picked her up; just keep her out of his sight."

After he disconnected, he said, "Wren…"

She interrupted and picked up her backpack. "I heard; I'm going with you."

He glowered. "No, you aren't. Civilians aren't allowed in the cruisers."

"That makes sense; it's better if we take my truck anyway: it's heavy duty, sits higher, and has better visibility than a car."

"You're right about the visibility; I'll take my truck."

"Mine has four doors, a back seat, and four-wheel drive; if we come across someone who needs to be rescued, we'll have room."

Justin crossed his arms. "No."

She shrugged. "Okay."

His eyes narrowed. "You're going to follow me, aren't you?"

She widened her eyes in her best 'I'm innocent' look. "No, I'm going to the ladies' room then hide out from Rick."

"I could arrest you for interfering with an investigation," he growled.

Wren's mouth quivered as she tried to control her smile. "My lawyer will have me out of here in two minutes."

"Will you do exactly as I say?"

"Of course."

"Okay, but I'm driving."

As he picked up his backpack and a rifle, he muttered under his breath, "Pat will accuse me of being a soft touch for a pretty face."

That didn't sound strictly professional; he's really irritated.

Wren had to hurry to keep up with his fast stride to the front desk; Rascal trotted along beside her.

"I'm taking her truck; she's going with me," Justin growled.

The man with a ruddy face grinned. "Good choice, Marshal."

"And Rascal too," Wren added.

"Fine; Rascal too. Anything else, Ms. Weaver?" Justin crossed his arms.

When Wren smiled her sweetest smile and shook her head, Justin pulled out a tan camouflaged, cotton balaclava from his back pocket. Wren hid her self-satisfied smile by putting on her bandana over her face bandit-style.

Justin donned his head gear then held out his hand. "Give me the keys then put on your sunglasses."

Wren pushed the fob and stood between him and the door while she put on her sunglasses. After she handed over the keys, she pushed on the door, but it didn't budge. Justin smirked as he leaned past her, turned the doorknob, and opened the door.

The man at the desk chuckled. "You two are evenly matched, aren't you?"

"I'll arrest her for blackmail when we get back, Pat."

Pat guffawed as Justin grabbed onto Wren's belt to keep her from being blown down as they rushed out the door to her truck. Rascal leapt past Wren and into the front seat then jumped to the back as she climbed in. Wren slammed the passenger's door shut while Justin started the engine.

He glared at her while she fastened her seat belt. "Hang on."

As Justin crept away from the building, Wren held her breath while the wind buffeted the truck, and the blowing sand cocooned the windows obliterating any visibility of their surroundings. *How does he know where we're going?*

She turned her head to glance at him. *He turned down the side mirror before he climbed in.* Wren leaned forward in her seat and used her side mirror to look at the side of the road. *He's following the line in the middle of the road. I sure hope no one has stopped in front of us.*

When he came to a white line across the road, Justin stopped. "Close your eyes, Rascal, and cover your nose with your paws.

Wren, I'm going to lower our windows just a crack. We need to listen for any traffic."

When her window opened, the sand pelted her. "I don't hear anything."

Justin closed their windows as he turned left. *I am really glad I was smart enough to let him drive.*

She leaned to peer through the blowing sand for Rick's car on the side of the road as Justin picked up his speed. She glanced at the speedometer. *Fifteen miles an hour; feels like we're zooming.*

After what felt to her like hours, the sand ahead of them looked darker. "Slow down."

Justin tapped the brake.

When a dark form appeared in her side window, she flinched in surprise. "We're next to it."

"Let me know when we've cleared it, and I'll pull over."

Wren watched as the truck crawled past the dark form. "We're clear."

Justin pulled to the side of the road then dropped into four-wheel drive. "Hang on; we're going four-wheeling."

The truck bounced, rolled, and bucked as Justin continued.

When he stopped, he patted the steering wheel. "Good job, truck."

He turned to the back. "How are you doing, Rascal?"

Rascal whined and yipped then grinned.

"You got that right." Justin laughed. "What about you, Wren? Which did you enjoy more: the journey or the destination?"

"I've never ridden a bucking bronco before." Wren giggled. "Stopping without hitting anyone was the highlight of my day."

"I wanted to come out here and get the license tag number before Rick left. Why were you all afire to come here? You know a sure sign of a perpetrator is the obsessive draw to revisit the scene of their crime. Is that why Rascal came along: to keep you from covering your tracks?"

Wren snorted. "Is that my cue to confess? Miranda told me I should write fiction; maybe that's your calling."

Justin rhythmically tapped his thumbs on the steering wheel.

Is that his version of pacing when he's forced to sit? While she waited for him to speak, she hummed a tune to herself to match the beat of Justin's tapping.

When Justin suddenly stopped, Wren sighed. *That was fun.*

"I want to check the car in case it isn't Rick's. I have to know whether there's a family or someone alone who is stuck on the side of the road in the storm."

She furrowed her brow. "I have a long rope in the compartment under the driver's side backseat. The young man who picked me up at the airport told me it would come in handy, and the service manager showed me the compartment and gave me the long rope as a gift from the dealership when I asked him if I would need one. You can wrap one end around you, and I'll tie the other end to the truck bumper. I think climbers do something like to stay together in a snowstorm; I know cavers do."

Justin sighed. "Tell me why you can't wait in the truck."

"If you need help, you can tug on the rope. I can't monitor the rope if I'm inside the truck."

"Okay, if you'll promise you'll get inside the truck if you have any trouble breathing."

"I will if you will."

"That's not unreasonable at all."

Wren narrowed her eyes as she inspected his face. *I'm not sure that counts as a promise.*

Justin glanced away from her. "Can you climb into the back seat and open the compartment? I'll grab the rope before I get out."

Wren slid over the seat to the back and removed the rope then handed it to Justin. "I'll get out on the driver's side from here, so I won't get turned around."

Justin pulled up his mask over his face. "Rascal, close your eyes, cover your nose, and hold your breath when we get out. Your count, Wren."

Wren stayed in the back seat as she pulled up her bandana and grabbed her backpack. "One, two, three, go!"

It took all of Wren's strength to open her door; Justin waited for her before he opened his. They jumped out of the truck, and the wind simultaneously slammed their doors. The wind immediately pushed Wren against the side of the pickup; Justin pulled her away from the truck and held onto her as he tied one end of the rope to the back of her belt. He held onto her as they walked together to the back of the pickup.

Justin pressed his mouth close to her ear. "I'll have to tie you to the truck, so you won't blow away; are you sure this is the right thing to do?"

After Wren wrapped her arms around his neck as the wind tried to tear her away from him, she shouted, "I was wrong; I'll have to stay inside the truck."

Justin held onto her as they returned to the driver's door. After he untied the rope from her belt, he held her with one arm, opened the driver's door, and tossed in her backpack then lifted Wren around her thighs and heaved her into the pickup; she landed on her stomach with a face plant on the passenger's seat. The door slammed shut behind her when he stepped away.

Wren struggled to get up; after she was sitting on the passenger's seat, she pulled off her bandana. "That was not the most graceful entrance I've ever made, but it was definitely the most expedient. I misjudged the strength of the wind and forgot to factor in my weight with my brilliant solution, but the embarrassing part is I was too pigheaded to listen to Justin. He's supposed to be the one who is too stuck in his ways to consider a perfectly valid solution."

She turned around and rose to her knees to peer out the back window. "I can't see a thing, Rascal."

Wren grunted in frustration as she sat then picked up her phone and sent a text to Betsy. "Any idea when the haboob will be past you?"

Betsy replied, "Hasn't yet. Will check."

Wren climbed into the back seat with Rascal and hugged him. "I hate that I can't see anything or even be outside to monitor the rope."

Betsy sent a new text. "Another 30-45 min. ugh. Are you okay?"

"Yes. Thanks."

While she fretted about not being able to monitor the rope for Justin, the map of the original Hidden Gulch popped into her head, and Wren frowned. *Why did Miranda point out that Socorro's property included mineral rights?*

That's why she waited for me: the mineral rights are the reason for the sudden interest in the property.

"Seems to me, Rascal, if Jeff Reed discovered something important about the property, then I can too."

When her phone rang, Wren didn't recognize the number; she shrugged. *It's an Arizona area code.*

"Miss Weaver? It's Pat at the marshal's office; I got your number from our dispatcher because I sent Justin a text, but I'm not sure he got it."

"He's checking the car, but I'm sitting in the truck, so I don't know if he did or not. Do you want me to tell him to call you when he's back in the pickup?"

"That would be good. Thanks."

When something slammed against the driver's side of the truck, Wren jumped and squealed, and Rascal barked.

Justin tugged open the driver's door and fell onto the seat then quickly rolled and bent his knees, and as the door slammed, it trapped the rope that was still tied securely around his waist.

"Hi honey, I'm home," he gasped then coughed.

Wren opened a bottle of water and leaned over the seat. "Can you sit up? I have a bottle of water for you."

Justin tried to sit up, but the rope was too tight. Wren grabbed her multitool from her backpack and cut the rope; Justin pushed against the door with his feet and sat up.

After Wren handed him the bottle of water, he took a sip then another. After he removed his head gear, he drank half the bottle before he inhaled a long, slow breath then exhaled.

"You have small cuts on your face around your eyes and near your wrists. Your sleeves must have slid up to expose your skin to the sand," Wren said.

"Thanks for the water; my throat feels like sandpaper." Justin examined his arms. "I didn't notice, but I felt the stings on my face around my sunglasses."

He took another long drink. "I'm glad we came out here."

"Pat from your office called; he sent you a text and wants you to call him."

Justin pulled out his phone from his back pocket. "I thought I had a text, but there was no way I could have read it."

He called Pat. "I'm glad you made that call. Scan the video to see if he called anyone. I found a few things under the front seat, but I haven't checked them yet. Have a couple of deputies search the building; call me after you review the video."

After he put down his phone, Justin gulped down the rest of the water then unbuttoned three of the buttons on his shirt; he reached inside and pulled out identification cards.

"Pat called a friend of his at the FBI office in Phoenix; our buddy Rick is an imposter, and he's gone. I can't imagine that he'd be so reckless that he would take off on foot, so some other foolhardy person must have picked him up. Pat's going to check on that."

"What video?" Wren asked.

Justin faked a cough; Wren giggled.

He finished his bottle of water. "Do you have any more water?"

Wren handed him another bottle of water.

"Thanks." He took a sip then continued to pick at the knot.

Wren leaned over the seat and watched him.

He glanced at her then frowned at the knot as he tugged at it. "Don't you have anything else to do?"

Wren rolled her eyes. "I put everything on hold, so you have my undivided attention."

Justin finally loosened the knot and untied the rope then slipped over to the driver's seat; Wren climbed over the seat to sit up front with him. She sat cross-legged with her elbows on her knees and her chin propped between her hands while she stared at him.

He chuckled. "Mr. Rick Edgerton was in our interrogation room; it's the only private room we have besides my office. When you asked me how long I'd known Rick, the alarm bells went off, and I asked Pat to record him. There's a sign on the wall that says that all conversations are recorded at all times; I've found that most people assume the sign does not mean them."

Justin narrowed his eyes as he scrutinized each of the ID cards then handed them to Wren. "What do you see?"

She straightened her back as she examined each card. "All the first names are essentially forms of the same name: Richard, Ricardo, Dick, and Rico; Rick is the man in the photo for all four. It's interesting that all four have Virginia addresses, but these are towns I've never heard of, and none of the licenses are expired. The last names are interesting: I can line them up alphabetically: A, B, C, and D with Rick Edgerton fitting right in."

Wren's eyes widened.

Justin quickly put his hand on her knee as he peered at her with concern. "Are you okay? What's wrong?"

"I just realized the man who came to the campground on Tuesday morning to meet with Jeff was named Edrick Foster, but his wife was Audrey, which messes up my alphabetic order."

"Is he still there?"

"No, they left sometime early on Thursday in their car; a towing company picked up their RV later in the day."

Justin furrowed his brow and absently tapped her knee with his thumb as he put his other hand on the steering wheel and tapped.

Wren smiled. *I feel like I'm helping him to think.* She watched as his facial expression changed from concerned to thoughtful then determined.

The last thing Miss Miranda said to her floated across her mind like a stray cloud. *"You really need to ask Justin about that photo."*

When he exhaled then smiled as he moved his hand from her knee, Wren returned his smile. "Can I ask you something?"

"I'm taller than you are."

She giggled. "Thank you, but I already figured that one out by myself."

She peered at his face. "You have a photo on your visor. I saw it because you left your visor down after the fire. Who is it?"

Wren's heart ached at the depth of sadness that swept over him.

"Her name was Ashley. We were married the week after I graduated from the academy. A month later, a drunk driver crashed into her. I'd always had a bad feeling about that stretch of the interstate..."

Wren moved close to him and leaned against his shoulder.

He put his arm around her with a weak smile. "I was on duty and was first on the scene. She died in my arms. The drunk driver went on a rant and claimed she ran into him. A truck driver who witnessed the crash was enraged and beat him to a pulp then knelt next to me, and we cried together."

"You didn't report the truck driver, did you?"

"No, I know his name and where he lives, but my report showed two fatalities in the crash. I decided I didn't deserve to be in law enforcement, but the marshal at Hidden Gulch came to visit me while I was on leave. He told me I'd never forget, and I haven't; he also told me that eventually I'd forgive myself for not saving her."

Wren smiled. "You're working on it."

He nodded. "Thanks, Wren. I've never talked about it; I've always thought Thomas knew but held no judgment against me."

"Ashley's the reason you left Maricopa County."

"Yes," Justin said quietly.

Wren nodded. *Thomas must have told Miranda.*

"Sometime maybe you can tell me about Ashley: what she liked and what made her laugh."

"Maybe I can sometime."

Justin's phone rang, and he sighed as he removed his arm and answered.

"Whatcha got, Pat?" he asked.

Justin shook his head as he listened. "You can't be everywhere; he must have been watching for an opportunity. I have four IDs with his photo, which will be a big help for us, but there's not much we can do until the storm passes by. As soon as it lightens up here, we'll head that way."

After he hung up, Justin shook his head. "Rick walked out the front door while Pat was giving report. The rookie at the desk told Rick to be careful."

Justin sighed. "Tell me about your experience with guns."

Wren smiled. "My dad was a competitive shooter. Mom and I went with him to all his competitions. He was amazing. I pestered him to let me shoot competitively when I was eight, and he finally started my training when I was twelve. Mom kind of dropped out of going with us after a while; I'm sure it was boring for her, but it was exciting to me. When I was in high school, Dad slowed down on going to competitions because he had become a senior partner at his law office and didn't have much spare time at all. I kept up competitive shooting all through college. I loved it."

"That is really interesting. I've never shot competitively, but it does sound like it would be fun. Seems like our range hosts competitive shoots from time to time, but I've never really paid attention."

A few minutes later, Wren's phone buzzed a text from Betsy. "Storm past us."

"Betsy said the dust storm has cleared the campground."

Justin started the engine then turned to head toward the road.

As the pickup lurched through the desert brush to the shoulder, Wren sighed. *We were close because of the storm; it was only a moment in time when two lonely souls reached out before they quietly drifted away. It was nice.* She rolled her eyes. *That was overly mushy; I must be sand-shocked.*

Chapter Fifteen

After the sand suddenly cleared, Justin headed toward town. "It's lunchtime, and I'm suddenly starving; what about you? May I buy you lunch, Ms. Weaver?"

Wren giggled. "Of course you may, Marshal."

On their way into town, Wren received a text from Charlie. "Sent you an email."

Wren groaned then replied, "Will check it after lunch. Thanks."

"That didn't sound good." Justin glanced at her.

"My publisher, Charlie, sent me a text to tell me he sent me an email. I'll check it after I return to the campground because I have a feeling it's feedback from the editor."

"I don't understand why that's not good."

"So far, the editor has every symptom of a frustrated writer who wants to rewrite everything I submit into his own voice."

"I'm not sure I understand the true implication of what you just said, but I suspect you can always quit and freelance while you live at the campground."

"That's actually a great safety net for me; thanks for the reminder." Wren smiled. "I've freelanced before; I can freelance again."

Justin chuckled. "Your motto? I like that."

Wren sent a text to Betsy. "I'm having lunch with the marshal."

Betsy replied. "Ooo la la. He's cute."

Wren quickly stuck her phone in her pocket, so Justin wouldn't accidently see the text.

Justin side-glanced Wren. "I'd like to talk to Pat before we go to lunch; are you in a rush to get back to the campground?"

"Not at all; do you want to meet me somewhere, or shall I wait?"

He turned off the highway to go to his office. "If you don't mind, I'd rather you waited, so I won't get pulled into something that can wait until after lunch."

Wren nodded. "I understand that; I may have the world championship title for 'one more thing.'"

Justin shook his head as he parked. "I don't know; I'm pretty good at it."

She rolled her eyes. "Is it okay if we save the competition for another day, so we can actually eat lunch?"

He smiled. "If you insist."

Before they went inside, Justin said, "Do you think Rascal will feel comfortable staying with Pat? We can eat in my office, if that would be better; I promise I'll turn off my phone."

"Do you want to be Pat's advisor, Rascal?"

Rascal grinned.

"I guess he does." Justin smiled.

While Justin and Pat talked quietly, Wren sat in one of the four straight-back chairs for visitors along the wall within sight of the front door. When her phone rang, she hurried outside to answer.

"Where are you? Are you having lunch with the marshal?" Betsy asked. "I should have texted you to call me."

"I'm waiting while he talks to Pat, then we'll go to lunch. What's up?"

"Francine, Miranda's niece, called me; the county records department has copies of the documents they located from the document numbers Miranda gave them before she died. A woman in records called Francine, and she told them that you would pick up the copies; Francine called me and asked if I'd relay the message to you because Miranda told her the documents were for you."

"Is the county records department in the courthouse? I could stop by there after lunch."

"That's it; enjoy your lunch, and I expect full details of your lunch date this afternoon."

It isn't a date; it's just lunch. Wren furrowed her brow as she went inside then smiled. *Betsy was joking.*

"Come on, Rascal," Pat said. "Let's find you some water, then I'll make a few phone calls."

"Do you want me to follow you?" Wren asked as they headed to the door.

"No, leave the cruiser here," Pat called out from the hallway.

Justin shrugged. "We'll take your truck; I owe you gas anyway."

"Why do you owe me gas? Where are we going?"

"Whoever drives gets to pick; it's the impromptu lunch rule."

"I pick wherever you had in mind." Wren jumped into the driver's seat.

"We could drag this out another ten minutes, or I could just give you directions, right?" Justin asked as he climbed in then closed the passenger's door.

"Right." Wren started the truck.

When Wren parked where Justin pointed, she peered at the small café. "I've never even noticed it before: it has a quaint, Old West look."

"Food's really good; I don't come here very often because I usually just grab a quick bite at the gas station."

When they went inside, Wren's eyes widened; after they were seated at a table, she whispered, "We just traveled back in time two hundred plus years, didn't we?"

"Don't you expect Thomas to come out of those swinging doors any minute and scowl at us? At least, that's what he does most of the time when I see him at the saloon."

Wren studied her menu. "He's probably irritated because you won't listen to him. What's a saloon lady burger? Sounds like exactly what I want."

Justin chuckled. "It has green chile, so it's a little spicy, just like you; perfect match."

Wren's eyes widened at the unusual menu. "I have to try the homemade root beer, and sweet potato fries sound good, but then I wouldn't have enough room for dessert."

"Wise choice, my friend." The server approached their table. "Saloon lady burger and root beer. Marshal, your usual?"

"No reason to change perfection," Justin said.

After their server left, Wren asked, "What's your usual?"

"Lawman burger and root beer; the burger is like yours except it has jalapenos instead of green chile."

"Super-hot lawman."

Justin stuck out his chest and saluted Wren with two fingers. "That's what they tell me, ma'am."

Wren giggled.

"So, tell me about this fella in Georgia who couldn't get away to be here with you and Rascal."

"The fella in Georgia dropped me for a tall blonde with political aspirations." Wren told him about Blake. "That was three years ago."

The server brought their food, and they dug in.

Justin finished his burger first. "Nobody's had the sense to stake a claim?"

After Wren ate half of her burger, she stared at the other half. "I think I'll have to save this for supper, so I can have dessert."

The server reappeared and whisked her plate away. "I'll box it up and bring dessert."

Wren smiled. "I threw myself into my assignments. I loved the freedom of freelancing and making my way, even though my first year was rough while I was getting established. My dad kept sneaking money into my bank account until I threatened to disinherit him."

"I'm sure he believed you and stopped."

"Of course, he did. My second year, word started getting around that I'd take the jobs that everyone else considered impossible, and my reputation grew. By the beginning of my third year, publishers and editors were calling me."

"So, you haven't had time for anybody since good ole Blake; sounds like it was on purpose, Wren."

She nodded. "It was probably just as well because the assignments took all my time and attention; I don't think I'd be here if I'd done anything else."

The server put their desserts in front of them. "Warm blueberry pie with freshly churned vanilla ice cream."

The ice cream oozed over the hot pastry, leaving a beautiful creamy blue lake surrounding the pie.

"I see why our pie is in a bowl, not a plate." She picked up her spoon and took a small bite. "I could burn my mouth and get a brain freeze at the same time if I'm not careful."

"If that's what brought you here, then I'm glad you went after what you wanted. What about this assignment?"

"I really don't know; it's not freelance, so it's different. I'll see it to the end because that's what I always do, but I'm not sure it's right for me."

"Didn't you say that Miranda thought you should write fiction? Why is that out?"

"She did, but I've never considered it seriously before. I would be starting over a second time."

Justin smiled. "You're definitely tenacious enough to carry it off."

After Justin paid the bill, they returned to the marshal's office; Justin ran inside and brought Rascal out to the truck. After Justin opened the door, Rascal jumped inside.

"Pat said he enjoyed Rascal's company and wanted to know when he'll be back."

Rascal yipped then grinned.

Justin continued, "Thanks for going with me to check the car. I wouldn't have done nearly as well on my own."

Wren smiled. "Thanks for lunch; it's nice to have a chance to relax."

Wren went to the county courthouse; Rascal appeared to be on guard duty as he sat near the door while Wren found the records department.

A woman rose from her desk and handed a file folder to Wren. "I have your copies right here. I understand you were very close to Miranda; I'm very sorry for your loss."

"Thank you; Miranda was a town treasure, wasn't she?"

The woman nodded. "Now, you let us know if there is anything else we can do to help you."

"Thank you." Wren felt her eyes misting and hurried out to join Rascal.

"Let's get back to the campground. I suspect I have work to do, and I still haven't done any laundry."

She drove straight to her site then sent Betsy a text. "We're back and will be there in a bit."

Wren powered on her computer; before she opened her email, she received two texts.

The first one was from Betsy. "OK."

The second text was from Cody. "Call when you can."

She called Cody. "We're at the campground; what's going on?"

"Socorro was just released from the hospital; Sheridan will stay with her at her house. They moved the wedding to tomorrow. Big shock, right? Socorro wants you to have dinner with us tonight; I think it's supposed to be a rehearsal dinner or something. Sheridan is going to pick up fried chicken from the grocery store deli and the fixings for his famous potato salad. I'm making guacamole, at Socorro's request. I suspect we'll be eating around six."

"I thought it would be a couple more days before Socorro would be released, but I'm not surprised by the wedding tomorrow."

"I don't know what time or any other details quite yet; I'll let you know. Customer's here. See you later."

As Wren opened her email, she said, "If I spend another week here, I'm going to need all new pants with stretchy waistbands. I can't remember a time that I ever ate three full meals a day."

Wren scanned the email from Charlie. "According to Charlie, the enclosed document has a few suggestions from the editor for my consideration. Listen to this, Rascal: 'Please return your revised article by today or early tomorrow morning at the latest because our deadline is Sunday.'"

Wren slammed her hand on the table. "I'm not the one who has held onto it for two days, Charlie."

After she saved the document to her laptop, she mumbled, "That incompetent worm had better have sent me a reviewed document that shows me where his comments and edits are; if he sent me a revised document that I have to compare to my original, I will quit on the spot."

She opened the edited document and her document she had sent to Charlie then checked the edited document for changes and comments.

"So far, my most heinous crime is the case of the misplaced commas; I'm a frequent offender because the words in my head go faster than my fingers."

Wren revised her document based on the editing corrections on the first page. "If this is what the rest of the document is like, I'll owe Charlie and his editor an apology; of course, they'll never get it, but I'll owe them."

When she got to the second page, Wren stared. "Get this, Rascal. I'll read the editor's comment to you. 'The saloon lady seems very improbable in terms of being a spirit; she's too passive. You need to rewrite with a more period-appropriate, active, malevolent ghost.'"

Wren glowered at the screen. "Is he trying to say he wants me to change the ghost to an outlaw? I don't write fiction, and if I did, guess who wouldn't be my editor. The revisions show his initials as B.P. You're definitely getting my blood pressure up, mister."

She exhaled. "I'll fix the punctuation then send my corrected article back to Charlie. I might explain the difference between fiction and nonfiction for his uneducated editor's enlightenment."

Wren carefully resumed correcting her punctuation then renamed and saved her article. After she attached the article to her email to Charlie, she added a comment then read it to Rascal. "I considered the suggestion to change the local legend to one that is more acceptable to one man's narrow view of Arizona, but after discussing it with the local residents, I'm afraid there would be a number of disappointed readers who were looking forward to reading the well-known story of the haunted campground and the saloon lady, the famous heroine of Hidden Gulch."

After Wren sent her email, she said, "Let's go see Betsy, then I absolutely have to get my dirty clothes into a washer."

Betsy smiled as Rascal rushed to her for a treat and a face rub. "Where did you spend the haboob?" she asked.

"With the marshal; that's why we went to lunch."

"So, you hide out in the marshal's office, and the only way he can get rid of you is to take you to lunch. Do I have it right?" Betsy grinned.

Wren giggled. "Something like that, but I like your version better. What was it like here?"

"I'm going to ask Socorro to build a haboob shelter for our guests. By the time the dust settled, pun intended," Betsy raised an eyebrow. "You may interrupt me with a chuckle at any time."

Wren rolled her eyes.

Betsy continued, "Good enough; by the time the dust settled, I was ready to toss them all outside in the hopes they'd blow far, far away."

"Cody called and told me Socorro is coming home, and Sheridan is moving in." Wren frowned. "Did I speak out of turn? You knew that, right?"

Betsy smiled. "Yes, and I know about the wedding tomorrow too. It's too bad you never made it to Tucson for your flower girl outfit, but I have a shirt that a friend gave me a long time ago. It's a really cute shirt, and I was highly flattered that she thought

I was so small, but the last time I wore a shirt that tiny, I was four years old."

"Wow, that's great, Betsy; I mean that you have something I can borrow. I thought I was packing smart, but I didn't pack anything for a wedding."

"I brought it with me; I'll show it to you."

Betsy went into the storeroom and returned with a dusty pink blouse that was dotted with tiny, embroidered, peach-colored roses.

"It's so elegant; I love it."

"I handwashed it to take out the sizing, so it's ready for you to wear."

Wren frowned. "It seems a little lowcut."

Betsy spoke with a firm voice. "It's perfect for you. Socorro will be the center of attention, anyway, and no, you can't wear a t-shirt under it."

"Can I borrow a safety pin?" Wren asked.

"Hush, and get over yourself; it's okay to look cute."

I'll see what Thomas says. If he laughs or sneers, I'm wearing a t-shirt.

"I suppose; I have to do laundry because I have nothing left to wear that is clean." Wren headed toward the door.

"Wait just a second. Someone might have inadvertently locked the door as they left; it wouldn't be the first time." Betsy opened a drawer then handed a key to Wren. "Here you go. Bring it back when you get the chance." Betsy's eyes twinkled. "Can I trust you with your shirt, or do I need to keep it for you until tomorrow?"

"That's more pressure than I can handle."

"Fine; I'll give it to you tomorrow."

"What if it's too small? I need to try it on."

Betsy sighed and held out the blouse to Wren.

Wren smiled. "Thanks; let's go, Rascal."

Rascal nudged Betsy's hand, and she gave him one more treat for the road, then he trotted to the door and grinned at Wren.

"You're such a smoothie, Rascal."

After they were back at the camper, Wren checked to be sure she had all her dirty clothes in her laundry basket then added her shampoo, body wash, and other shower things, a clean towel, the detergent, and her two repurposed plastic medicine bottles of quarters for the washer and dryer. She smiled. *Thanks for the bottles, Mom. They're the perfect size for quarters for the laundry, just like you said.*

"That's it; are you going or staying?"

Rascal tilted his head then flopped down on the floor.

"I don't blame you; I won't be long."

Wren carried her basket to the laundry room. After she unlocked the door, she caught a whiff of a pungent odor of rotting meat.

Something's dead. A rat must have been trapped in here.

When she bumped open the door with her hip, the stench became even more overpowering, and she gagged. Bile rose in her throat when she saw the body on the floor: Edrick Foster was on his back with his sunken, dead eyes staring at the ceiling.

Wren backed out and gagged again then dropped to her knees and dry heaved. She hyperventilated as she imagined the rank smell had attached itself to her.

She threw her basket away from the entrance to save it from the enveloping stench of death.

Her hands shook as she pulled out her phone and called the marshal.

When he answered, she bit her lip and forced away the hysteria. "I found Edrick Foster in the laundry room at the campground; he's been dead."

"On the way; where are you?"

"I'm here; on the ground. I can't..."

"It's okay, honey; I'll be right there."

Strictly professional; he wanted to calm me. She exhaled. *It worked; I'm calmer.*

When she tried to rise to her feet, her head spun. *I'll just stay right here.* She stared at her dirty clothes strewn around her. *If I keep my head low, I'll be fine.*

She righted her laundry basket then crawled on her hands and knees to toss her clothing and shower things into it. *I don't know if it was my vain side or my puritan side that didn't want the marshal seeing my underwear.*

She caught a whiff from the open laundry room door and put her hand over her nose and mouth. *I have to get farther from the door.*

She rose to her knees then slowly stood. After the waves of nausea stopped, she pulled her laundry basket farther away from the building to the nearest site, which was vacant, and leaned against the single fencepost with the site number on it.

She exhaled when she heard the siren approaching the campground. *How long have I been holding my breath?*

She smiled when the siren suddenly stopped and the sound of tires sliding on the gravel as a vehicle turned at the driveway.

Justin slammed to a stop next to her. When he opened the door, he winced. "Let's get you back to your camper."

He opened his passenger's side door on his cruiser, ran to the laundry room, and slammed the door before he picked up Wren's laundry basket and put it in the backseat.

After he slid into the driver's seat, he picked up his phone. "Pat, we have a body at the campground in the laundry room; he's been dead at least a day or two. I've closed the door, but we'll need a crime scene investigation team, the coroner, and eventually a biohazard team for clean up."

He listened while he slowly drove to Wren's campsite.

"All good. I'll talk to Butch." He nodded. "She's okay; just a little shook up."

Wren's knees wobbled as she got out of the cruiser; Justin helped her inside then guided her to the sofa. Rascal jumped up beside her and licked her face.

Wren smiled. "Thank you, Rascal; I feel much better now."

"Would you like something to drink?" Justin asked.

She nodded, and he pulled out a bottle of water from the refrigerator and opened it before he handed it to her then went outside.

He returned with Wren's laundry and set it down near the door. "I called Butch, so he'd know what's going on. Are you okay to talk? When was the last time you saw Foster?" he asked.

"I saw him yesterday morning. I was at the office with Betsy; he was angry about something and insisted on talking to Socorro. He called her Mrs. Reed. I looked him up on the internet..."

Justin raised his eyebrows.

Wren bit her lip. "It's critical for my career as a professional journalist to research, and I'm a natural-born snoop, so there's that."

Justin chuckled.

"Anyway, I must have mistyped or autocorrect took over because I found an article about Eric Foster who is the chef of a fine dining restaurant in D.C. called Edrick's. Later in the morning, I noticed the Fosters' car was gone."

Justin pulled out a small notebook from his pocket.

While he jotted down a few notes, Wren's eyes widened. "I just remembered the purse."

"What?" Justin stared at her.

"I found a purse in the shower yesterday evening. I was going to take it to the office this morning, but I left the campground before office hours, then I forgot about it. It's on my bed."

Justin strode to the small bedroom then returned with the purse. "It was in the shower? It doesn't look like it has been wet."

"The shower was completely dry when I found it."

He opened it and removed the wallet, and six identification cards fell out onto the floor.

Justin picked them up and glanced through them. "Here's Audrey Foster. The rest them have Audrey for the first name, then the last names are from A to E and match the ones that Rick used. I don't think they ever expected anyone to catch up with them, but these people don't have much imagination, do they?"

He searched the purse then dropped the cards into it.

"No phone, but it was a long shot anyway. This must be related to Edrick Foster's death, but how? I'm having trouble understanding why she left her purse in the shower. Do you have any ideas?"

"Not a single one."

Justin rubbed his forehead with his fingers. "What other tidbits and snippets do you have for me?"

"Socorro is coming home today."

He nodded. "Sheridan called me; he's thinking about ten o'clock for the wedding, but he's waiting for Socorro to decide before he makes it official."

"I'm having supper with them tonight; hopefully, Socorro will have told Sheridan by then."

Justin cleared his throat. "Is Cody going to be there?"

Chapter Sixteen

Wren peered at Justin's face. *What an odd question, but he doesn't ask idle questions; he must have a reason.*

"Yes, he will; why?"

He nodded. "I heard Cody is staying at one of the cabins; it makes sense. It was nice of him to drop everything to help out his brother."

Justin exhaled. "Guess I better get going; I have a lot to do. I'll see you at the wedding. Be safe; you're starting to worry Pat."

Wren listened to the crunch of Justin's tires on the sand while he drove away then snorted. "I guess that's a hint the marshal isn't losing any sleep on my account. I need to talk to Betsy."

As she picked up her phone to call, it rang. *Betsy.*

Wren smiled as she answered. "Hi, I was just getting ready to call you."

"Are you okay?"

"I'm fine now; it was a huge shock, but I still have laundry to do, and now I need a shower," Wren said.

Betsy chuckled. "Sheridan just called and asked me to have our cleaning crew straighten up Socorro's house before he brings her home; he's afraid she'll decide she has to clean before the wedding tomorrow. I'll dust and vacuum myself and actually called to ask you to keep me company. Sheridan expects to be here in two hours, but it won't take me that long to clean Socorro's already spotless house. Bring Rascal, your shower stuff, and your laundry."

After she hung up, Wren said, "Betsy wants us to join her at Socorro's, Rascal."

Rascal trotted to the door while Wren picked up the laundry basket. "I sure did just throw everything in here; I'll pull out my shower gear after we're there."

After Wren and Rascal reached Socorro's, Betsy gave Rascal a treat while Wren tossed her dirty clothes into the washer.

Before Wren started the machine, Betsy asked, "Did you bring something to wear after your shower?"

Wren sighed. "Everything I packed for my trip is dirty."

"In that case, I'll give you one of Socorro's coverups to wear until your clothes are dry, so you can wash what you're wearing."

"I don't know; I can wait to take my shower."

"That doesn't make sense; Socorro never wears her coverups because she never takes the time to go to the pool, so it's not like she'll even miss it when she gets here. I'll write a note that it was my idea if that would make you feel any better."

Wren shrugged. "It would be nice to have all of my clothes clean, especially what I'm wearing right now."

Wren sniffed her shirt. "Phew, it really stinks."

"It doesn't, but that's even more of a reason for you to wash your clothes rather than putting them back on while your nose still thinks there's a lingering odor."

"You're right."

"Of course I am; after you strip for your shower, throw your clothes into the hall, and I'll add them to the washer and get it going."

After her shower, Wren went into the kitchen holding up the cotton coverup with both hands to keep the fabric from dragging on the floor.

Betsy stood on a small stepstool while she swiped at the top of the refrigerator.

"I'm pretend-dusting." Betsy grinned. "That bright turquoise color suits you."

"I feel like a princess who has to hold up her fancy ball gown to keep from falling flat on her face."

"Whatever it takes," Betsy said.

"What if I have to run outside? I don't even have any clean socks to wear; I can't run on the sand barefooted."

"Look at the bright side: if we're caught in a flood, you're ready. I made my first batch of sweet tea; I'll pour you a glass, and you can tell me how wonderful I am."

Betsy put ice in a glass before she added tea. After she put it on the table, she crossed her arms and glared at Wren. "Well?"

"You're great at being bossy," Wren mumbled.

"Thank you, drink up."

Wren took a tiny sip then a larger one. "This is really good, Betsy. I feel much better, and you are wonderful."

"Told you."

While Betsy pretended to dust the fronts of the cabinets, Wren said, "I've been reading a book about the area that was written in 1845; it talks about the original prospectors who were looking for gold."

"That was what I always heard when I was growing up. They came here looking for Coronado's gold. Have you heard of that?" Betsy asked.

"From what I remember, Coronado led an expedition to find gold in the 1500s."

Betsy nodded. "The legend was that he found it; all of the early prospectors had their own ideas of where Coronado either found or hid his gold, but they all eventually moved on, except for one prospector who discovered silver. He filed the original claim on Hidden Gulch, which is what he named his claim."

The key is silver.

"Has anyone found the mine?" Wren asked.

Betsy shrugged. "Not many have tried because the desert is so vast and so unforgiving. Of the few that have, the lucky ones returned alive, but there have been only two or three of them."

Betsy poured herself a splash of sweet tea in a glass, took a sip, and shuddered as she poured out the contents then rinsed the glass.

"I tried it; sweet tea must be an acquired taste or genetic; it's all yours, Wren." Betsy refilled Wren's glass.

Before Betsy returned the pitcher to the refrigerator, she pulled out a small notepad and tape from a drawer and wrote on the paper. After she taped it to the pitcher, she put the sweet tea into the refrigerator.

"Did you label it?" Wren asked.

"Sure did; I'd be in big trouble if Sheridan gave Socorro a big, ol' glass of sweet tea."

Wren nodded as she furrowed her brow. "Was Jeff from here? I wonder if he'd found the silver mine or claimed he found it, so that's what the Fosters thought they were buying; they certainly didn't seem like the campground owner types."

"He grew up here, but he wasn't the outdoorsy type at all, so I can't imagine he'd ever have gone out looking for the mine; I can see him claiming he found it, though."

Betsy finished wiping down the cabinets. "I think the washer might be done, and I don't want you tripping over your ball gown."

Wren rolled her eyes, and Betsy chuckled as she left the kitchen.

As Wren peered out the back window at the desert behind Socorro's house, she smiled. *At least she didn't call me 'Princess'.*

After Betsy swept the kitchen, she vacuumed the living room and hall floors.

When she returned to the kitchen, Betsy said, "Sheridan said they'd be here in forty-five minutes and asked me to get a big pot of potatoes cooking for his potato salad. How are you at peeling potatoes?"

"I'm an expert."

"Good, I'll get you started. I want to clean the bathrooms then all that's left is to wash the baseboards, but I'm leaving that chore for Ms. Particular because I know I'd never do that right."

Betsy put a five pound sack of potatoes on the table. "Here's the potatoes; if you'll empty it, we'll use the potato sack for the peels." She pointed to a drawer. "You'll find knives and peelers in there. If you'll peel them, I'll cut and peel after I have the bathroom clean."

While Wren emptied the potatoes onto the counter, Betsy filled a large pot half-full with water at the sink. After she hefted the pot to carry it to the counter, she poured out half of the water.

"That would have been a big mistake; it still may take both of us to carry this to the stove after we get the potatoes peeled."

She put the pot on a counter close to the stove. "We'll work here. Grab yourself a few potatoes at a time."

After Wren organized herself near the pot, she began peeling then dropping the potatoes into the water. She had peeled a little over half when Betsy joined her.

After all the potatoes were peeled and cut, Betsy said, "I can slide the pot over to the stove. Why don't you check the dryer? Your clothes may be dry enough for you by now."

Wren pulled out the warm clothes and dropped them into her laundry basket. After she was dressed, she carried her basket to the kitchen where Betsy was dicing celery.

"I hung the coverup on the hook on the back of the bathroom door; if it's okay, I have a few things to do before supper."

"Thank you so much for your help; I hope I didn't keep you too long."

"Not at all; tell Sheridan to let me know when I'm supposed to come back." Wren headed toward the door with her basket, and Rascal followed her.

Betsy hurried ahead of her and opened the door. "I will, but I suspect Cody will drop by for you after he closes the store."

"I think he might have said something like that."

After they were back at the camper, Wren quickly folded and put away her clothes then turned on her laptop.

She opened the new email from Charlie; her eyes widened, and she clenched her jaw as she read.

"This is unbelievable. I'll read it to you, Rascal, then we'll walk out to the saloon to see Thomas, so I won't send a completely irate email in response that would make a pirate blush. Ready?"

Rascal tipped his head to the side as Wren read aloud.

"Listen to this: 'Wren, even though I love the article you wrote, the editor insists that you replace the section with the saloon lady with the following.' What follows is a long, confusing story about a budding writer who goes west to finish his self-proclaimed masterpiece of a novel and is kidnapped. The rest of it is how heroic this guy is and his tragic death while saving a child from drowning in a river in the middle of the desert. Unbelievable: in the middle of the desert. Let's go; I don't want to damage my laptop."

Rascal raced ahead as Wren stomped to the saloon. "What an egotistical slumgullion," she muttered. "He didn't even bother to edit his own work."

Wren mouth quivered and a small smile ruined her fiery mood. *I'm picking up the best words from that 1845 book.*

"Slumgullion?" Thomas asked. "What jackroller are you talking about?"

Jackroller? I'll have to look that up; I like it.

"I'm writing an article for a magazine and the dolt of an editor tried to completely take over and rewrite everything I wrote."

"So, what are you going to do, bird girl?"

Wren stared at Thomas. "I can withdraw my name from the article if the publisher insists on replacing most of my work with someone else's writing."

Thomas nodded. "Your name don't belong on somebody else's claim."

"That's exactly it, Thomas; thank you."

"Any time, bird girl; are you leaving soon?"

"Yes, one way or another."

"You'll be back; I'll wait." Thomas grinned.

Wren nodded. "That's what stagecoach guards do."

When she turned to leave, Thomas said, "Come tell me when you leave, so I'll know."

"I will."

"Good, it's what friends do."

Before Wren had gone more than a few steps, Thomas added, "The marshal is your friend, girl."

Wren turned and stared at Thomas. "Really?"

"If you'd quit acting like a silly girl, you might see it."

"What about Cody?" she asked.

"That lawyer guy? You tell me. People have more than one friend, but there is different kinds."

Wren walked slowly back to the campsite. *Thomas is prejudiced because the marshal can see him, but he's right: there are different kinds of friends.*

After they were inside the camper, Rascal flopped down on his rug and closed his eyes while Wren sat at her dining table with her laptop.

Before Wren opened Charlie's email, she searched for the meaning of jackroller. "I knew I liked this word, Rascal; in Thomas's day, a jackroller was someone who robbed an intoxicated or sleeping person. Sounds like a low-life to me; what do you think?"

Rascal opened one eye and wagged his tail.

Wren exhaled then quickly typed her response to Charlie. After she poured herself a glass of tea, she reread what she had typed.

We have an unfortunate blurring of the roles of the writer and the editor on this assignment. I have completed and submitted the article before the agreed-upon deadline. If you publish the editor's version of the article, remove my name and accept this as formal notification of my resignation; I will immediately return the camper to the dealership in Phoenix.

"Seems clear to me, Rascal. I'll set it aside for now; I have more interesting things to do."

She picked up the folder from the county records office and scoured each document. "I don't understand a lot of this, but it's pretty clear to me that the original claim was for a silver mine, and it was located well within that large circle that Miranda showed me."

Wren compared the dates on the claim and a land grant. "The prospector was smart and applied for the land grant first."

She furrowed her brow as she read the land grant more carefully. "I'm completely out of my realm of expertise, but the land grant was much larger than what I thought because I didn't understand the scale." Wren exhaled. "Thank goodness it isn't up to me to sort all this out. I'll take this folder and the other one that Miranda gave me with us when we go to Socorro's, Rascal; maybe I'll have an opportunity to share them."

Wren read her reply to Charlie. "I think I'll get a second opinion on my email, Rascal."

Wren sent Betsy a text. "Are you at the office?"

Wren's phone rang. *Betsy. I should have called her.*

Wren answered. "I'm okay; I've composed an email to Charlie and need a second opinion. Do you have a few minutes?"

"Sure do. I'm in the office waiting for guests to arrive who registered online yesterday. Are you going to read it to me?"

"I thought I'd walk to the office, so you can read it."

"I'll be here."

After she hung up, Rascal hopped up from his nap.

"I thought you were napping. Let's go."

After Wren opened the door, Rascal raced to the office. As she followed him, Wren smiled. *Going to the office for Rascal is like taking a kid to a candy shop.*

When she went inside, Rascal was at Betsy's side. Wren put her laptop on the counter and opened it to her email then turned it, so Betsy could see it. "Let me know what you think," Wren said.

Betsy read the reply twice. "You are much more polite than I could be. What if he moves forward with your article? What would be next?"

"I'd travel to the next haunted campground, drop off the camper, and pick up a new trailer to test for the manufacturer."

Betsy sighed. "What if he publishes your article with the editor's changes? Will you stay here after you turn in your camper?"

"I hadn't really thought that far ahead."

Rascal whined.

Wren smiled. "We know where Rascal stands, don't we? I can always go back to freelancing and being my own boss, which right now, is a lot more fun that dealing with an editor who oversteps his bounds."

"We have the cabins, so you have the option of staying here."

Wren furrowed her brow. "I thought one of the rules for the cabins was no pets."

Betsy snorted. "Rascal is not a pet; he's a campground resident."

Wren turned her laptop around and pressed send. "There; we'll see what Charlie says. Thanks, Betsy."

Before Wren and Rascal left, the campground phone rang.

"It's a remarkable day at our Forgotten Oasis Campground, how can I help you?" Betsy asked then listened and waved wildly for Wren to join her.

"I'm not sure, Mrs. Foster, but our assistant manager is here. Perhaps she can help you."

Betsy put the phone on mute then whispered, "It's Audrey Foster; she wants to know if her husband is here."

"Wow; give me one second to think."

Wren bit her lip. "I can't think; my mind is going ninety miles an hour. I'll talk to her anyway."

"How may I help you, Mrs. Foster?"

"Are you the assistant manager? My husband had a meeting at the campground, but I had an appointment in Tucson; now, I'm stranded because he hasn't returned. Have you seen him?"

"I haven't seen Mr. Foster since Wednesday, I believe. A tow truck picked up your RV sometime yesterday."

"I know about that; is his car there?" Audrey asked.

"I'm not sure; do you have the license number?"

"Of course not. It was a rental car with a Colorado license plate, and the rental place wants to extend the contract another month. I don't want to fork out that kind of money if he's on his way to return it." Audrey snorted. "How many cars could you have there with a Colorado license plate?"

"Why don't I check and call you back? You're in Tucson? Are you staying there?"

"I don't have a choice, do I? I'll give you the number of the hotel where I'm staying and my room number. Are you going to write this down?"

"Go ahead." Wren picked up a pen. "I'm ready."

After Audrey gave her the name of her hotel, the hotel phone number, and her room number, Wren asked, "Do you have a cell phone in case you aren't in your room when I call?"

Audrey snorted. "You don't trust them to get a message straight, do you? Here's my cell number."

Wren dutifully wrote it down. "I'll get back to you as soon as I can."

"I want to hear back from you today."

"I'll get right on it."

After Audrey hung up, Wren said, "I'm calling the marshal; is it okay if I go into my unofficial office?"

"Go right ahead; you got a lot more information than I would have, by the way. That was slick."

When Wren called Justin, he answered immediately.

"I'm okay," she automatically said. "Audrey Foster called the campground office and said she was looking for her husband. Betsy handed the call off to me."

"What?" Justin sighed. "I say that a lot, don't I? Sorry."

"She said she is in Tucson and is trying to find him. I have the name of the hotel, its phone number, her room number, and her cell phone number."

"The investigators have been trying to locate her. Give me the information, and I'll pass it on."

After she gave him the information, he said, "Thanks, Wren; y   o   u   '   r   e amazing."

"Thank you, but I was just in the right place at the right time to help Betsy."

As she headed out the door, Wren said, "It's not our problem; I handed it off to the marshal. He'll give her information to the investigators, so I suspect you won't be hearing from Mrs. Foster again."

Betsy hurried to Wren and hugged her. "Thank you for everything."

On the way back to the camper, Wren said, "It will be hard to leave Hidden Gulch if we go to our next assignment, won't it, Rascal?"

Rascal glanced at Wren with sad eyes.

"This is my favorite place too, Rascal; it's been nice to have friends."

Wren and Rascal sat on the sofa together; Rascal put his head on Wren's knee while she read the 1845 book.

When her phone buzzed a text, Wren realized she'd dozed off with Rascal asleep next to her.

She picked up the book that had fallen on the floor as she read the text from Justin. "Enjoyed lunch. What about dinner tomorrow?"

That's a surprise, but Thomas told me the marshal was my friend.

She replied, "Sounds great."

A new text immediately popped up. "We'll figure out details after the wedding tomorrow."

"Good."

Wren stared at her texts and groaned. "Rascal, I sound bored or worse yet, boring. I should have said I enjoyed lunch too or at least something that was warm and friendly, and what about that 'good'? Ugh. 'Looking forward to it' would have sounded more like I was actually interested. I suddenly hate texting; there's no personality, or maybe I have no personality. I didn't even say something teasing like...I can't think of anything."

Wren whined. "I am boring. I could at least have said I'd check with my social secretary. Wouldn't that have been funny?"

She received another text. "You can buy lunch tomorrow."

Wren giggled. "Game on, marshal."

She replied, "I'll pencil you in."

"Make it permanent ink."

"I'll chisel it in stone. Happy?"

"Am now."

"So am I. See you in the morning."

"You got it."

"That was definitely an improvement; I don't think Justin realizes he's bolstered my self-esteem by giving me a chance to redeem myself and my previous klutzy texts." Wren smiled. "I'll bet Sheridan is planning lunch tomorrow after the wedding, which is why Justin said I could buy lunch. That's sneaky; I need to think of a way to put my twist on that. I can't bake a cake or anything because I don't have an oven; besides, I don't have enough time to learn how to make a wedding cake."

Rascal quietly growled at a knock at the door. Wren hurried to the window and peeked out.

"Oh, for goodness' sake, Rascal, it's Cody." She opened the door. "Time got away from me; give me one second, and I'll be ready."

As they strolled to Socorro's, Cody asked, "Why were you on your way back to town this morning when you picked up Rick?"

The back of Wren's neck prickled. *How does he know about that?*

Chapter Seventeen

"On my way back to the campground, Betsy called to ask me where I was and told me to go back to town. I was closer to town anyway, and if I'd tried to go to the campground, I would have run right into the haboob. That was a wicked storm; I've never experienced anything like that before."

"I've only been in a couple, but that was plenty for me. Why did you go to the marshal's office? Why didn't you join us at the hardware store?"

"I seriously thought about it, but the sand was almost on top of me, and the marshal's office was closer."

He nodded. "That's right; I didn't think about that. Rick was lucky you came along."

"I didn't see his tire, of course, but he told me it blew. He was really frustrated. He was thinking he could finish changing the tire then keep driving. He didn't realize how bad the storm could be."

"He isn't from around here, is he? Where is he from?"

"I don't really know; we didn't talk much because I was so focused on my driving."

"I'm glad you made it to town okay," Cody said.

Wren exhaled. "Thanks; I felt like I was being chased by a hungry lion."

"That's a good description."

"I'm looking forward to seeing Socorro. I hope we don't wear her out, but she may be able to outlast me. It's been an exhausting day."

Cody nodded. "I know this is minor, but those puppies wore me out. They are fluffy balls of kinetic energy."

"I like that. Can I borrow that sometime?"

Cody chuckled. "Be my guest; I'll let you in on a secret. The puppy sitter will deliver the puppies to Socorro's house tomorrow morning."

"She'll be thrilled." Wren smiled.

When Cody tapped on the door, Sheridan called out, "Come on in."

Rascal dashed ahead to find Socorro.

She squealed. "Rascal! There's my boy."

Socorro sat at the kitchen table with Rascal leaning against her chair; Wren gently hugged her before she sat and slipped her backpack between her feet. Socorro's eyes were slightly puffy and blackened, and her face was greenish yellow.

"I'm a mess, but I can see." Socorro's split lip made her smile lopsided. "I never saw who attacked me; I think it was a rogue cousin of Bigfoot's. So, what's going on with you? How's the article and your publisher?"

"I put in the edits the publisher sent me, so he has the final. I'm waiting to hear whether he and his editor accept the article as is. The editor had some major changes to the article, but I declined."

Socorro chuckled.

"Why is that funny, sweetie?" Sheridan asked.

"I speak Wren. She's in a standoff with her publisher and the editor. My money's on Wren."

"I'm not taking that bet," Sheridan said.

"I'm not either." Cody added chopped onions and salsa to his mashed avocados. "You've been busted, Wren. Let's hear the lowdown."

Wren smiled. "A major part of my article was the legend of the saloon lady. The editor didn't care for her; my professional assessment is that he's a jerk. He rewrote the entire story with a dude from back east character; his story was poorly written and poorly edited, not to mention it was a confusing story that he obviously made up on the fly. We came to an impasse. I told the publisher to remove my name from the article if he included the editor's story, and I would return the camper to the dealership in Phoenix."

"What did he say? Are you going to stay here? This is really exciting news," Socorro said.

"I haven't heard from the publisher yet; he likes to hide from problems. I may not hear anything from him, but the magazine is scheduled for publication on Sunday, so I may subscribe to get an online copy to see what he decided."

"That is totally nuts," Sheridan said.

Socorro picked up a fork from the table and mimicked the voice of an old-time radio announcer. "It's a showdown at the Forgotten Oasis in Hidden Gulch."

"Now that's a story I could write." Wren giggled.

"I'd read it," Cody said.

"We all would," Sheridan said.

"The saloon lady would still be in it, wouldn't she?" Socorro asked.

"It wouldn't be a story without her."

"As soon as Cody puts his finishing touches on the guacamole, our supper is ready." Sheridan pulled out a large bowl of potato salad and set it in the middle of the table. "Nobody's driving anywhere this evening. Socorro is still on pain meds, so she's our token teetotaler. Will that be three beers?"

"I'd like sweet tea; Betsy made some earlier today," Wren said.

"Cody?" Sheridan asked.

"Sure, and I'll get the sweet tea for our Georgia flower girl."

Socorro snickered. "I wondered how long it would be before you brought that up."

Sheridan stood behind Socorro; he raised his eyebrows at Wren. She smiled and nodded.

"Speaking of which, what time is the wedding tomorrow, Socorro?" Wren asked.

"Ten o'clock."

Sheridan beamed.

"That's perfect," Wren said.

Cody narrowed his eyes. "Why is that?"

"Not too early, and not too hot," Sheridan said. "We'll still have the wedding at the saloon, but Socorro will be arriving in her chariot; it's too far for her to walk from here. We won't have a reception, but I'll make a coffee cake this evening, so we can have what they call a continental breakfast before the wedding. I've invited our guests to be here at nine for coffee and a light breakfast. Betsy's going to make scones. Cody, I ordered a fruit platter from the grocery store deli; Justin will pick it up in the morning and bring it with him."

"Justin? Why is he coming?"

"His dad and I served in the Army together. Justin's my family too; you know that, Cody."

"You're right." Cody's face was dark.

Socorro side-glanced Wren.

While they ate, Cody received a phone call. He glanced at his phone. "Sorry, I have to take this." He hurried out the front door.

"Cody doesn't know how to allow time off for leisure; he's always working." Sheridan shook his head. "Why don't you two relax in the living room, so I won't be critiqued when I load the dishwasher?"

"Okay, honey," Socorro said.

"I'll help you," Sheridan rushed to her side.

After Socorro and Wren were in the living room, Socorro said, "I knew we'd have a few minutes or more alone together, so I could explain the Cody and Justin thing. Cody was the golden boy in Hidden Gulch from the time he could talk; becoming a lawyer was the perfect career for him because people are drawn to his charm. When Justin showed up, the attention shifted to the new marshal. Cody had never had competition before, but the fact that Justin wasn't interested in competing was beyond his comprehension. He couldn't attack Justin even indirectly because Cody would look petty, and he's very much into appearances. Cody has harbored a grudge against Justin for so many years that I wonder if he even remembers why."

"I can see how that could happen because Cody does tend to divert any focus to himself," Wren said. "It's my observation, not a criticism."

Socorro snickered. "I'm not his brother, so you don't have to tiptoe around my feelings. Some people are open books; Cody is not one of them, even though that's the persona he cultivates."

Socorro furrowed her brow. "We never made it to Tucson. Are you okay with the wedding tomorrow?"

"Betsy gave me a shirt to wear; I'm pretty sure it is too lowcut for a flower girl. Do you have a safety pin I can borrow?"

Socorro laughed. "Betsy told you no, didn't she? I don't have one either."

Sheridan joined them. "What's so funny?"

"Socorro laughed at my ..."

Socorro interrupted Wren. "Girl stuff."

Sheridan nodded. "I picked up some ice cream. Anybody ready for dessert?"

"You know I am," Socorro said.

"Not really, but I'd like to have a small scoop anyway," Wren said.

"In here or in the kitchen?" Sheridan asked.

"We'll go with you to the kitchen," Socorro said. "I might want seconds."

Sheridan helped Socorro out of her chair then put his arm around her waist to steady her; Wren and Rascal followed them into the kitchen.

Wren ate half of her ice cream. "That's the best I can do; I'm sorry to eat and waddle, but I'm exhausted."

"I'm supposed to give Butch a shout when you're ready to go home. Your ride will be here in two minutes."

While Sheridan sent a text, Cody came inside. "Ice cream? That's great."

"It's in the freezer; help yourself." Sheridan handed Cody the ice cream scoop and a bowl.

As Cody filled his bowl, he asked, "What did I miss?"

Wren and Socorro exchanged glances then giggled.

"Girl stuff," Sheridan said.

Cody nodded.

Butch opened the front door and strode inside. "Ready, Wren?"

"Sure am."

"Wait, what's going on?"

"Eat your ice cream, Cody. Wren has had a long day, so Butch is giving her a ride," Sheridan said.

"I thought I'd walk her home," he said.

"Maybe another time," Socorro said. "We'll see you in the morning for breakfast, sweet girl."

"Thanks for the thought, Cody; I'll see you tomorrow." Wren hugged Socorro, then she and Rascal left with Butch.

Rascal ran ahead and was waiting for them when they reached her camper.

Before she climbed out, Butch said, "Unless you want Cody to drop by, leave your lights off. If he knocks, don't answer because Betsy said you need your rest."

"That's going to be easy for me but thank you and tell Betsy thank you too because I might have tried to read for a while."

After Wren and Rascal were in the trailer, she said, "I'll check real quick to see if I've heard anything from Charlie."

When she opened her email, she sighed. "I hoped I'd have an email from Charlie, but I'm torn about what I want it to say." She closed her computer.

"I'm really exhausted, but I'm too wired to go to sleep."

Wren brushed her teeth and put on a clean pair of pajamas.

Her phone buzzed a text from Justin. "Are you still at Socorro's?"

She propped herself with pillows on her bed and smiled as she replied, "No; too tired to be good company; too wired to go to sleep."

"Terrible combination; same for me. Okay if I call?"

"Yes."

When her phone rang, she answered.

"How was your evening?" he asked.

"Socorro's bruises are really colorful; her eyes are still swollen, but she can see. I enjoyed spending the evening with her. Sheridan hovered and Cody spent much of his time outside on the phone."

"He did? That's too bad."

"You need to work on your sincerity: that was terrible."

Justin chuckled. "What's going on with your publisher?"

"He sent me an email that said the editor insisted that I remove the Saloon Lady and replace her with the editor's poorly written tripe with an unbelievable character. Can I read you my reply?"

"I can't wait to hear it."

Wren opened her computer and read her reply email. After she finished, she said, "Socorro called it the 'showdown at the Forgotten Oasis in Hidden Gulch.'"

Justin chuckled. "That would make a great story, wouldn't it? I like your reply; it has absolutely no smidgeon of ambiguity in it. If I'd heard that from anyone else, I would have said, 'Good bluff', but you'll follow through. Have you heard back from him?"

"No; I checked as soon as I got back to the camper a few minutes ago. I honestly didn't expect to hear until tomorrow, but I had to see."

"I don't know much about publishing, but doesn't your publisher own the magazine? I don't understand why he doesn't tell the editor to back off, especially since he likes your article. I mean, isn't he the boss?"

"He's supposed to be. I can't figure it out either. The publisher and Mom have been friends for a long time; maybe she might know why he has an aversion to taking charge."

Justin cleared his throat. "I'd like your opinion on a law enforcement item. I don't mean to be like Cody and drag in work stuff while we're supposed to be relaxing, though; shall I ask you tomorrow?'

Wren rolled her eyes. *You could never be like Cody.* "No, go right ahead."

"Two investigators went to the hotel where Audrey Foster told you she was staying to tell her about the death of her husband. They found her in the room's bathroom, hung by the neck on the shower rod."

"That's terrible."

"The investigators declared it a suicide, but I wanted your opinion because you know what Audrey Foster was like firsthand. Do you think she would have taken her own life?"

"I'm not an expert, but from my interaction and observations of her, absolutely not."

"Not even if she already knew her husband was dead? Would she have become despondent in her grief?"

"Not at all; she might have been angry with him for inconveniencing her, but despondent? I seriously doubt it."

"That's what I told them. I offered to get a second opinion from someone who had personal interaction with her, and the chief investigator liked the idea."

"I suppose she could have been putting on an act when she was here, but I seriously doubt it. She was genuinely snooty and unpleasant. I don't mean to be insensitive, but doesn't it seem like all our bad guys are showing up dead: Jeff Reed, Edrick Foster, and now Audrey Foster? When do we run out? Do we have a vigilante loose? Just a hint: it's not me."

Justin chuckled. "You just knocked out my number one suspect; I should have known you'd be too wily to confess. While we're entertaining unanswered questions, we have another unknown piece to the murders: what is the motive?"

"I think I might have the answer to that. I went to the county records today to pick up copies of documents that Miranda had requested. I think there is an old silver mine on Socorro's property."

"If that was true, it makes more sense of Reed's murder and the attack on Socorro, wouldn't it?"

"If it isn't true, it could have possibly been sold as true."

When Justin was quiet, Wren smiled. *He's pacing.*

"Where are the documents?" he asked.

"In my backpack."

"I'm coming to get them."

"I don't think that's a good idea, but I'm not sure why. I'll give them to you in the morning."

"Are you worried about someone at the campground seeing me?" Justin asked.

"If you're specifically suggesting Cody, I might be; if he's involved, it would tip our hand or at least expose a level of communication between us that he may fear or suspect, but I don't think we're quite ready for that."

"I agree, and we still don't know where Rick fits in," Justin said.

"Butch told me to keep my inside lights off because he was certain Cody would check and stop by to talk if they were on. Maybe I should turn on my lights."

"No."

"You're right; it's a bad idea."

"Darn straight, I'm right."

While Wren quickly changed into jeans and a T-shirt, she said, "Betsy gave me a shirt to wear for the wedding tomorrow, but I'm afraid it would be too revealing. Maybe I'm old-fashioned, but it seems wrong to draw attention away from the bride."

"I'm definitely no expert on wedding apparel or traditions, but I think Sheridan will have eyes only for Socorro, and who else matters?"

Wren furrowed her brow. "You know, you're right. I'll wear a T-shirt under it and quit stressing."

"Don't do that; you'll hurt Betsy's feelings. Have you tried on the shirt?"

"Are you suggesting I haven't even tried on the shirt?"

Justin chuckled. "What a good idea; have you?"

Wren smiled. *Justin is much more fun that Cody.* "Don't you need to pace or something, so you can think about what you are saying?"

"You are absolutely right. I need to pace because I almost let you divert us from our previous discussion of Cody and lights on inside your camper."

"I agreed with you that it was a bad idea; what else do we need to discuss?"

"I've actually gained a little insight into your thought process. While you agreed it was a bad idea, you're examining any benefits, so what are they?"

"You mentioned Rick, and you're right that we don't know where he fits in. It's a stretch, but could he be a client at Cody's firm?"

When Justin remained quiet, Wren sat on her sofa, put her feet up and listened. *He's pacing.*

"Cody's reckless enough to have driven from the hardware store to the office to pick up Rick."

"I hadn't thought of that; Rick could have stayed in the hardware storeroom in the back until the storm left and he could leave."

"Right; are we at an impasse?"

"Possibly; I haven't decided yet," Wren said.

"I'll stay up all night until you let me know that Cody's not there."

"Now, that sounds like blackmail," Wren grumbled.

"Call it what you will; I'll wait, and don't wear a T-shirt tomorrow."

After they hung up, Wren hurried to her bedroom. "If I'm reading to relax, I should look relaxed, right, Rascal?"

Wren quickly changed back from her clothes to her pajamas then flipped on the light next to the sofa and opened the 1845 book to the page where she'd left off.

Rascal growled low at the light tap on the door. Cody whispered, "Wren? Are you awake?"

"It's showtime," Wren muttered as she rose then strolled to the door with her book in her hand.

She yawned as she opened the door but left the screen door closed. "Hi; sorry, I didn't expect any company."

"I didn't mean to wake you; I saw your light and stopped by to say good night."

Wren giggled. "Good night."

Cody squinted at her book. "What are you reading?"

"It's a novel written in 1845. I used it to steep myself in the 1800s culture for the article, but I have to finish it because it's a great story. Unfortunately, I read it late at night and fall asleep, but it's not the story's fault."

Cody chuckled. "I have a law book that I absolutely love; sounds crazy, doesn't it? I read it when I'm too wound up to fall asleep. Are you excited about the wedding tomorrow?"

"I really am," she said. *When are you going to get to the point, Cody? I'm appropriately relaxed and not wary. How about a nudge?*

She yawned again. "I guess I'll see you in the morning at Socorro's for breakfast; thanks for dropping by."

As she stepped back to close the door, he said, "One more thing; I was picking up some records at the courthouse and heard you'd picked up a folder that Miranda had requested for you."

"Right; Miranda thought I'd be interested in the records of the businesses in the 1800s during the heyday of the Hidden Oasis saloon. I reviewed them, but there wasn't anything that I could use in my article; I returned them and asked the clerk at the records department to give them to the town historical society."

"I didn't know there was a town historical society."

Wren shrugged. "Really? I assumed there was when the clerk took them back."

"Too bad you couldn't use them. Did they give you any other records?"

"No, like what? Are you looking for some records?"

"Not really; just curious. See you in the morning; good night, again."

Wren closed and locked the door then turned off the light and listened as Cody hurried from her camper to his cabin. She changed to all dark clothes then quietly crept from her camper to the first cabin. She heard two voices coming from the second cabin. *Bingo.* She moved closer.

"The records she picked up were lists of business receipts in the early 1800s, which are totally useless; she's not a threat at all," Cody said. "Wait a minute; I heard something outside."

Wren froze, then Thomas whispered, "Come over this way, girl."

Before Cody opened the cabin door, Wren crept toward Thomas's voice then crouched behind an old, broken-down hay wagon with no wheels.

Cody took a few steps away from the cabin; a whippoorwill called, then a gust of wind slammed the cabin door closed.

Cody returned to the cabin and chuckled as he opened the door. "I'm not used to the night noises out here in the desert anymore; did you jump when the door slammed? I did too."

"Go to bed, girl," Thomas said. "You need your rest for tomorrow."

After she returned to her camper, Rascal whined. She took him outside for a few minutes, then they went inside, and she locked up.

She sent a text to Justin. "Cody asked about the records I got from the records office. I was boring, so he left."

"Lights out? Going to sleep?"

"Yes, and yes."

"Good; see you in the morning, so I can hear the real story."

Wren changed back into her pajamas. *I've lost count of how many times I've changed into pajamas and back.*

After she settled under her sheet and fluffed and punched her pillow into her favorite sleeping position, she sighed. *Too bad I couldn't hear the voice of whoever was in the cabin with Cody.* She frowned. *Cody totally downplayed what I told him. Why?*

Chapter Eighteen

When Wren woke, the sky was streaked with orange as the sun rose. She hurried to start her coffee maker, then she and Rascal stepped outside.

Wren sat on her camp chair while Rascal explored the area around the camper then leaned against her leg.

"I slept hard, Rascal; coffee should almost be done. I'll drink a cup before I take a shower in the camper's tiny shower booth." While Rascal ate his breakfast, Wren sipped her coffee and opened her computer.

Her eyes widened. "I have an email from Charlie, Rascal."

She read the email, then sighed. "Well, we have an answer, but I'm not impressed at all."

She drained her cup then refilled it before she sent Justin a text. "I heard from Charlie. Call after you'd had some coffee."

Before she'd taken a sip of her second cup, her phone rang.

When she answered, Justin said, "Good morning. Read the email to me, then I'll come to the campground, so we can talk about it in person."

Wren exhaled. "Thank you, but it might be better if you come here because there are definitely some interesting discussion points."

"Okay; did he accept your article?"

"Yes."

"I get it; he said yes, but. I'll be there in ten minutes."

"I have plenty of coffee; I'll see you then."

After they hung up, Wren said, "I can't shower in ten minutes. I'll just get dressed."

She quickly dressed, brushed her teeth, and brushed her hair then hurried to the door and opened it as Justin slammed on the brakes next to her camper.

"Good morning." He strode inside and hugged her; her eyes widened, and her cheeks warmed, but she quickly retuned his hug.

"Hey, Rascal; how's the boy?" Justin bent down and scratched Rascal's ears.

"I'm glad you're here. Have a seat, and I'll pour your coffee," Wren said.

"I can't sit because I might have to pace; read it to me."

She poured his cup then read. "I appreciate your patience while I sorted through my options. As the publisher, I see no reason not to accept your article as you wrote it, and I am pleased to inform you that your article has been formatted for the scheduled publication. I will send you the link to your free electronic copy of the magazine as soon as I receive it, and I will send a packet of magazines to your mother, so she can share them with your friends in Georgia."

"This is what you wanted, right?" Justin peered at her face.

"I'm going to ask Mom to send copies of the magazine to you, Socorro, and Betsy; there's more."

Wren continued reading. "I apologize for the inexcusable delay that occurred while I pondered the proposal of our young editor. He has taken a short vacation for the weekend and will be returning to work on Monday. I will inform him that the article is published, so we can move on."

"Wait." Justin frowned. "He's going behind the editor's back? Do you think he's publishing two different copies of the magazine? Never mind, that's insane."

"Yes it is, but hold that thought." Wren read the next section.

"I'm excited to tell you about your next haunted campground: Lonesome Trail Campground in Dry Creek, Texas. Turn your camper in at the RV dealership in El Paso, Texas, this afternoon and pick up your next one there; the RV dealership has a campground, so it is your first stop. You're expected at the Lonesome Trail Campground on Monday. I look forward to hearing your feedback on your new camper and reading your first draft next Friday; as a reminder more for me than you, you have two weeks to write the final article, unless you need an extension. Thank you so much for your hard work."

"What? When did he send that? You're supposed to pack up and leave this morning? Right now? Has he lost his ever-loving mind? Where is Dry Creek, Texas? How long will it take to get there?"

Justin stopped pacing and pulled out his phone to check. "Dry Creek, Texas, is over nine hundred miles from here. That would take you three days to drive, and you're supposed to leave immediately? I take it back: this isn't insane, he's insane. When did he send this?"

Wren refilled his cup. "Ten o'clock last night; but that was his time, and he's in California."

"So, it arrived in your inbox at eleven o'clock last night. No wonder you didn't see it until this morning. Do you know what you want to do?"

"I want to write the four articles about haunted campgrounds. Miranda gave me a box of short stories she had written over the years because she wanted me to rewrite them into novels for her. Writing four articles about four different haunted campgrounds will be the perfect writing exercise for me because of the fiction element in each article."

Wren bit her lip. *And I want to come back.*

Justin exhaled then sat next to Wren at the table. "I think I just walked to Tucson and back, so what are you thinking you will do?"

"First thing, I'm not leaving today; if I leave, the earliest would be Sunday morning."

"Would that throw off the magazine schedule?"

"Not at all. This is a monthly magazine, so the next haunted campground installment will be next month."

"We'll talk every day, right?" Justin asked.

"I'd like that; if you're too busy, though, you have to tell me," Wren said.

"Same for you; I don't want you to feel obligated to talk to me because you're afraid you'll hurt my feelings if it's not working for you anymore. You know you'll have the same fight with the editor when you turn in your next article, don't you?"

"You're right. I may ask Betsy if I can send the articles for her to review before I send it to Charlie. She read my saloon lady story and gave me some great feedback."

"What about the editor? Did he add any valuc at all?"

Wren sighed. "I hate to admit it, but he's an excellent copy editor and proofreader."

"I know what a proofreader does, but what's a copy editor?" Justin asked.

"A copy editor focuses on the mechanics: punctuation and standard English in the language."

"Why don't you remind Charlie that the editor is an excellent copy editor? Maybe that will give Charlie some ammunition to boost the ego of his editor for your next project."

"That is an absolutely great suggestion."

Justin's eyes twinkled. "How great?"

"Did I say great? I meant to say brilliant." Wren giggled.

"Sexy too?" Justin smirked as he side-glanced her.

Wren laughed. "You're pushing it, Marshal. I'll give that a maybe."

Justin looked at his phone. "Wow, it's eight o'clock. We're supposed to be at Socorro's in an hour. Can you make it?"

"I need to take a shower. Can you pick up some safety pins for me at the grocery store?"

Justin laughed. "Sheridan already warned me about the safety pin."

"Dang it; I don't think I even have a paper clip or a stapler."

Justin headed toward the door. "You're gorgeous in whatever you wear; don't worry about it."

Justin grinned, then when she wrapped her arms around him, he held her for a few minutes. "I wish I could ask you to promise to come back, but you will if it's right." He kissed the top of her head and left.

Wren's eyes misted. "Did you hear that, Rascal? Justin thinks I'm gorgeous and wants me to come back. When he asked me what I wanted to do, all I could think of is that I wanted to come back. I miss him already." Wren sighed. "I'll shower then go see Thomas. Maybe he'll agree it's too much and find me a safety pin."

After Wren stepped out of the shower and dried off, she put on her cotton slacks, her dressy boots, and the shirt Betsy loaned her. "This shirt is really comfortable; I love how soft it is."

She stood in front of the mirror. "I don't love this part: it's positively indecent; we have to go see Thomas."

She removed her waist band holster from her blue jeans and slipped it inside her cotton slacks then examined herself in the mirror again. "Now I feel dressed to go outside while a crazed killer is running around killing bad guys. I'm afraid he's running out of bad guys, Rascal, and might decide I'm a good target."

When Wren and Rascal reached the old saloon, Thomas was standing on the façade. Wren blinked then squinted at Thomas's hair that was parted in the middle and slicked down. "Are you dressed up for the wedding?"

"Course, bird girl. Ain't every day the Saloon Lady gets married, is it?" He narrowed his eyes as he examined Wren. "You're downright fancy yerself. You look right purdy, 'ceptin it wouldn't hurt if you put on some of that thar face paint like the Saloon Lady wears."

Wren's face felt like it caught on fire. "Thank you for the compliment, Thomas; I was a little worried whether I looked okay for a wedding."

"Well, that's dumb. Where'd you get such a notion in your head?"

Wren furrowed her brow, then her mouth twitched into a slight smile. "I can't rightly say."

"You and the marshal going to meet up after the wedding? You know he took the whole day off to be with you, girl, so don't you go be mean to him."

Wren's jaw tightened, and she stomped her foot for emphasis. "I'm never mean to him."

"Well, he's sure pining away like you been ignorin' him all week."

"That's good because that's how I feel too."

"Girls never make sense; then how come he doesn't know that? Did you tell him?"

"Kind of."

"You think about that; I'll see you at the wedding." Thomas grinned then disappeared.

"Just maddening," Wren muttered as she turned to leave.

"Talking about yerself, bird girl?" Thomas cackled.

Wren stomped back to her camper. *Thomas is an annoying matchmaker.*

She smiled as she reached her camper. *He did say I was pretty, though, so I don't feel quite as anxious about the shirt Betsy gave me.*

Before she opened the door, her phone rang; she smiled as she answered.

"I've run into a small problem at the grocery store," Justin said. "They wrote down the wrong time for the wedding, so they're scrambling to pull together the fruit tray that Sheridan ordered. It might be better if you go now to Socorro's; she'll probably appreciate the moral support. I'll be there as soon as I can."

He sounds really tense.

"I'll see you there," Wren said.

Thomas's voice drifted to her along with a light breeze. "Say something nice, bird girl."

She added, "I'm looking forward to spending the day with you."

Justin exhaled. "Thanks, you just made my day."

I guess Justin needed a little moral support too.

Wren went inside to pick up her backpack. While she brushed her hair again, she inspected her face.

Maybe Thomas is right.

She turned her head side to side. *I look a little washed-out.*

Wren painstakingly lined her upper lid then applied mascara and brushed a little blush on her cheeks. *Too pink.*

She scrubbed off the blush and brushed on a blush that was closer to peach. "That's better, don't you think, Rascal? It kind of has to be because it's my only other choice."

She pulled out her one lipstick and showed it to Rascal. "The color kind of looks like my blush to me. What do you think?"

Rascal whined.

"You're right; I didn't think about being too matchy, but it's the only color I have. I should change back to the pink blush, shouldn't I?"

After Wren scrubbed off the blush, she said, "Maybe I'll leave my cheeks natural; they have a little color to them, so I should be okay."

She applied the lipstick; she looked in the mirror then pretended to gag. "Now the lipstick makes my face look washed out. Oh, cruddleduds; I'll just put a dab of the pink blush on without looking at the mirror."

Wren flicked the brush across her cheeks with her back to the mirror. "Done; now Thomas won't have any reason to complain."

She picked up her backpack and opened the camper door. "Are you ready to go to Socorro's house, Rascal? Rumor has it the puppies will be there."

Wren giggled as Rascal leapt out of the camper straight to the ground and raced toward Socorro's house. When she stepped out, Cody was sitting at the picnic table.

He chuckled. "I take it you told Rascal the puppies would be at Socorro's."

Wren smiled. "Sure did. Have you been waiting long? I didn't realize you were out here."

"I was just walking past your trailer. When I saw the door open, I thought you might like a little company."

Hard to believe, but whatever.

"Have you been able to clear your plate for this morning? It seems like you're on call for your job around the clock."

"It does, doesn't it? I'm the lead on a couple of big court cases coming up, so they're consuming more of my time than usual."

While Cody continued talking about his important role on the cases and how no one else could handle the work as well as he did, Wren thought about her choice of leaving or staying.

Justin and I are just beginning to get acquainted; if I leave, whatever is between us may wither and die, and I'd always wonder about what could have been.

She sighed. *If I stay, I'll never write the remaining three articles; I'm not sure I could live with myself because I'd always remember the project I abandoned.*

"Life is hard," she muttered.

"Did you say something?" Cody asked as they reached Socorro's house.

Wren smiled. "Not really."

Cody raised his arm to knock, and Betsy jerked open the door.

"You have to talk to Socorro, Wren. She's having second thoughts."

"Really? Where is she?"

"In her bathroom; follow me."

"Justin's running a little late at the grocery store," Wren said as they hurried down the short hallway to Socorro's bedroom.

"He just called; he'll be here in ten minutes. Somebody has to be nice to him when he gets here because he sounded really frazzled. I pick you."

Wren smiled. "I'll try."

When Betsy and Wren went into Socorro's bathroom, Socorro wailed, "Wren, this is a major disaster; we have to call off the wedding. I'm flashing the world with my immodest shirt. Look at this."

Socorro bent over at the waist and raised her shoulders with her arms out, and the neckline of her shirt slightly gapped. "See?" she growled.

"Stand up a second." Wren climbed on top of the toilet seat. "Okay, now stand up straight next to me, so I can see if any leering is a possibility."

Socorro stared up at Wren. "Nobody's going to stand on a toilet to look down my shirt."

"Everybody's taller than me; I need a different perspective, so I can be objective."

Socorro rolled her eyes as she stood next to the toilet.

"Turn to the left then to the right." Wren said.

After Socorro turned left then right, Wren said, "Okay, now face me and shake your arms."

Betsy's eyes widened. "Oh, lordy." She put her hands over her mouth and ran out of the room.

"Now, you've upset Betsy," Socorro whined.

Wren climbed down. "As long as you don't walk bent over with your arms swinging like a monkey, nobody can see anything they shouldn't."

"Oh." Socorro exhaled. "I think I had bride jitters, so I'll remember no walking like a monkey."

Wren giggled. "What about my shirt? What do you think?"

"It's cute, and you can't walk like a monkey either." Socorro hugged Wren. "Thanks for the help."

Wren smiled as she left the bedroom.

When she joined Betsy in the kitchen, Betsy burst out laughing. "I had to leave, Wren. When you told the bride to turn to the left, turn to the right, and shake, all I could think of was the Hokey Pokey."

Betsy began singing the Hokey Pokey song and dancing while she put scones on a platter; Wren laughed and joined in with her. Butch walked into the kitchen and stared then left. Socorro came into the kitchen and joined in the dance.

After Betsy ended the song, the three women laughed and hugged.

Socorro sighed. "You two have made a wonderful day even better; thank you so much."

Betsy glanced at the doorway to the kitchen. "Okay, fellas; it's safe to come in for breakfast."

"Oh good," Justin said. "Sheridan and I were afraid to interrupt. Here's the fruit."

"Grab a plate and serve yourself," Betsy said.

"May I serve you breakfast, my beautiful bride?" Sheridan smiled as he hugged Socorro.

"I'll serve you, Flower Girl," Cody said.

"Cody, I need for you to pour coffee," Betsy said.

Justin hugged Wren and whispered, "You are so beautiful."

Cody sneered as he poured the coffee until Socorro glared at him. He cleared his throat. "Coffee's up."

When Rascal whined, Wren said, "Thank you."

She tilted her head and examined Justin. "You look dashing in your uniform."

He kissed her cheek. "Thanks."

The wedding guests began arriving a few minutes later, and the small crowd spilled over into the living room.

After breakfast, Butch announced, "The priest is here; if the rest of you folks would walk to the saloon, I'll bring the bride, groom, and the priest in the wedding golf cart." When Wren and Justin went outside, Wren giggled at the horseshoes that hung along the sides of the golf cart.

"That is absolutely the most perfect wedding golf cart I've ever seen," Wren said.

Betsy beamed. "We didn't have any flowers except for a fake Christmas wreath, and it had to be special."

After everyone gathered at the saloon to wait for the wedding golf cart, Wren waved to Thomas, and he solemnly nodded as he stood at the peak of the roof and held his battered hat over his heart.

When the golf cart arrived, the priest took his place in front of the saloon facing the small group. He smiled and motioned for the group to part to make an aisle in front of him, and everyone obliged. Sheridan and Cody took their places on the priest's left and faced the group.

Betsy handed Wren a small basket of dried flowers. Wren rolled her eyes, then solemnly strolled the aisle with Rascal at her side as she dropped flowers until she reached the priest. She and Rascal joined Justin on the first row of the group on the priest's right.

Betsy came down the aisle, then Socorro followed her.

The group groaned, "Ahh," with interjected whispers, "She's so beautiful," as Socorro walked down the aisle and smiled at Sheridan.

Wren's eyes widened at Socorro's beautiful bouquet of black-eyed Susans with yellow and oranges ribbons streaming from it.

Justin leaned close and whispered, "That was a surprise for her from us."

A tear slipped down Wren's face; she whispered, "You're amazing." She gazed at him; he returned her gaze and beamed.

When the priest pronounced Sheridan and Socorro husband and wife, everyone cheered as Sheridan kissed Socorro.

Wren smiled as she watched Thomas dancing on the roof. *Thomas is cheering the loudest of all.*

Justin elbowed Wren then pointed to Socorro who furtively waved to Thomas. When Thomas solemnly bowed to Socorro, the tears in Wren's eyes overflowed.

"That is the sweetest thing I've ever seen," she whispered as she tried to brush away the tears.

When Justin handed her his handkerchief, her tears flowed even faster.

That was the nicest gesture imaginable. What a kind-hearted man.

Wren sniffled to keep from blubbering. *I've gone totally off the deep end emotionally, and I can't help it.*

After the ceremony was over and the wedding couple and the priest were whisked away in the wedding chariot, Wren and Justin strolled behind the rest of the group.

On their way to Wren's camper, Justin said, "I'd like to show you my house before lunch. Would that be okay?"

"I'd like that. I'd like to respond to Charlie's email first to get it done and off my list."

"Why don't you change and start working on it; there are a few things I can do to help Butch then I'll come get you, or you can come to Socorro's house."

"Perfect."

He kissed her cheek then left.

Wren lightly touched her cheek where he'd kissed it then practiced quickly turning her head. *I'll be ready next time.*

Chapter Nineteen

Wren stared at the email Charlie sent. "I need to be sure the RV dealership is open tomorrow."

When she called the dealership she asked, "What are your hours tomorrow?"

"Honey, we're open seven days a week from nine in the morning to six at night. Is there something I can help you with?"

"My name is Wren Weaver. I am supposed to drop off a camper trailer there today and pick up another one then stay overnight at the campground, but I can't be there until tomorrow."

"Don't worry about a thing; we got you, darlin'. I'll alert the service department to watch for you, and I'll switch that reservation for you. Your publisher didn't call us until late yesterday, and I questioned him about the timing. Some people just don't realize how far it is between here and Tucson, which is close to where he said you are. Is that right?"

"Yes, ma'am, it is."

"You just be safe and call right away if you need any help along the way."

After she hung up, more tears ran down Wren's face. "Rascal, I'm overwhelmed by all the nice people today. It must be wedding magic or something."

Wren sighed then opened her laptop and typed her reply to Charlie. When she was satisfied, she read it to Rascal.

"I didn't receive your email until this morning because of the time difference. I will leave here on Sunday morning for El Paso; I've spoken to the El Paso dealership, and they are expecting me tomorrow. I'll leave it to you to adjust the reservation at the Lonesome Trail Campground. Please let me know immediately if there is any problem or if this is not acceptable to you.

"Even though we ran into a major issue that could have killed the project, I appreciated that you recognized the crucial difference between the role of an author and the role of an editor and have clarified the definition with your editor.

"I was very pleased by the excellent copyediting skills. I hope your editor will continue to provide that critical copyediting service for my articles."

Rascal yipped.

"I think it's good too. I'll wait until after Justin reads it before I send it, though."

Wren quickly changed clothes; she hung up her new shirt, so she'd remember to handwash it because of the embroidery.

Wren put her computer into her backpack, so she could share her email with Justin. When they went outside, Wren chuckled as Rascal raced toward Socorro's.

After she was only two rows from her camper, she heard footsteps to her left. When she glanced toward the sound, she stopped. *Cody.*

"Were you on your way to my camper?" she asked.

"Why didn't you tell me about the silver mine, Wren? You've really complicated things more than you can imagine," Cody said. "I have friends at the courthouse records, and one of them called me to be sure you got your records that Miranda had requested for you. My friends are very chatty."

"I thought you were hiding something from me." Rick's drawl was almost absent as he stepped out from the front of the large RV to Wren's right with a drawn gun that he first pointed at Wren then shifted to aim at Cody. "You told me she had only business reports."

Wren gasped and staggered backwards several feet as she dropped her backpack. *I hope that looked like I was startled; now I can see both of them without moving my head. Cody has his right hand on his waist.*

"That's what she told me last night; my friend called me this morning, but I haven't had a chance to talk to you," Cody said. "What are you being so hostile about?"

Cody narrowed his eyes. "Foster must have been working for you because he claimed he just took orders."

"He did until he decided he could call the shots better than me. Before you ask, Audrey was too smart for her own good and figured everything out and wanted a cut."

"What about Jeff Reed?"

"He was an idiot." Rick sneered.

Wren shuddered. *He looks like a cobra about to strike. I guess I'm the mongoose here. No, Cody is; he's keeping Rick's attention on him.*

"So, how are you going to spin shooting both of us?" Cody asked.

Rick snorted. "Easy; you killed Wren, so I shot you. I'm the hero."

"What about ballistics?"

"You are such a dimwit." Rick looked down at his waistband. "I have..."

Smooth and easy.

In one motion, just like her dad taught her, Wren pulled out her pistol, aimed, and shot Rick. His pistol flew out of his hand as he collapsed to the ground.

Wren whirled to aim at Cody, but his hands were raised over his head.

"Wren, don't shoot!" he shouted. "My hands are up."

"Wren!" Justin shouted as he ran to her.

"Dang good shot, bird girl!" Thomas hollered.

"Thanks." Wren giggled.

Cody stared at her. "Are you okay, Wren?"

"She's better than okay, she's a genu-wine sharpshooter!" Thomas yelled.

Wren beamed.

When Justin was close, he continued at a saunter and spoke in a soothing voice. "Honey, put your pistol on the ground unless you're going to shoot Cody; it's your choice. I'll back you up either way."

Wren slowly lowered her pistol.

"Justin!" Cody glowered and started to lower his hands, and Wren automatically resumed her aim.

Cody glared at Justin as he quickly raised his hands. "Sorry, Wren; the marshal enjoys irritating me."

Wren watched Cody closely as she slowly put her pistol in front of her on the ground.

Justin wrapped his arms around her. "Cody's a good guy. I learned this morning he's undercover and has been trying to catch Rick for months. I don't happen to agree with his methods, but it's not my call."

Cody exhaled. "It's a good thing it isn't. Anybody going to check Rick?"

Justin shrugged. "He's all yours. I called the ambulance when I heard the shot."

"I'm going to miss an important call," Cody grumbled.

"Maybe not; I have a deputy coming too. He'll keep the scene intact for you while you make your call."

"You might be the big shot, but I saved Wren." Cody jutted out his jaw.

Wren raised her eyebrows. "Excuse me?"

"Well, you know; I kept his attention on me, so you could take him down."

An ambulance and a deputy cruiser joined them.

The deputy stepped out and strode to Justin while the ambulance crew rushed to Rick.

"Cody is an undercover agent and in charge of the investigation," Justin said. "He has some calls to make; we're assisting him by keeping the scene secure. You can leave in thirty minutes; just remind him you're leaving."

Justin picked up Wren's backpack. "Are you ready for a tour and lunch, Ms. Sharpshooter?"

As they strolled to Socorro's house with their arms around each other, Wren said, "That's what Thomas called me. Did you hear him?"

"Genu-wine sharpshooter," Justin repeated with a twinkle in his eye.

Wren giggled. "I guess you did. Why don't you like Cody?"

"No particular reason," Justin said.

"That's not a reason."

Justin shrugged. "Tell me about Rick."

"Rick reminded me of a cobra, and Cody was a mongoose, darting around at least verbally, and keeping Rick's attention on him. I was shocked at how brazen Cody's questions were. Rick bragged about killing Jeff, Edrick, and Audrey and explained his plan was to kill both of us and make it look like Cody shot me, and Rick shot Cody in his attempt to save me."

"Was his motive the silver mine?" Justin asked.

"I'm not sure; Cody would know better than me, but I think Rick's original plan was to sell the concept of a silver mine; in other words, sell the bogus mine and disappear with all the money before anyone caught onto what he was doing. I guess he got tired of the crooks around him, which seems either totally ironic or idiotic to me."

"Cody would have been the perfect lawyer for him: semi-shady, but not criminal," Justin said.

"That's why you don't like him."

"Probably."

Betsy opened the door. "Are you here for Rascal? Sheridan's going to miss Rascal. I let Socorro and Sheridan know you're leaving, Wren, but you'll be back."

Wren tilted her head. "How did you know?"

"Nothing else makes sense, does it?"

"Not really."

After they were in the cruiser, Justin said, "There's a loose end I'd like to take care of before we leave."

Wren side-glanced Justin as he drove back to the scene and stopped near Cody.

"Do you need Wren's pistol for any reason?" Justin asked.

"No, she can take it," Cody grumbled. "Don't shoot me, Wren."

Cody winced as Wren picked up her pistol and put it back into her holster.

"Where did you aim, Wren?" Cody asked.

"His knee. I wanted him to go down."

"You got it. He claimed that you were aiming for his heart, and he held his breath, so you'd think he was dead. He had the gall to announce he was lucky you were a bad shot. The deputy told Rick he was lucky Wren was so kind-hearted because she could have taken both knees if she'd felt like it. Rick shut up." Cody chuckled.

Justin grinned. "Sharpshooter."

"That's the truth," Cody said. "Be safe, Wren."

On the way to town, Justin said, "I've never heard a sincere word come out of Cody's mouth before this. I think he genuinely cares about you." Justin side-glanced Wren.

"Honey, he's just afraid I'll shoot him."

Justin beamed. "You called me honey."

"So? You've called me honey."

"I like how it sounds when you say it with your Georgia accent."

Wren gasped when she saw the adobe house that was surrounded by small mesquite trees, sage brush, and cactus on the five acres north of downtown Hidden Gulch.

"This is beautiful, Justin."

"It belonged to the marshal who retired; he built it himself years ago. I told him it was too much house for a single guy, but he told me it would sit vacant for a long time, and that would break his wife's heart."

"He got you there, didn't he?"

Justin chuckled. "Sure did. Come on in."

As they went inside, Justin said, "It has what they call an open floor plan; there are three bedrooms, an office, and two and a half bathrooms."

Rascal wandered off to explore while Wren gazed at the large room in wonder. "I love the arches and the dark wooden beams. This is pueblo revival style, isn't it?"

"That's what Mom calls it. Dad, Mom, and I went on a shopping spree in Tucson to furnish it because I didn't want to move any of my furniture from Phoenix to here."

Wren nodded.

"I gave the furniture that Ashley loved to her family; I didn't realize at the time how much that would mean to them, but Mom told me later it did."

Rascal trotted back to them and grinned.

"I think I have the seal of approval from Rascal." Justin scratched Rascal's ear.

"My computer is in my backpack; can we look at my reply?"

"I've got a dining table, but no sweet tea; I can offer you a glass of cold water."

"That would be perfect." Wren set her computer on the table.

Justin read it twice. "This is what you want, right?"

"I have to complete the project; I'll hate being away from you."

"You will?"

"Thomas accuses me of being dense all the time."

"I'm dense?"

"As dense as I am if you don't know how much I'll miss you."

Justin chuckled. "I get it. We're both dense, and you'll miss me almost as much as I'll miss you."

Wren glared at him and growled, "It is not a competition."

She sniffed. "I win because I said it first."

Justin smiled. "You're fun; send the email and come back soon."

Wren sent the email.

"Let's have lunch then go for a ride; there are some beautiful old homes to see, and we can go to a park that has a dog-friendly trail."

After they drove a circuit that included several large homes, Wren said, "I've seen more trucks than cars; kind of makes me feel at home."

"A truck is more versatile, especially a four-wheel drive truck. My cruiser's getting old; the county's talking about replacing it with a four-wheel drive truck kind of like yours. It would be an advantage if we had at least one vehicle that could pull out cars that got stuck in the sand, which happens more often than people realize."

While they were at the park on the trail, Justin said, "Stand next to that rock; I want to take a picture of you."

"Why don't we take a selfie? I'd like to have a photo of us together."

"All three of us," Justin added.

They found a bench in front of a saguaro cactus and sat down. Wren coaxed Rascal to sit between them. As Wren and Justin leaned close to Rascal, Justin raised his phone to snap the photo. Wren glanced at him, and he was looking at her. He smiled, and she returned his smile as he snapped the photo.

"I wasn't ready," she grumbled. "I was looking at you, not your phone. You're supposed to look at the phone to take a selfie."

"Oh, would you listen to Miss 'I Break Every Rule' try to quote a selfie rule." Justin showed Wren the photo. "I like it."

Wren smiled. "So do I; send it to me."

After supper, they sat on the patio and watched the sun go down while they sipped wine and talked about everything except Wren leaving.

As it neared nine o'clock, Wren said, "I don't have much to do to get ready to leave, but I'd like to be on the road not long after sunrise."

Justin nodded, and they rode to the campground in silence.

Justin parked and waited while Wren unlocked the camper door.

Wren stood on the first step; Justin smiled as he wrapped his arms around her waist. After a lingering, sweet kiss, Justin said, "One more for old times' sake."

Wren laughed then put her arms around his neck and pulled him close for a kiss worth remembering.

When she released him, he said, "I'll be here at sunrise with breakfast."

When her alarm went off while it was still dark, Wren groaned, "Whose idea was it to get up so stinking early, Rascal? Was that yours?"

Rascal whined; Wren let him outside for his morning break then fed him breakfast.

She dressed and prepped the inside of the camper for travel before she unhooked the utilities and hitched the camper to the truck. While she was checking her lights, Justin parked at the site next to hers. He hopped out of his cruiser with two cups, a large thermos, and a lunch sack.

"I brought you coffee and a breakfast taco, honey."

"I need to tell Thomas I'm leaving," she said. "Is it okay if we go now?"

"That's fine; let's go."

As they strolled hand in hand to the saloon, the sky lightened.

Thomas waited on the front façade. "Time for you to go, bird girl, but we'll wait for you, won't we, Marshal?"

"That we will, Thomas," Justin said.

"Be safe, Wren." Thomas disappeared.

Wren gaped at the saloon. "Thomas has never called me Wren."

"It's your name, silly bird girl." Thomas laughed.

Justin chuckled.

"It's not funny." Wren stuck her nose in the air and headed back to her camper.

"Was too, and you know it." Justin caught up with her.

After they had breakfast at the picnic table, Justin hugged her. "I hate this."

"Six weeks; we can do it." Wren gazed at Justin, and he kissed her; she returned his kiss then he held her tight.

After he released her, he whispered, "We can do it."

Wren opened the truck door with tears streaming down her face; Rascal jumped in, then she climbed into the driver's seat and gave a tiny wave.

Justin led the way to the exit then parked at the office. Wren's eyes widened. Betsy, Socorro, Sheridan, and Butch stood at the exit waving small Arizona flags and blowing New Year's Eve horns.

Wren laughed through her tears and waved.

I'll be back.

Next to read:

WHACKED IN THE WOODS: WREN AND RASCAL COZY MYSTERY, BOOK 2

Wren and Rascal leave Arizona and Justin for her second writing assignment: a haunted campground in Texas. A killer wants her dead.

Wren and Rascal, her protective, mostly Labrador Retriever, discover a dead man in the woods. It's obvious who the killer is, isn't it? Even the ghost tells her not everyone is who they seem.

Wren and Justin might be farther apart in miles, but they're growing closer...

Check BARRETT BOOK SHOP to find WHACKED IN THE WOODS and other exciting JUDITH A. BARRETT BOOKS!

Browse, shop, read, enjoy!

Acknowledgements

Huge thanks to my husband for his patience, support, talented technical expertise, and guidance. Thanks to my editor, family, friends, and faithful readers for their awesome support and encouragement.

Thank you for reading. You keep reading; I'll keep writing!

Tell a friend how much you love Wren and Rascal and leave a short review with Barrett Book Shop or your favorite retailer. Authors can always use a few sparkles to brighten the gloomiest days.

PRO TIP: Post a five-star rating or recommend a book: both count the same as reviews!

Ready for news about what's next?
Look for the NEWSLETTER tab on
JUDITHABARRETT.COM to subscribe to my
not-your-typical newsletter for stories, new releases, and VIP
Reader bargains!

About the Author

Judith A. Barrett, award-winning author, lives on a farm in Georgia with her husband, two dogs, and chickens. She writes series for her readers: post-apocalyptic science fiction, thriller, mystery, and cozy mystery novels. Stories with a twist: not your typical characters from not your typical author!

When she isn't writing, Judith is working on farm chores, hiking or camping with her husband and dogs, or rocking on her front porch while she watches the sunset.

You keep reading; I'll keep writing!

Website   www.judithabarrett.com

BARRETT BOOK SHOP
Browse, shop, read, enjoy!
BarrettBookShop.com
Subscribe to the eNewsletter via her website
Let's keep in touch!

Also By Judith A. Barrett

Wren and Rascal Cozy Mystery Series

Donut Lady Cozy Mystery Series

Riley Malloy Mystery Series

Maggie Sloan Thriller Series

Grid Down Survival Series